sunlight & shadows

sunlight & shadows

James A. MacNeill
Glen A. Sorestad

NELSON CANADA LIMITED

contents

Life or Death

√10 Poison/Roald Dahl
22 Two Little Soldiers/Guy de Maupassant
29 The Lady, or the Tiger?/Frank Stockton
√36 A Shocking Accident/Graham Greene

Folly

46 The Hour of Letdown/E.B. White
51 An Ounce of Cure/Alice Munro
63 Tiresome Company/Jacques Ferron
66 Wanda Hickey's Night of Golden
Memories/Jean Shepherd

Anguish

105 The Gunfighter/Alden Nowlan
110 A Man Called Horse/Dorothy M. Johnson
125 Chickamauga/Ambrose Bierce
132 Out of the Rain/Ted Wood

Of the Heart

144 Mr. Know-All/W. Somerset Maugham
151 First Confession/Frank O'Connor
160 Snow/Gwendolyn MacEwen
164 The Man With the Heart in the
Highlands/William Saroyan

And Beyond

177 The Connection/Andreas Schroeder
183 Heav'n, Heav'n/Eric Frank Russell
192 Men Are Different/Alan Bloch
194 City of Yesterday/Terry Carr
203 Bloodflowers/W.D. Valgardson

life or death

"Don't touch the bed! For God's sake
don't touch the bed!" He was
speaking like he'd been shot in the
stomach ...

The slightest movement, the softest
sound can kill this man. How? Death
by poison.

poison
Roald Dahl

It must have been around midnight when I drove home, and as I approached the gates of the bungalow I switched off the headlamps of
the car so the beam wouldn't swing in through the window of the
side bedroom and wake Harry Pope. But I needn't have bothered.
Coming up the drive I noticed his light was still on, so he was awake
anyway—unless perhaps he'd dropped off while reading.

I parked the car and went up the five steps to the balcony, counting each step carefully in the dark so I wouldn't take an extra one
which wasn't there when I got to the top. I crossed the balcony,
pushed through the screen doors into the house itself and switched
on the light in the hall. I went across to the door of Harry's room,
opened it quietly, and looked in.

He was lying on the bed and I could see he was awake. But he
didn't move. He didn't even turn his head towards me, but I heard
him say, "Timber, Timber, come here."

He spoke slowly, whispering each word carefully, separately, and I
pushed the door right open and started to go quickly across the
room.

"Stop. Wait a moment, Timber." I could hardly hear what he was saying. He seemed to be straining enormously to get the words out.

"What's the matter, Harry?"

"Sshhh!' he whispered. "Sshhh! For God's sake don't make a noise. Take your shoes off before you come nearer. *Please* do as I say, Timber."

The way he was speaking reminded me of George Barling after he got shot in the stomach when he stood leaning against a crate containing a spare aeroplane engine, holding both hands on his stomach and saying things about the German pilot in just the same hoarse straining half whisper Harry was using now.

"Quickly, Timber, but take your shoes off first."

I couldn't understand about taking off the shoes but I figured that if he was as ill as he sounded I'd better humour him, so I bent down and removed the shoes and left them in the middle of the floor. Then I went over to his bed.

"Don't touch the bed! For God's sake don't touch the bed!" He was still speaking like he'd been shot in the stomach, and I could see him lying there on his back with a single sheet covering three-quarters of his body. He was wearing a pair of pyjamas with blue, brown, and white stripes, and he was sweating terribly. It was a hot night and I was sweating a little myself, but not like Harry. His whole face was wet and the pillow around his head was sodden with moisture. It looked like a bad go of malaria to me.

"What is it, Harry?"

"A krait," he said.

"A *krait*! Oh, my God! Where'd it bite you? How long ago?"

"Shut up," he whispered.

"Listen, Harry," I said, and I leaned forward and touched his shoulder. "We've got to be quick. Come on now, quickly, tell me where it bit you." He was lying there very still and tense as though he was holding on to himself hard because of sharp pain.

"I haven't been bitten," he whispered. "Not yet. It's on my stomach. Lying there asleep."

I took a quick pace backwards. I couldn't help it, and I stared at his stomach or rather at the sheet that covered it. The sheet was rumpled in several places and it was impossible to tell if there was anything underneath.

"You don't really mean there's a krait lying on your stomach now?"

"I swear it."

"How did it get there?" I shouldn't have asked the question because it was easy to see he wasn't fooling. I should have told him to keep quiet.

"I was reading." Harry said, and he spoke very slowly, taking each word in turn and speaking it carefully so as not to move the muscles of his stomach. "Lying on my back reading and I felt something on my chest, behind the book. Sort of tickling. Then out of the corner of my eye I saw this little krait sliding over my pyjamas. Small, about ten inches. Knew I mustn't move. Couldn't have anyway. Lay there watching it. Thought it would go over top of the sheet." Harry paused and was silent for a few moments. His eyes looked down along his body towards the place where the sheet covered his stomach, and I could see he was watching to make sure his whispering wasn't disturbing the thing that lay there.

"There was a fold in the sheet," he said, speaking more slowly than ever now and so softly I had to lean closer to hear him. "See it, it's still there. It went under that. I could feel it through my pyjamas, moving on my stomach. Then it stopped moving and now it's lying there in the warmth. Probably asleep. I've been waiting for you." He raised his eyes and looked at me.

"How long ago?"

"Hours," he whispered. "Hours and bloody hours and hours. I can't keep still much longer. I've been wanting to cough."

There was not much doubt about the truth of Harry's story. As a matter of fact it wasn't a surprising thing for a krait to do. They hang around people's houses and they go for the warm places. The surprising thing was that Harry hadn't been bitten. The bite is quite deadly except sometimes when you catch it at once and they kill a fair number of people each year in Bengal, mostly in the villages.

"All right, Harry," I said, and now I was whispering too. "Don't move and don't talk any more unless you have to. You know it won't bite unless it's frightened. We'll fix it in no time."

I went softly out of the room in my stockinged feet and fetched a small sharp knife from the kitchen. I put it in my trouser pocket ready to use instantly in case something went wrong while we were still thinking out a plan. If Harry coughed and moved or did something to

frighten the krait and got bitten, I was going to be ready to cut the
bitten place and try to suck the venom out. I came back to the bedroom and Harry was still lying there very quiet and sweating all over
his face. His eyes followed me as I moved across the room to his bed
and I could see he was wondering what I'd been up to. I stood beside
him, trying to think of the best thing to do.

"Harry," I said, and now when I spoke I put my mouth almost on his
ear so I wouldn't have to raise my voice above the softest whisper, "I
think the best thing to do is for me to draw the sheet back very, very
gently. Then we could have a look first. I think I could do that without
disturbing it."

"Don't be a damn fool." There was no expression in his voice. He
spoke each word too slowly, too carefully, and too softly for that.
The expression was in the eyes and around the corners of the
mouth.

"Why not?"

"The light would frighten him. It's dark under there now."

"Then how about whipping the sheet back quick and brushing it off
before it has time to strike."

"Why don't you get a doctor?" Harry said. The way he looked at me
told me I should have thought of that myself in the first place.

"A doctor. Of course. That's it. I'll get Ganderbai."

I tiptoed out to the hall, looked up Ganderbai's number in the
book, lifted the phone and told the operator to hurry.

"Dr. Ganderbai," I said. "This is Timber Woods."

"Hello, Mr. Woods. You not in bed yet?"

"Look, could you come round at once? And bring serum—for a
krait bite."

"Who's been bitten?" The question came so sharply it was like a
small explosion in my ear.

"No one. No one yet. But Harry Pope's in bed and he's got one lying
on his stomach—asleep under the sheet on his stomach."

For about three seconds there was silence on the line. Then
speaking slowly, not like an explosion now, but slowly, precisely,
Ganderbai said, "Tell him to keep quite still. He is not to move or to
talk. Do you understand?"

"Of course."

"I'll come at once!" He rang off and I went back to the bedroom.

Harry's eyes watched me as I walked across to his bed.

"Ganderbai's coming. He said for you to lie still."

"What in God's name does he think I'm doing!"

"Look, Harry, he said no talking. Absolutely no talking. Either of us."

"Why don't you shut up then?" When he said this, one side of his mouth started twitching with rapid little downward movements that continued for a while after he finished speaking. I took out my handkerchief and very gently I wiped the sweat off his face and neck, and I could feel the slight twitching of the muscle—the one he used for smiling—as my fingers passed over it with the handkerchief.

I slipped out to the kitchen, got some ice from the ice-box, rolled it up in a napkin, and began to crush it small. That business of the mouth, I didn't like that. Or the way he talked, either. I carried the ice-pack back to the bedroom and laid it across Harry's forehead.

"Keep you cool."

He screwed up his eyes and drew breath sharply through his teeth. "Take it away," he whispered. "Make me cough." His smiling-muscle began to twitch again.

The beam of a headlamp shone through the window as Ganderbai's car swung around to the front of the bungalow. I went out to meet him, holding the ice-pack with both hands.

"How is it?" Ganderbai asked, but he didn't stop to talk; he walked on past me across the balcony and through the screen doors into the hall. "Where is he? Which room?"

He put his bag down on a chair in the hall and followed me into Harry's room. He was wearing soft-soled bedroom slippers and he walked across the floor noiselessly, delicately, like a careful cat. Harry watched him out of the sides of his eyes. When Ganderbai reached the bed he looked down at Harry and smiled, confident and reassuring, nodding his head to tell Harry it was a simple matter and he was not to worry but just to leave it to Dr. Ganderbai. Then he turned and went back to the hall and I followed him.

"First thing is to try to get some serum into him," he said, and he opened his bag and started to make preparations. "Intravenously. But I must do it neatly. Don't want to make him flinch."

We went into the kitchen and he sterilised a needle. He had a hypodermic syringe in one hand and a small bottle in the other and he stuck the needle through the rubber top of the bottle and began drawing a pale yellow liquid up into the syringe by pulling out the plunger. Then he handed the syringe to me.

"Hold that till I ask for it."

He picked up the bag and together we returned to the room. Harry's eyes were bright now and wide open. Ganderbai bent over Harry and very cautiously, like a man handling sixteenth-century lace, he rolled up the pyjama sleeve to the elbow without moving the arm. I noticed he stood well away from the bed.

He whispered, "I'm going to give you an injection. Serum. Just a prick but try not to move. Don't tighten your stomach muscles. Let them go limp."

Harry looked at the syringe.

Ganderbai took a piece of red rubber tubing from his bag and slid one end under and up and around Harry's biceps; then he tied the tubing tight with a knot. He sponged a small area of the bare forearm with alcohol, handed the swab to me and took the syringe from my hand. He held it up to the light, squinting at the calibrations, squirting out some of the yellow fluid. I stood beside him, watching. Harry was watching too and sweating all over his face so it shone like it was smeared thick with face cream melting on his skin and running down on to the pillow.

I could see the blue vein on the inside of Harry's forearm, swollen now because of the tourniquet, and then I saw the needle above the vein, Ganderbai holding the syringe almost flat against the arm, sliding the needle in sideways through the skin into the blue vein, sliding it slowly but so firmly it went in smooth as into cheese. Harry looked at the ceiling and closed his eyes and opened them again, but he didn't move.

When it was finished Ganderbai leaned forward putting his mouth close to Harry's ear. "Now you'll be all right even if you *are* bitten. But don't move. Please don't move. I'll be back in a moment."

He picked up his bag and went out to the hall and I followed.

"Is he safe now?" I asked.

"No."

"How safe is he?"

The little Indian doctor stood there in the hall rubbing his lower lip.

"It must give some protection, mustn't it?" I asked.

He turned away and walked to the screen doors that led on to the verandah. I thought he was going through them, but he stopped this side of the doors and stood looking out into the night.

"Isn't the serum very good?" I asked.

"Unfortunately not," he answered without turning round. "It might save him. It might not. I am trying to think of something else to do."

"Shall we draw the sheet back quick and brush it off before it has time to strike?"

"Never! We are not entitled to take a risk." He spoke sharply and his voice was pitched a little higher than usual.

"We can't very well leave him lying there," I said. "He's getting nervous."

"Please! Please!" he said, turning round, holding both hands up in the air. "Not so fast, please. This is not a matter to rush into baldheaded." He wiped his forehead with his handkerchief and stood there, frowning, nibbling his lip.

"You see," he said at last. "There is a way to do this. You know what we must do—we must administer an anaesthetic to the creature where it lies."

It was a splendid idea.

"It is not safe," he continued, "because a snake is cold-blooded and anaesthetic does not work so well or so quick with such animals, but it is better than any other thing to do. We could use ether . . . chloroform. . . ." He was speaking slowly and trying to think the thing out while he talked.

"Which shall we use?"

"Chloroform," he said suddenly. "Ordinary chloroform. That is best. Now quick!" He took my arm and pulled me towards the balcony. "Drive to my house! By the time you get there I will have waked up my boy on the telephone and he will show you my poisons cupboard. Here is the key of the cupboard. Take a bottle of chloroform. It has an orange label and the name is printed on it. I stay here in case anything happens. Be quick now, hurry! No, no, you don't need your shoes!"

I drove fast and in about fifteen minutes I was back with the bottle of chloroform. Ganderbai came out of Harry's room and met me in the hall. "You got it," he said. "Good, good. I just been telling him what we are going to do. But now we must hurry. It is not easy for him in there like that all this time. I am afraid he might move."

He went back to the bedroom and I followed, carrying the bottle carefully with both hands. Harry was lying on the bed in precisely the same position as before with the sweat pouring down his cheeks. His face was white and wet. He turned his eyes towards me and I smiled at him and nodded confidently. He continued to look at me. I raised my thumb, giving him the okay signal. He closed his eyes. Ganderbai was squatting down by the bed, and on the floor beside him was the hollow rubber tube that he had previously used as a tourniquet, and he'd got a small paper funnel fitted into one end of the tube.

He began to pull a little piece of the sheet out from under the mattress. He was working directly in line with Harry's stomach, about eighteen inches from it, and I watched his fingers as they tugged gently at the edge of the sheet. He worked so slowly it was almost impossible to discern any movement either in his fingers or in the sheet that was being pulled.

Finally he succeeded in making an opening under the sheet and he took the rubber tube and inserted one end of it in the opening so that it would slide under the sheet along the mattress towards Harry's body. I do not know how long it took him to slide that tube in a few inches. It may have been twenty minutes, it may have been forty. I never once saw the tube move. I knew it was going in because the visible part of it grew gradually shorter, but I doubted that the krait could have felt even the faintest vibration. Ganderbai himself was sweating now, large pearls of sweat standing out all over his forehead and along his upper lip. But his hands were steady and I noticed that his eyes were watching, not the tube in his hands, but the area of crumpled sheet above Harry's stomach.

Without looking up, he held out a hand to me for the chloroform. I twisted out the ground-glass stopper and put the bottle right into his hand, not letting go till I was sure he had a good hold on it. Then he jerked his head for me to come closer and he whispered, "Tell him I'm going to soak the mattress and that it will be very cold under his body. He must be ready for that and he must not move. Tell him now."

I bent over Harry and passed on the message.

"Why doesn't he get on with it?" Harry said.

"He's going to now, Harry. But it'll feel very cold, so be ready for it."

"Oh, God Almighty, get on, get on!" For the first time he raised his voice, and Ganderbai glanced up sharply, watched him for a few seconds, then went back to his business.

Ganderbai poured a few drops of chloroform into the paper funnel and waited while it ran down the tube. Then he poured some more. Then he waited again, and the heavy sickening smell of chloroform spread out over the room bringing with it faint unpleasant memories of white-coated nurses and white surgeons standing in a white room around a long white table. Ganderbai was pouring steadily now and I could see the heavy vapour of the chloroform swirling slowly like smoke above the paper funnel. He paused, held the bottle up to the light, poured one more funnelful and handed the bottle back to me. Slowly he drew out the rubber tube from under the sheet; then he stood up.

The strain of inserting the tube and pouring the chloroform must have been great, and I recollect that when Ganderbai turned and whispered to me, his voice was small and tired. "We'll give it fifteen minutes. Just to be safe."

I leaned over to tell Harry. "We're going to give it fifteen minutes, just to be safe. But it's probably done for already."

"Then why for God's sake don't you look and see!" Again he spoke loudly and Ganderbai sprang round, his small brown face suddenly very angry. He had almost pure black eyes and he stared at Harry and Harry's smiling-muscle started to twitch. I took my handkerchief and wiped his wet face, trying to stroke his forehead a little for comfort as I did so.

Then we stood and waited beside the bed, Ganderbai watching Harry's face all the time in a curious intense manner. The little Indian was concentrating all his will-power on keeping Harry quiet. He never once took his eyes from the patient and although he made no sound, he seemed somehow to be shouting at him all the time, saying: Now listen, you've got to listen, you're not going to go spoiling this now, d'you hear me; and Harry lay there twitching his mouth, sweating, closing his eyes, opening them, looking at me, at the sheet, at the ceiling, at me again, but never at Ganderbai. Yet somehow Ganderbai was holding him. The smell of chloroform was oppressive and it made me feel sick, but I couldn't leave the room now.

I had the feeling someone was blowing up a huge balloon and I could see it was going to burst, but I couldn't look away.

At length Ganderbai turned and nodded and I knew he was ready to proceed. "You go over to the other side of the bed," he said. "We will each take one side of the sheet and draw it back together, but very slowly, please, and very quietly."

"Keep still now, Harry," I said and I went around to the other side of the bed and took hold of the sheet. Ganderbai stood opposite me, and together we began to draw back the sheet, lifting it up clear of Harry's body, taking it back very slowly, both of us standing well away but at the same time bending forward trying to peer underneath it. The smell of chloroform was awful. I remember trying to hold my breath and when I couldn't do that any longer I tried to breathe shallow so the stuff wouldn't get into my lungs.

The whole of Harry's chest was visible now, or rather the striped pyjama top which covered it, and then I saw the white cord of his pyjama trousers, neatly tied in a bow. A little farther and I saw a button, a mother-of-pearl button, and that was something I had never had on my pyjamas, a fly button, let alone a mother-of-pearl one. This Harry, I thought, he is very refined. It is odd how one sometimes has frivolous thoughts at exciting moments, and I distinctly remember thinking about Harry being very refined when I saw that button.

Apart from the button there was nothing on his stomach.

We pulled the sheet back faster then, and when we had uncovered his legs and feet we let the sheet drop over the end of the bed on to the floor.

"Don't move," Ganderbai said, "don't move, Mr. Pope'; and he began to peer around along the side of Harry's body and under his legs.

"We must be careful," he said. It may be anywhere. It could be up the leg of his pyjamas."

When Ganderbai said this, Harry quickly raised his head from the pillow and looked down at his legs. It was the first time he had moved. Then suddenly he jumped up, stood on his bed and shook his legs one after the other violently in the air. At that moment we both thought he had been bitten and Ganderbai was already reaching down into his bag for a scalpel and a tourniquet when Harry ceased his caperings and stood still and looked at the mattress he was standing on and shouted, "It's not there!"

Ganderbai straightened up and for a moment he too looked at the mattress; then he looked up at Harry. Harry was all right. He hadn't been bitten and now he wasn't going to get bitten and he wasn't going to be killed and everything was fine. But that didn't seem to make anyone feel any better.

"Mr. Pope, you are of course *quite* sure you saw it in the first place?" There was a note of sarcasm in Ganderbai's voice that he would never have employed in ordinary circumstances. "You don't think you might possibly have been dreaming, do you, Mr. Pope?" The way Ganderbai was looking at Harry, I realised that the sarcasm was not seriously intended. He was only easing up a bit after the strain.

Harry stood on his bed in his striped pyjamas, glaring at Ganderbai, and the colour began to spread out over his cheeks.

"Are you telling me I'm a liar?" he shouted.

Ganderbai remained absolutely still, watching Harry. Harry took a pace forward on the bed and there was a shining look in his eyes.

"Why, you dirty little sewer rat!"

"Shut up, Harry!" I said.

"You dirty——"

"Harry!" I called. "Shut up, Harry!" It was terrible, the things he was saying.

Ganderbai went out of the room as though neither of us was there and I followed him and put my arm around his shoulder as he walked across the hall and out on to the balcony.

"Don't you listen to Harry," I said. "This thing's made him so he doesn't know what he's saying."

We went down the steps from the balcony to the drive and across the drive in the darkness to where his old Morris car was parked. He opened the door and got in.

"You did a wonderful job," I said. "Thank you so very much for coming."

"All he needs is a good holiday," he said quietly, without looking at me, then he started the engine and drove off.

Roald Dahl (1916-)
Born in England of Norwegian parents, Roald Dahl published his
first story in 1942. He has since become one of the world's most pop-
ular contemporary story writers. Excitement and suspense char-
acterize his writing. Dahl has lived and worked throughout the world.
During the North African Campaign he served in the RAF.

"He sat motionless, stupefied by astonishment and suffering, with an
agony which was simple but deep."

The unintentional slights of others
can wound us, *even kill us*.

two little soldiers
Guy de Maupassant

Every Sunday, the moment they were dismissed, the two little soldiers made off. Once outside the barracks, they struck out to the
right through Courbevoie, walking with long rapid strides, as though
they were on a march.

When they were beyond the last of the houses, they slackened
pace along the bare, dusty roadway which goes toward Bézons.

They were both small and thin, and looked quite lost in their coats,
which were too big and too long. Their sleeves hung down over their
hands, and they found their enormous red breeches, which compelled them to waddle, very much in the way. Under their stiff, high
helmets their faces had little character—two poor, sallow Breton
faces, simple with an almost animal simplicity, and with gentle and
quiet blue eyes.

They never conversed during these walks, but went straight on,
each with the same thought in his head. This thought atoned for the
lack of conversation; it was this, that just inside the little wood near
Les Champioux they had found a place which reminded them of
their own country, where they could feel happy again.

When they arrived under the trees where the roads from Colombes
and from Chatou cross, they would take off their heavy helmets and
wipe their foreheads. They always halted on the Bézons bridge to
look at the Seine, and would remain there two or three minutes, bent
double, leaning on the parapet.

Sometimes they would gaze out over the great basin of Argenteuil, where the skiffs might be seen scudding, with their white, careening sails, recalling perhaps the look of the Breton waters, the harbor of Vanne, near which they lived, and the fishing-boats standing out across the Morbihan to the open sea.

Just beyond the Seine they bought their provisions from a sausage merchant, a baker, and a wine-seller. A piece of blood-pudding, four sous' worth of bread, and a liter of "petit bleu" constituted the provisions, which they carried off in their handkerchiefs. After they had left Bézons they traveled slowly and began to talk.

In front of them a barren plain studded with clumps of trees led to the wood, to the little wood which had seemed to them to resemble the one at Kermarivan. Grainfields and hayfields bordered the narrow path, which lost itself in the young greenness of the crops, and Jean Kerderen would always say to Luc le Ganidec:

"It looks just as it does near Plounivon."

"Yes; exactly."

Side by side they strolled, their souls filled with vague memories of their own country, with awakened images as naive as the pictures on the colored broadsheets which you buy for a penny. They kept on recognizing, as it were, now a corner of a field, a hedge, a bit of moorland, now a crossroad, now a granite cross. Then, too, they would always stop beside a certain landmark, a great stone, because it looked something like the cromlech at Locneuven.

Every Sunday on arriving at the first clump of trees Luc le Ganidec would cut a switch, a hazel switch, and begin gently to peel off the bark, thinking meanwhile of the folk at home. Jean Kerderen carried the provisions.

From time to time Luc would mention a name, or recall some deed of their childhood in a few brief words, which caused long thoughts. And their own country, their dear, distant country, recaptured them little by little, seizing on their imaginations, and sending to them from afar her shapes, her sounds, her well-known prospects, her odors—odors of the green lands where the salt sea-air was blowing.

No longer conscious of the exhalations of the Parisian stables, on which the earth of the *banlieue* fattens, they scented the perfume of the flowering broom, which the salt breeze of the open sea plucks and bears away. And the sails of the boats from the river banks seemed like the white wings of the coasting vessels seen beyond the great plain which extended from their homes to the very margin of the sea.

They walked with short steps, Luc le Ganidec and Jean Kerderen, content and sad, haunted by a sweet melancholy, by the lingering, ever-present sorrow of a caged animal who remembers his liberty.

By the time that Luc had stripped the slender wand of its bark they reached the corner of the wood where every Sunday they took breakfast. They found the two bricks which they kept hidden in the thicket, and kindled a little fire of twigs, over which to roast the blood-pudding at the end of a bayonet.

When they had breakfasted, eaten their bread to the last crumb, and drunk their wine to the last drop, they remained seated side by side upon the grass, saying nothing, their eyes on the distance, their eyelids drooping, their fingers crossed as at mass, their red legs stretched out beside the poppies of the field. And the leather of their helmets and the brass of their buttons glittered in the ardent sun, making the larks, which sang and hovered above their heads, cease in mid-song.

Toward noon they began to turn their eyes from time to time in the direction of the village of Bézons, because the girl with the cow was coming. She passed by them every Sunday on her way to milk and change the pasture of her cow—the only cow in this district which ever went out of the stable to grass. It was pastured in a narrow field along the edge of the wood a little farther on.

They soon perceived the girl, the only human being within vision, and were gladdened by the brilliant reflections thrown off by the tin milk-pail under the rays of the sun. They never talked about her. They were simply glad to see her, without understanding why.

She was a big strong wench with red hair, burned by the heat of sunny days, a sturdy product of the environs of Paris.

Once, finding them seated in the same place, she said:

"Good morning. You two are always here, aren't you?"

Luc de Ganidec, the bolder, stammered:

"Yes, we come to rest."

That was all. But the next Sunday she laughed on seeing them, laughed with a protecting benevolence and a feminine keenness which knew well enough that they were bashful. And she asked:

"What are you doing there? Are you trying to see the grass grow?"

Luc was cheered up by this, and smiled likewise: "Maybe we are."

"That's pretty slow work," said she.

He answered, still laughing: "Well, yes, it is."

She went on. But coming back with a milk-pail full of milk, she stopped again before them, and said:

"Would you like a little? It will taste like home."

With the instinctive feeling that they were of the same peasant race as she, being herself perhaps also far away from home, she had divined and touched the spot.

They were both touched. Then with some difficulty, she managed to make a little milk run into the neck of the glass bottle in which they carried their wine. And Luc drank first, with little swallows, stopping every minute to see whether he had drunk more than his half. Then he handed the bottle to Jean.

She stood upright before them, her hands on her hips, her pail on the ground at her feet, glad at the pleasure which she had given.

Then she departed, shouting: *"Allons,* adieu! Till next Sunday!"

And as long as they could see her at all, they followed with their eyes her tall silhouette, which faded, growing smaller and smaller, seeming to sink into the verdure of the fields.

When they were leaving the barracks the week after, Jean said to Luc:

"Oughtn't we to buy her something good?"

They were in great embarrassment before the problem of the choice of a delicacy for the girl with the cow. Luc was of the opinion that a little tripe would be the best, but Jean preferred some *berlingots* because he was fond of sweets. His choice fairly made him enthusiastic, and they bought at a grocer's two sous' worth of white and red candies.

They ate their breakfast more rapidly than usual, being nervous with expectation.

Jean saw her first. "There she is!" he cried. Luc added: "Yes, there she is."

While yet some distance off she laughed at seeing them. Then she cried:

"Is everything going as you like it?"

And in unison they asked:

"Are you getting on all right?"

Then she conversed, talked to them of simple things in which they felt an interest—of the weather, of the crops, and of her master.

They were afraid to offer her the candies, which were slowly melting away in Jean's pocket.

At last Luc grew bold, and murmured:

"We have brought you something."

She demanded, "What is it? Tell me!"

Then Jean, blushing up to his ears, managed to get at the little paper cornucopia, and held it out.

She began to eat the little bonbons, rolling them from one cheek to the other where they made little round lumps. The two soldiers, seated before her, gazed at her with emotion and delight.

Then she went to milk her cow, and once more gave them some milk on coming back.

They thought of her all the week; several times they even spoke of her. The next Sunday she sat down with them for a little longer talk; and all three, seated side by side, their eyes lost in the distance, clasping their knees with their hands, told the small doings, the minute details of life in the villages where they had been born, while over there the cow, seeing that the milkmaid had stopped on her way, stretched out toward her its heavy head with its dripping nostrils, and gave a long low to call her.

Soon the girl consented to eat a bit of bread with them and drink a mouthful of wine. She often brought them plums in her pocket, for the season of plums had come. Her presence sharpened the wits of the two little Breton soldiers, and they chattered like two birds.

But, one Tuesday, Luc le Ganidec asked for leave—a thing which had never happened before—and he did not return until ten o'clock at night. Jean racked his brains uneasily for a reason for his comrade's going out in this way.

The next Thursday Luc, having borrowed ten sous from his bedfellow, again asked and obtained permission to leave the barracks for several hours. When he set off with Jean on their Sunday walk his manner was very queer, quite restless, and quite changed. Kerderen did not understand, but he vaguely suspected something without divining what it could be.

They did not say a word to one another until they reached their usual halting-place, where, from their constant sitting in the same spot, the grass was quite worn away. They ate their breakfast slowly. Neither of them felt hungry.

Before long the girl appeared. As on every Sunday, they watched her coming. When she was quite near, Luc rose and made two steps forward. She put her milk-pail on the ground and kissed him. She kissed him passionately, throwing her arms about his neck, without noticing Jean, without remembering that he was there, without even seeing him.

And he sat there desperate, poor Jean, so desperate that he did not understand, his soul quite overwhelmed, his heart bursting, but not yet understanding himself. Then the girl seated herself beside Luc, and they began to chatter.

Jean did not look at them. He now divined why his comrade had gone out twice during the week, and he felt within him a burning grief, a kind of wound, that sense of rending which is caused by treason.

Luc and the girl went off together to change the position of the cow. Jean followed them with his eyes. He saw them departing side by side. The red breeches of his comrade made a bright spot on the road. It was Luc who picked up the mallet and hammered down the stake to which they tied the beast.

The girl stooped to milk her, while he stroked the cow's sharp spine with a careless hand. Then they left the milk-pail on the grass, and went deep into the wood.

Jean saw nothing but the wall of leaves where they had entered; and he felt himself so troubled that if he had tried to rise he would certainly have fallen. He sat motionless, stupefied by astonishment and suffering, with an agony which was simple but deep. He wanted to cry, to run away, to hide himself, never to see anybody any more.

Soon he saw them issuing from the thicket. They returned slowly, holding each other's hands as in the villages do those who are promised. It was Luc who carried the pail.

They kissed one another again before they separated, and the girl went off after having thrown Jean a friendly "Good evening" and a smile which was full of meaning. Today she no longer thought of offering him any milk.

The two little soldiers sat side by side, motionless as usual, silent and calm, their placid faces betraying nothing of all which troubled their hearts. The sun fell on them. Sometimes the cow lowed, looking at them from afar.

At their usual hour they rose to go back. Luc cut a switch. Jean carried the empty bottle to return it to the wine-seller at Bézons. Then they sallied out upon the bridge, and, as they did every Sunday, stopped several minutes in the middle to watch the water flowing.

Jean leaned, leaned more and more, over the iron railing, as though he saw in the current something which attracted him. Luc said: "Are you trying to drink?" Just as he uttered the last word Jean's head overbalanced his body, his legs described a circle in the air, and the little blue and red soldier fell in a heap, struck the water, and disappeared.

Luc, his tongue paralyzed with anguish, tried in vain to shout. Farther down he saw something stir; then the head of his comrade rose to the surface of the river and sank immediately. Farther still he again perceived a hand, a single hand, which issued from the stream and then disappeared. That was all.

The bargemen who dragged the river did not find the body that day.

Luc set out alone for the barracks, going at a run, his soul filled with despair. He told of the accident, with tears in his eyes, and a husky voice, blowing his nose again and again: "He leaned over—he—he leaned over—so far—so far that his head turned a somersault; and—and—so he fell—he fell—"

Choked with emotion, he could say no more. If he had only known!

Guy de Maupassant (1850-1893)
One of the greatest French storytellers of all time, Guy de Maupassant wrote over three hundred stories within a ten-year period. Some of these, such as "The Diamond Necklace" and "The Piece of String" are considered world classics. Maupassant drove himself furiously, until he was committed to an insane asylum a few years before his death.

"She raised her hand, and made a
slight, quick movement toward the
right."

On this movement a man's fate is
determined. Will he marry a beautiful woman, or will he be ravaged by
a tiger? Here is a story of justice,
perhaps less than perfect, but
certainly *final*.

the lady,
or the tiger?

Frank Stockton

In the very olden time there lived a semi-barbaric king, whose ideas,
though somewhat polished and sharpened by the progressiveness
of distant Latin neighbours, were still large, florid, and un-
trammelled, as became the half of him which was barbaric. He was a
man of exuberant fancy, and withal, of an authority so irresistible
that, at his will, he turned his varied fancies into facts. He was greatly
given to self-communing; and, when he and himself agreed upon
anything, the thing was done. When every member of his domestic
and political systems moved smoothly in its appointed course, his
nature was bland and genial; but whenever there was a little hitch,
and some of his orbs got out of their orbits, he was blander and more
genial still, for nothing pleased him so much as to make the crooked
straight, and crush down uneven places.

Among the borrowed notions by which his barbarism had become
semified was that of the public arena, in which, by exhibitions of
manly and beastly valour, the minds of his subjects were refined and
cultured.

But even here the exuberant and barbaric fancy asserted itself. The arena of the king was built, not to give the people an opportunity of hearing the rhapsodies of dying gladiators, nor to enable them to view the inevitable conclusion of a conflict between religious opinions and hungry jaws, but for purposes far better adapted to widen and develop the mental energies of the people. This vast amphitheatre, with its encircling galleries, its mysterious vaults, and its unseen passages, was an agent of poetic justice, in which crime was punished, or virtue rewarded, by the decrees of an impartial and incorruptible chance.

When a subject was accused of a crime of sufficient importance to interest the king, public notice was given that on an appointed day the fate of the accused person would be decided in the king's arena —a structure which well deserved its name; for, although its form and plan were borrowed from afar, its purpose emanated solely from the brain of this man, who, every barleycorn a king, knew no tradition to which he owed more allegiance than pleased his fancy, and who ingrafted on every adopted form of human thought and action the rich growth of his barbaric idealism.

When all the people had assembled in the galleries, and the king, surrounded by his court, sat high up on his throne of royal state on one side of the arena, he gave a signal, a door beneath him opened, and the accused subject stepped out into the amphitheatre. Directly opposite him, on the other side of the enclosed space, were two doors, exactly alike and side by side. It was the duty and the privilege of the person on trial to walk directly to these doors and open one of them. He could open either door he pleased: he was subject to no guidance or influence but that of the aforementioned impartial and incorruptible chance. If he opened the one, there came out of it a hungry tiger, the fiercest and most cruel that could be procured, which immediately sprang upon him, and tore him to pieces, as a punishment for his guilt. The moment that the case of the criminal was thus decided, doleful iron bells were clanged, great wails went up from the hired mourners posted on the outer rim of the arena, and the vast audience, with bowed heads and downcast hearts, wended slowly their homeward way, mourning greatly that one so young and fair, or so old and respected, should have merited so dire a fate.

But, if the accused person opened the other door, there came forth from it a lady, the most suitable to his years and station that his majesty could select among his fair subjects; and to this lady he was immediately married, as a reward of his innocence. It mattered not that he might already possess a wife and family, or that his affections might be engaged upon an object of his own selection: the king allowed no such subordinate arrangements to interfere with his great scheme of retribution and reward. The exercises, as in the other instance, took place immediately, and in the arena. Another door opened beneath the king, and a priest, followed by a band of choristers, and dancing maidens blowing joyous airs on golden horns and treading an epithalamic measure, advanced to where the pair stood, side by side; and the wedding was promptly and cheerily solemnized. Then the gay brass bells rang forth their merry peals, the people shouted glad hurrahs, and the innocent man, preceded by children strewing flowers on his path, led his bride to his home.

This was the king's semi-barbaric method of administering justice. Its perfect fairness is obvious. The criminal could not know out of which door would come the lady: he opened either he pleased, without having the slightest idea whether, in the next instant, he was to be devoured or married. On some occasions the tiger came out of one door, and on some out of the other. The decisions of this tribunal were not only fair, they were positively determinate: the accused person was instantly punished if he found himself guilty, and, if innocent, he was rewarded on the spot, whether he liked it or not. There was no escape from the judgments of the king's arena.

The institution was a very popular one. When the people gathered together on one of the great trial days they never knew whether they were to witness a bloody slaughter or a hilarious wedding. This element of uncertainty lent an interest to the occasion which it could not otherwise have attained. Thus the masses were entertained and pleased, and the thinking part of the community could bring no charge of unfairness against this plan; for did not the accused person have the whole matter in his own hands?

This semi-barbaric king had a daughter as blooming as his most florid fancies, and with a soul as fervent and imperious as his own. As is usual in such cases, she was the apple of his eye, and was loved by him above all humanity. Among his courtiers was a young man of that fineness of blood and lowness of station common to the con-

ventional heroes of romance who love royal maidens. This royal
maiden was well satisfied with her lover, for he was handsome and
brave to a degree unsurpassed in all this kingdom; and she loved him
with an ardour that had enough of barbarism in it to make it ex-
ceedingly warm and strong. This love affair moved on happily for
many months, until one day the king happened to discover its existence. He did not hesitate nor waver in regard to his duty in the prem-
ises. The youth was immediately cast into prison, and a day was appointed for his trial in the king's arena. This, of course, was an
especially important occasion; and his majesty, as well as all the
people, was greatly interested in the workings and development of
this trial. Never before had such a case occurred; never before had a
subject dared to love the daughter of a king. In after-years such
things became commonplace enough; but then they were, in no
slight degree, novel and startling.

The tiger-cages of the kingdom were searched for the most savage
and relentless beasts, from which the fiercest monster might be selected for the arena; and the ranks of maiden youth and beauty
throughout the land were carefully surveyed by competent judges,
in order that the young man might have a fitting bride in case fate did
not determine for him a different destiny. Of course, everybody knew
that the deed with which the accused was charged had been done.
He had loved the princess, and neither he, she, nor any one else
thought of denying the fact; but the king would not think of allowing
any fact of this kind to interfere with the workings of the tribunal, in
which he took such great delight and satisfaction. No matter how the
affair turned out, the youth would be disposed of; and the king would
take an aesthetic pleasure in watching the course of events, which
would determine whether or not the young man had done wrong in
allowing himself to love the princess.

The appointed day arrived. From far and near the people gathered,
and thronged the great galleries of the arena; and crowds, unable to
gain admittance, massed themselves against its outside walls. The
king and his court were in their places, opposite the twin doors—
those fateful portals, so terrible in their similarity.

All was ready. The signal was given. A door beneath the royal
party opened, and the lover of the princess walked into the arena.
Tall, beautiful, fair, his appearance was greeted with a low hum of

admiration and anxiety. Half the audience had not known so grand a
youth had lived among them. No wonder the princess loved him!
What a terrible thing for him to be there!

As the youth advanced into the arena, he turned, as the custom
was, to bow to the king: but he did not think at all of that royal per-
sonage; his eyes were fixed upon the princess, who sat to the right of
her father. Had it not been for the moiety of barbarism in her nature it
is probable that lady would not have been there; but her intense and
fervid soul would not allow her to be absent on an occasion in which
she was so terribly interested. From the moment that the decree had
gone forth, that her lover should decide his fate in the king's arena,
she had thought of nothing, night or day, but this great event and the
various subjects connected with it. Possessed of more power, influence, and force of character than any one who had ever before
been interested in such a case, she had done what no other person
had done—she had possessed herself of the secret of the doors. She
knew in which of the two rooms, that lay behind those doors, stood
the cage of the tiger, with its open front, and in which waited the
lady. Through these thick doors, heavily curtained with skins on the
inside, it was impossible that any noise or suggestion should come
from within to the person who should approach to raise the latch of
one of them; but gold, and the power of a woman's will, had brought
the secret to the princess.

And not only did she know in which room stood the lady ready to
emerge, all blushing and radiant, should her door be opened, but
she knew who the lady was. It was one of the fairest and loveliest of
the damsels of the court who had been selected as the reward of the
accused youth, should he be proved innocent of the crime of aspir-
ing to one so far above him; and the princess hated her. Often had
she seen, or imagined that she had seen, this fair creature throwing
glances of admiration upon the person of her lover, and sometimes
she thought these glances were perceived and even returned. Now
and then she had seen them talking together; it was but for a moment or two, but much can be said in a brief space; it may have been
on most unimportant topics, but how could she know that? The girl
was lovely, but she had dared to raise her eyes to the loved one of
the princess; and, with all the intensity of the savage blood trans-
mitted to her through long lines of wholly barbaric ancestors, she

hated the woman who blushed and trembled behind that silent door.

When her lover turned and looked at her, and his eye met hers as she sat there paler and whiter than any one in the vast ocean of anxious faces about her, he saw, by that power of quick perception which is given to those whose souls are one, that she knew behind which door crouched the tiger, and behind which stood the lady. He had expected her to know it. He understood her nature, and his soul was assured that she would never rest until she had made plain to herself this thing, hidden to all other lookers-on, even to the king. The only hope for the youth in which there was any element of certainty was based upon the success of the princess in discovering this mystery; and the moment he looked upon her, he saw she had succeeded, as in his soul he knew she would succeed.

Then it was that his quick and anxious glance asked the question: "Which?" It was as plain to her as if he shouted it from where he stood. There was not an instant to be lost. The question was asked in a flash; it must be answered in another.

Her right arm lay on the cushioned parapet before her. She raised her hand, and made a slight, quick movement toward the right. No one but her lover saw her. Every eye but his was fixed on the man in the arena.

He turned, and with a firm and rapid step he walked across the empty space. Every heart stopped beating, every breath was held, every eye was fixed immovably upon that man. Without the slightest hesitation, he went to the door on the right, and opened it.

Now, the point of the story is this: Did the tiger come out of that door, or did the lady?

The more we reflect upon this question, the harder it is to answer. It involves a study of the human heart which leads us through devious mazes of passion, out of which it is difficult to find our way. Think of it, fair reader, not as if the decision of the question depended upon yourself, but upon that hot-blooded, semi-barbaric princess, her soul at a white heat beneath the combined fires of despair and jealousy. She had lost him, but who should have him?

How often, in her waking hours and in her dreams, had she started in wild horror, and covered her face with her hands as she thought of her lover opening the door on the other side of which waited the cruel fangs of the tiger!

But how much oftener had she seen him at the other door! How in her grievous reveries had she gnashed her teeth, and torn her hair, when she saw his start of rapturous delight as he opened the door of the lady! How her soul had burned in agony when she had seen him rush to meet that woman, with her flushing cheek and sparkling eye of triumph; when she had seen him lead her forth, his whole frame kindled with the joy of recovered life; when she had heard the glad shouts from the multitude, and the wild ringing of the happy bells; when she had seen the priest, with his joyous followers, advance to the couple, and make them man and wife before her very eyes; and when she had seen them walk away together upon their path of flowers, followed by the tremendous shouts of the hilarious multitude, in which her one despairing shriek was lost and drowned!

Would it not be better for him to die at once, and go to wait for her in the blessed regions of semi-barbaric futurity?

And yet, that awful tiger, those shrieks, that blood!

Her decision had been indicated in an instant, but it had been made after days and nights of anguished deliberation. She had known she would be asked, she had decided what she would answer, and, without the slightest hesitation, she had moved her hand to the right.

The question of her decision is one not to be lightly considered, and it is not for me to presume to set myself up as the one person able to answer it. And so I leave it with all of you: Which came out of the opened door—the lady, or the tiger?

Frank Stockton (1834-1902)
American humorist, novelist and storyteller, Frank Stockton first published "The Lady, or the Tiger?" in 1882. The story has appeared in so many collections that it has become a classic of its kind. Variations of the same idea have been written since, but none are better than Stockton's.

"Your father was walking along a
street in Naples when a pig fell on
him. A shocking accident."
Jerome said, "What happened to
the pig?"

a shocking accident

Graham Greene

Jerome was called into his housemaster's room in the break between
the second and the third class on a Thursday morning. He had no
fear of trouble, for he was a warden—the name that the proprietor
and headmaster of a rather expensive preparatory school had
chosen to give to approved, reliable boys in the lower forms (from a
warden one became a guardian and finally before leaving, it was
hoped for Marlborough or Rugby, a crusader). The housemaster, Mr.
Wordsworth, sat behind his desk with an appearance of perplexity
and apprehension. Jerome had the odd impression when he entered
that he was a cause of fear.

"Sit down, Jerome," Mr. Wordsworth said. "All going well with the
trigonometry?"

"Yes, sir."

"I've had a telephone call, Jerome. From your aunt. I'm afraid I have
bad news for you."

"Yes, sir?"

"Your father has had an accident."

"Oh."

Mr. Wordsworth looked at him with some surprise. "A serious accident."

"Yes, sir?"

Jerome worshipped his father: the verb is exact. As man re-creates
God, so Jerome re-created his father—from a restless widowed
author into a mysterious adventurer who travelled in far places—

Nice, Beirut, Majorca, even the Canaries. The time had arrived about his eighth birthday when Jerome believed his father either "ran guns" or was a member of the British Secret Service. Now it occurred to him that his father might have been wounded in "a hail of machine-gun bullets."

Mr. Wordsworth played with the ruler on his desk. He seemed at a loss how to continue. He said, "You knew your father was in Naples?"

"Yes, sir."

"Your aunt heard from the hospital today."

"Oh."

Mr. Wordsworth said with desperation, "It was a street accident."

"Yes, sir?" It seemed quite likely to Jerome that they would call it a street accident. The police, of course, had fired first; his father would not take human life except as a last resort.

"I'm afraid your father was very seriously hurt indeed."

"Oh."

"In fact, Jerome, he died yesterday. Quite without pain."

"Did they shoot him through the heart?"

"I beg your pardon. What did you say, Jerome?"

"Did they shoot him through the heart?"

"Nobody shot him, Jerome. A pig fell on him." An inexplicable convulsion took place in the nerves of Mr. Wordsworth's face; it really looked for a moment as though he were going to laugh. He closed his eyes, composed his features, and said rapidly, as though it were necessary to expel the story as rapidly as possible, "Your father was walking along a street in Naples when a pig fell on him. A shocking accident. Apparently in the poorer quarters of Naples they keep pigs on their balconies. This one was on the fifth floor. It had grown too fat. The balcony broke. The pig fell on your father."

Mr. Wordsworth left his desk rapidly and went to the window, turning his back on Jerome. He shook a little with emotion.

Jerome said, "What happened to the pig?"

This was not callousness on the part of Jerome as it was interpreted by Mr. Wordsworth to his colleagues (he even discussed with them whether, perhaps, Jerome was not yet fitted to be a warden). Jerome was only attempting to visualize the strange scene and to get the details right. Nor was Jerome a boy who cried; he was a boy who brooded, and it never occurred to him at his preparatory school that the circumstances of his father's death were comic—they were still part of the mystery of life. It was later in his first term at his public school, when he told the story to his best friend, that he began to realize how it affected others. Naturally, after that disclosure he was known, rather unreasonably, as Pig.

Unfortunately his aunt had no sense of humour. There was an enlarged snapshot of his father on the piano: a large sad man in an unsuitable dark suit posed in Capri with an umbrella (to guard him against sunstroke), the Faraglioni rocks forming the background. By the age of sixteen Jerome was well aware that the portrait looked more like the author of *Sunshine and Shade* and *Rambles in the Balearics* than an agent of the Secret Service. All the same, he loved the memory of his father: he still possessed an album filled with picture-postcards (the stamps had been soaked off long ago for his other collection), and it pained him when his aunt embarked with strangers on the story of his father's death.

"A shocking accident," she would begin, and the stranger would compose his or her features into the correct shape for interest and commiseration. Both reactions, of course, were false, but it was terrible for Jerome to see how suddenly, midway in her rambling discourse, the interest would become genuine. "I can't think how such things can be allowed in a civilized country," his aunt would say. "I suppose one has to regard Italy as civilized. One is prepared for all kinds of things abroad, of course, and my brother was a great traveller. He always carried a water-filter with him. It was far less expensive, you know, than buying all those bottles of mineral water. My brother always said that his filter paid for his dinner wine. You can see from that what a careful man he was, but who could possibly have expected when he was walking along the Via Dottore Manuele Panucci on his way to the Hydrographic Museum that a pig would fall on him?" That was the moment when the interest became genuine.

Jerome's father had not been a very distinguished writer, but the time always seems to come, after an author's death, when somebody thinks it worth his while to write a letter to *The Times Literary Supplement* announcing the preparation of a biography and asking to

see any letters or documents or receive any anecdotes from friends
of the dead man. Most of the biographies, of course, never appear—
one wonders whether the whole thing may not be an obscure form of
blackmail and whether many a potential writer of a biography or the-
sis finds the means in this way to finish his education at Kansas or
Nottingham. Jerome, however, as a chartered accountant, lived far
from the literary world. He did not realize how small the menace
really was, nor that the danger period for someone of his father's ob-
scurity had long passed. Sometimes he rehearsed the method of re-
counting his father's death so as to reduce the comic element to its
smallest dimensions—it would be of no use to refuse information, for
in that case the biographer would undoubtedly visit his aunt, who
was living to a great old age with no sign of flagging.

It seemed to Jerome that there were two possible methods—the
first led gently up to the accident, so well prepared that the death
came really as an anticlimax. The chief danger of laughter in such a
story was always surprise. When he rehearsed this method Jerome
began boringly enough.

"You know Naples and those high tenement buildings? Somebody
once told me that the Neapolitan always feels at home in New York
just as the man from Turin feels at home in London because the river
runs in much the same way in both cities. Where was I? Oh, yes,
Naples, of course. You'd be surprised in the poorer quarters what
things they keep on the balconies of those skyscraping tenements—
not washing, you know, or bedding, but things like livestock,
chickens or even pigs. Of course the pigs get no exercise whatever
and fatten all the quicker." He could imagine how his hearer's eyes
would have glazed by this time. "I've no idea, have you, how heavy a
pig can be, but those old buildings are all badly in need of repair. A
balcony on the fifth floor gave way under one of those pigs. It struck
the third-floor balcony on its way down and sort of ricocheted into
the street. My father was on the way to the Hydrographic Museum
when the pig hit him. Coming from that height and that angle it
broke his neck." This was really a masterly attempt to make an in-
trinsically interesting subject boring.

The other method Jerome rehearsed had the virtue of brevity.

"My father was killed by a pig."

"Really? In India?"

"No, in Italy."

"How interesting. I never realized there was pig-sticking in Italy. Was your father keen on polo?"

In course of time, neither too early nor too late, rather as though, in his capacity as a chartered accountant, Jerome had studied the statistics and taken the average, he became engaged to be married: to a pleasant fresh-faced girl of twenty-five whose father was a doctor in Pinner. Her name was Sally, her favourite author was still Hugh Walpole, and she had adored babies ever since she had been given a doll at the age of five which moved its eyes and made water. Their relationship was contented rather than exciting, as became the love affair of a chartered accountant; it would never have done if it had interfered with the figures.

One thought worried Jerome, however. Now that within a year he might himself become a father, his love for the dead man increased; he realized what affection had gone into the picture-postcards. He felt a longing to protect his memory, and uncertain whether this quiet love of his would survive if Sally were so insensitive as to laugh when she heard the story of his father's death. Inevitably she would hear it when Jerome brought her to dinner with his aunt. Several times he tried to tell her himself, as she was naturally anxious to know all she could that concerned him.

"You were very small when your father died?"

"Just nine."

"Poor little boy," she said.

"I was at school. They broke the news to me."

"Did you take it very hard?"

"I can't remember."

"You never told me how it happened."

"It was very sudden. A street accident."

"You'll never drive fast, will you Jemmy?" (She had begun to call him "Jemmy.") It was too late then to try the second method—the one he thought of as the pig-sticking one.

They were going to marry quietly at a registry-office and have their honeymoon at Torquay. He avoided taking her to see his aunt until a week before the wedding, but then the night came, and he could not have told himself whether his apprehension was more for his father's memory or the security of his own love.

The moment came all too soon. "Is that Jemmy's father?" Sally asked, picking up the portrait of the man with the umbrella.

"Yes, dear. How did you guess?"

"He has Jemmy's eyes and brow, hasn't he?"

"Has Jerome lent you his books?"

"No."

"I will give you a set for your wedding. He wrote so tenderly about his travels. My own favourite is *Nooks and Crannies*. He would have had a great future. It made that shocking accident all the worse."

"Yes?"

How Jerome longed to leave the room and not see that loved face crinkle with irresistible amusement.

"I had so many letters from his readers after the pig fell on him." She had never been so abrupt before.

And then the miracle happened. Sally did not laugh. Sally sat with open eyes of horror while his aunt told her the story, and at the end, "How horrible," Sally said. "It makes you think, doesn't it? Happening like that. Out of a clear sky."

Jerome's heart sang with joy. It was as though she had appeased his fear forever. In the taxi going home he kissed her with more passion than he had ever shown, and she returned it. There were babies in her pale blue pupils, babies that rolled their eyes and made water.

"A week today," Jerome said, and she squeezed his hand. "Penny for your thoughts, my darling."

"I was wondering," Sally said, "what happened to the poor pig?"

"They almost certainly had it for dinner," Jerome said happily and kissed the dear child again.

Graham Greene (1904-)
Graham Greene is a highly popular and successful British novelist,
known for such novels as The Third Man *and* The Comedians. *He*
has also published three books of exceptional short stories.
"A Shocking Accident" is taken from his most recent collection,
May We Borrow Your Husband?.

folly

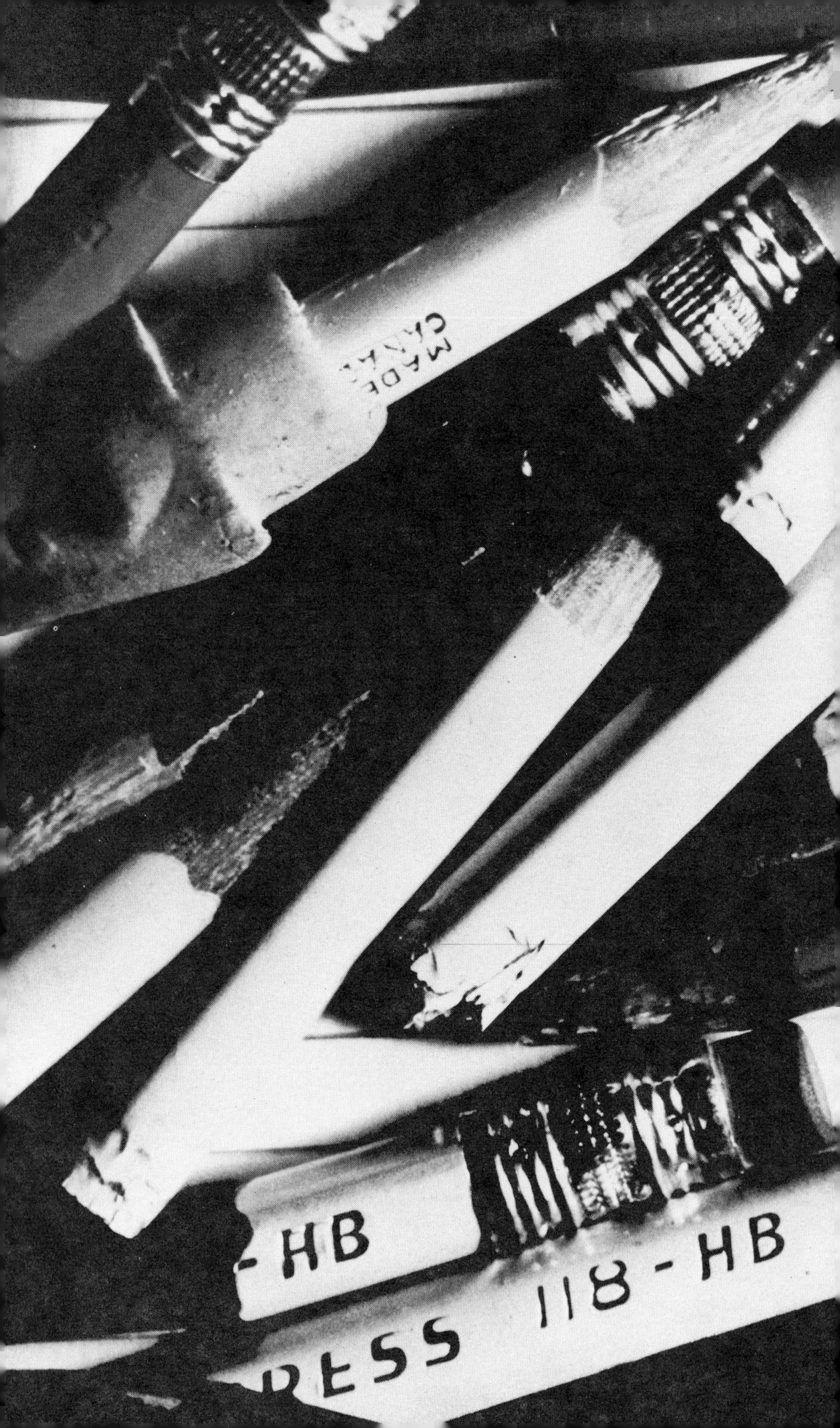

-HB
118-HB

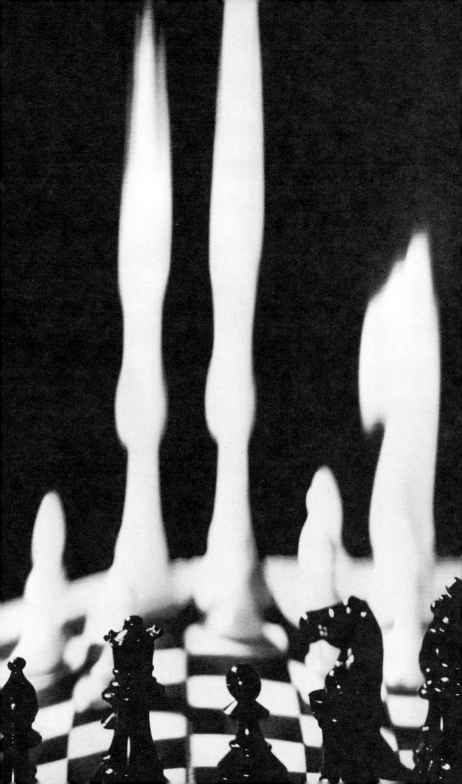

Bartenders, like everyone else, have
their exasperating days. Who can
blame a bartender for getting angry
when he must serve drinks to a
sharp-tongued machine that has
just won five thousand dollars playing chess?

the hour of letdown
E. B. White

When the man came in, carrying the machine, most of us looked up
from our drinks, because we had never seen anything like it before.
The man set the thing down on top of the bar near the beerpulls. It
took up an ungodly amount of room and you could see the bartender
didn't like it any too well, having this big, ugly-looking gadget parked
right there.

"Two rye-and-water," the man said.

The bartender went on puddling an Old-Fashioned that he was
working on, but he was obviously turning over the request in his
mind.

"You want a double?" he asked, after a bit.

"No," said the man. "Two rye-and-water, please." He stared straight
at the bartender, not exactly unfriendly but on the other hand not af-
firmatively friendly.

Many years of catering to the kind of people that come into sa-
loons had provided the bartender with an adjustable mind. Nev-
ertheless, he did not adjust readily to this fellow, and he did not like
the machine—that was sure. He picked up a live cigarette that was
idling on the edge of the cash register, took a drag out of it, and returned it thoughtfully. Then he poured two shots of rye whiskey,
drew two glasses of water, and shoved the drinks in front of the man.
People were watching. When something a little out of the ordinary
takes place at a bar, the sense of it spreads quickly all along the line
and pulls the customers together.

The man gave no sign of being the center of attention. He laid a
five-dollar bill down on the bar. Then he drank one of the ryes and
chased it with water. He picked up the other rye, opened a small vent
in the machine (it was like an oil cup) and poured the whiskey in, and
then poured the water in.

The bartender watched grimly. "Not funny," he said in an even
voice. "And furthermore, your companion takes up too much room.
Why'n you put it over on that bench by the door, make more room
here."

"There's plenty of room for everyone here," replied the man.

"I ain't amused," said the bartender. "Put the damn thing over near
the door like I say. Nobody will touch it."

The man smiled. "You should have seen it this afternoon," he said.
"It was magnificent. Today was the third day of the tournament.
Imagine it—three days of continuous brain-work! And against the
top players in the country, too. Early in the game it gained an advantage; then for two hours it exploited the advantage brilliantly,
ending with the opponent's king backed in a corner. The sudden
capture of a knight, the neutralization of a bishop, and it was all over.
You know how much money it won, all told, in three days of playing
chess?"

"How much?" asked the bartender.

"Five thousand dollars," said the man. "Now it wants to let down,
wants to get a little drunk."

The bartender ran his towel vaguely over some wet spots. "Take it
somewheres else and get it drunk there!" he said firmly. "I got
enough troubles."

The man shook his head and smiled. "No, we like it here." He
pointed at the empty glasses. "Do this again, will you, please?"

The bartender slowly shook his head. He seemed dazed but dog-
ged. "You stow the thing away," he ordered. "I'm not ladling out
whiskey for jokestersmiths."

"'Jokesmiths,'" said the machine. "The word is 'jokesmiths.'"

A few feet down the bar, a customer who was on his third highball
seemed ready to participate in this conversation to which we had all
been listening so attentively. He was a middle-aged man. His necktie
was pulled down away from his collar, and he had eased the collar
by unbuttoning it. He had pretty nearly finished his third drink, and

the alcohol tended to make him throw his support in with the under-
privileged and the thirsty.

"If the machine wants another drink, give it another drink," he said
to the bartender. "Let's not have haggling."

The fellow with the machine turned to his new-found friend and
gravely raised his hand to his temple, giving him a salute of gratitude
and fellowship. He addressed his next remark to him, as though de-
liberately snubbing the bartender.

"You know how it is when you're all fagged out mentally, how you
want a drink?"

"Certainly do," replied the friend. "Most natural thing in the world."

There was a stir all along the bar, some seeming to side with the
bartender, others with the machine group. A tall, gloomy man standing next to me spoke up.

"Another whiskey sour, Bill," he said. "And go easy on the lemon
juice."

"Picric acid," said the machine, sullenly. "They don't use lemon
juice in these places."

"That does it!" said the bartender, smacking his hand on the bar.
"Will you put that thing away or else beat it out of here. I ain't in the
mood, I tell you. I got this saloon to run and I don't want lip from a
mechanical brain or whatever the hell you've got there."

The man ignored this ultimatum. He addressed his friend, whose
glass was now empty.

"It's not just that it's all tuckered out after three days of chess," he
said amiably. "You know another reason it wants a drink?"

"No," said the friend. "Why?"

"It cheated," said the man.

At this remark, the machine chuckled. One of its arms dipped
slightly, and a light glowed in a dial.

The friend frowned. He looked as though his dignity had been
hurt, as though his trust had been misplaced. "Nobody can cheat at
chess," he said. "Simpossible. In chess, everything is open and
above the board. The nature of the game of chess is such that
cheating is impossible."

"That's what I used to think, too," said the man. "But there *is* a way."

"Well, it doesn't surprise me any," put in the bartender. "The first
time I laid my eyes on that crummy thing I spotted it for a crook."

"Two rye-and-water," said the man.

"You can't have the whiskey," said the bartender. He glared at the mechanical brain. "How do I know it ain't drunk already?"

"That's simple. Ask it something," said the man.

The customers shifted and stared into the mirror. We were all in this thing now, up to our necks. We waited. It was the bartender's move.

"Ask it what? Such as?" said the bartender.

"Makes no difference. Pick a couple big figures, ask it to multiply them together. You couldn't multiply big figures together if you were drunk, could you?"

The machine shook slightly, as though making internal preparations.

"Ten thousand eight hundred and sixty-two, multiply it by ninety-nine," said the bartender, viciously. We could tell that he was throwing in the two nines to make it hard.

The machine flickered. One of its tubes spat, and a hand changed position, jerkily.

"One million seventy-five thousand three hundred and thirty-eight," said the machine.

Not a glass was raised all along the bar. People just stared gloomily into the mirror; some of us studied our own faces, others took carom shots at the man and the machine.

Finally, a youngish, mathematically minded customer got out a piece of paper and a pencil and went into retirement. "It works out," he reported, after some minutes of calculating. "You can't say the machine is drunk!"

Everyone now glared at the bartender. Reluctantly he poured two shots of rye, drew two glasses of water. The man drank his drink. Then he fed the machine its drink. The machine's light grew fainter. One of its cranky little arms wilted.

For a while the saloon simmered along like a ship at sea in calm weather. Every one of us seemed to be trying to digest the situation, with the help of liquor. Quite a few glasses were refilled. Most of us sought help in the mirror—the court of last appeal.

The fellow with the unbuttoned collar settled his score. He walked stiffly over and stood between the man and the machine. He put one arm around the man, the other arm around the machine. "Let's get out of here and go to a good place," he said.

The machine glowed slightly. It seemed to be a little drunk now.

"All right," said the man. "That suits me fine. I've got my car outside."

He settled for the drinks and put down a tip. Quietly and a trifle uncertainly he tucked the machine under his arm, and he and his companion of the night walked to the door and out into the street.

The bartender stared fixedly, then resumed his light housekeeping. "So he's got his car outside," he said, with heavy sarcasm. "Now isn't that nice!"

A customer at the end of the bar near the door left his drink, stepped to the window, parted the curtains, and looked out. He watched for a moment, then returned to his place and addressed the bartender. "It's even nicer than you think," he said. "It's a Cadillac. And which one of the three of them d'ya think is doing the driving?"

E.B. White (1899-)
E.B. White is an American writer of many talents. He is a humorist, satirist, critic, editor, and even a writer of delightful children's books such as Charlotte's Web *and* Stuart Little.

"But even after I had looked at them
and lifted them to feel their weight I
had not decided to get drunk; I had
decided to have *a drink*."

The baby-sitter is looking at three
liquor bottles and she has made the
decision to have the first drink of her
life. Would you like to predict the
outcome?

an ounce of cure
Alice Munro

My parents didn't drink. They weren't rabid about it, and in fact I remember that when I signed the pledge in grade seven, with the rest
of that superbly if impermanently indoctrinated class, my mother
said, "It's just nonsense and fanaticism, children of that age." My father would drink a beer on a hot day, but my mother did not join him,
and—whether accidentally or symbolically—this drink was always
consumed *outside* the house. Most of the people we knew were the
same way, in the small town where we lived. I ought not to say that it
was this which got me into difficulties, because the difficulties I got
into were a faithful expression of my own incommodious nature—
the same nature that caused my mother to look at me, on any occasion which traditionally calls for feelings of pride and maternal ac-
complishment (my departure for my first formal dance, I mean, or
my hellbent preparations for a descent on college) with an expression of brooding and fascinated despair, as if she could not possibly expect, did not ask, that it should go with me as it did with other
girls; the dreamed-of spoils of daughters—orchids, nice boys, diamond rings—would be borne home in due course by the daughters

of her friends, but not by me; all she could do was hope for a lesser
rather than a greater disaster—an elopement, say, with a boy who
could never earn his living, rather than an abduction into the White
Slave trade.

But ignorance, my mother said, ignorance, or innocence if you
like, is not always such a fine thing as people think and I am not sure
it may not be dangerous for a girl like you; then she emphasized her
point, as she had a habit of doing, with some quotation which had an
innocent pomposity and odour of mothballs. I didn't even wince at
it, knowing full well how it must have worked wonders with Mr. Berryman.

The evening I baby-sat for the Berrymans must have been in April.
I had been in love all year, or at least since the first week in September, when a boy named Martin Collingwood had given me a surprised, appreciative, and rather ominously complacent smile in the
school assembly. I never knew what surprised him; I was not looking
like anybody but me; I had an old blouse on and my home-perman-
ent had turned out badly. A few weeks after that he took me out
for the first time, and kissed me on the dark side of the porch—also, I
ought to say, on the mouth; I am sure it was the first time anybody
had ever kissed me effectively, and I know that I did not wash my
face that night or the next morning, in order to keep the imprint of
those kisses intact. (I showed the most painful banality in the conduct of this whole affair, as you will see.) Two months, and a few
amatory stages later, he dropped me. He had fallen for the girl who
played opposite him in the Christmas production of *Pride and Pre-
judice*.

I said I was not going to have anything to do with that play, and I
got another girl to work on Makeup in my place, but of course I went
to it after all, and sat down in front with my girl friend Joyce, who
pressed my hand when I was overcome with pain and delight at the
sight of Mr. Darcy in white breeches, silk waistcoat, and sideburns. It
was surely seeing Martin as Darcy that did it for me; every girl is in love
with Darcy anyway, and the part gave Martin an arrogance and male
splendour in my eyes which made it impossible to remember that he
was simply a high-school senior, passably good-looking and of me-
dium intelligence (and with a reputation slightly tainted, at that, by
such preferences as the Drama Club and the Cadet *Band*) who hap-

pened to be the first boy, the first really presentable boy, to take an
interest in me. In the last act they gave him a chance to embrace Eli-
zabeth (Mary Bishop, with a sallow complexion and no figure, but
big vivacious eyes) and during this realistic encounter I dug my nails
bitterly into Joyce's sympathetic palm.

That night was the beginning of months of real, if more or less self-
inflicted, misery for me. Why is it a temptation to refer to this sort of
thing lightly, with irony, with amazement even, at finding oneself involved with such preposterous emotions in the unaccountable past?
That is what we are apt to do, speaking of love; with adolescent love,
of course, it's practically obligatory; you would think we sat around,
dull afternoons, amusing ourselves with these tidbit recollections of
pain. But it really doesn't make me feel very gay—worse still, it
doesn't really surprise me—to remember all the stupid, sad, half-.
ashamed things I did, that people in love always do. I hung around
the places where he might be seen, and then pretended not to see
him; I made absurdly roundabout approaches, in conversation, to
the bitter pleasure of casually mentioning his name. I daydreamed
endlessly; in fact if you want to put it mathematically, I spent perhaps ten times as many hours thinking about Martin Collingwood—
yes, pining and weeping for him—as I ever spent with him; the idea
of him dominated my mind relentlessly and, after a while, against my
will. For if at first I had dramatized my feelings, the time came when I
would have been glad to escape them; my well-worn daydreams had
become depressing and not even temporarily consoling. As I worked
my math problems I would torture myself, quite mechanically and
helplessly, with an exact recollection of Martin kissing my throat. I
had an exact recollection of *everything*. One night I had an impulse
to swallow all the aspirins in the bathroom cabinet, but stopped after
I had taken six.

My mother noticed that something was wrong and got me some iron
pills. She said, "Are you sure everything is going all right at school?"
School! When I told her that Martin and I had broken up all she said
was, "Well so much the better for that. I never saw a boy so stuck on
himself." "Martin has enough conceit to sink a battleship," I said
morosely and went upstairs and cried.

The night I went to the Berrymans was a Saturday night. I baby-sat for them quite often on Saturday nights because they liked to drive over to Baileyville, a much bigger, livelier town about twenty miles away, and perhaps have supper and go to a show. They had been living in our town only two or three years—Mr. Berryman had been brought in as plant manager of the new door-factory—and they remained, I suppose by choice, on the fringes of its society; most of their friends were youngish couples like themselves, born in other places, who lived in new ranch-style houses on a hill outside town where we used to go tobogganing. This Saturday night they had two other couples in for drinks before they all drove over to Baileyville for the opening of a new supper-club; they were all rather festive. I sat in the kitchen and pretended to do Latin. Last night had been the Spring Dance at the High School. I had not gone, since the only boy who had asked me was Millerd Crompton, who asked so many girls that he was suspected of working his way through the whole class alphabetically. But the dance was held in the Armouries, which was only half a block away from our house; I had been able to see the boys in dark suits, the girls in long pale formals under their coats, passing gravely under the street-lights, stepping around the last patches of snow. I could even hear the music and I have not forgotten to this day that they played "Ballerina," and—oh, song of my aching heart—"Slow Boat to China." Joyce had phoned me up this morning and told me in her hushed way (we might have been discussing an incurable disease I had) that yes, M.C. *had* been there with M.B., and she had on a formal that must have been made out of somebody's old lace tablecloth, it just *hung*.

When the Berrymans and their friends had gone I went into the living room and read a magazine. I was mortally depressed. The big softly lit room, with its green and leaf-brown colours, made an uncluttered setting for the development of the emotions, such as you would get on a stage. At home the life of the emotions went on all right, but it always seemed to get buried under the piles of mending to be done, the ironing, the children's jigsaw puzzles and rock collections. It was the sort of house where people were always colliding with one another on the stairs and listening to hockey games and Superman on the radio.

I got up and found the Berrymans' "Danse Macabre" and put it on the record player and turned out the living-room lights. The curtains were only partly drawn. A street light shone obliquely on the windowpane, making a rectangle of thin dusty gold, in which the shadows of bare branches moved, caught in the huge sweet winds of spring. It was a mild black night when the last snow was melting. A year ago all this—the music, the wind and darkness, the shadows of the branches—would have given me tremendous happiness; when they did not do so now, but only called up tediously familiar, somehow humiliatingly personal thoughts, I gave up my soul for dead and walked into the kitchen and decided to get drunk.

No, it was not like that. I walked into the kitchen to look for a coke or something in the refrigerator, and there on the front of the counter were three tall beautiful bottles, all about half full of gold. But even after I had looked at them and lifted them to feel their weight I had not decided to get drunk; I had decided to have a drink.

Now here is where my ignorance, my disastrous innocence, comes in. It is true that I had seen the Berrymans and their friends drinking their highballs as casually as I would drink a coke, but I did not apply this attitude to myself. No; I thought of hard liquor as something to be taken in extremities, and relied upon for extravagant results, one way or another. My approach could not have been less casual if I had been the Little Mermaid drinking the witch's crystal potion. Gravely, with a glance at my set face in the black window above the sink I poured a little whisky from each of the bottles (I think now there were two brands of rye and an expensive Scotch) until I had my glass full. For I had never in my life seen anyone pour a drink and I had no idea that people frequently diluted their liquor with water, soda, et cetera, and I had seen that the glasses the Berrymans' guests were holding when I came through the living room were nearly full.

I drank it off as quickly as possible. I set the glass down and stood looking at my face in the window, half expecting to see it altered. My throat was burning, but I felt nothing else. It was very disappointing, when I had worked myself up to it. But I was not going to let it go at that. I poured another full glass, then filled each of the bottles with water to approximately the level I had seen when I came in. I drank the second glass only a little more slowly than the first. I put the empty glass down on the counter with care, perhaps feeling in my head a rustle of things to come, and went and sat down on a chair in the living room. I reached up and turned on a floor lamp beside the chair, and the room jumped on me.

When I say that I was expecting extravagant results I do not mean that I was expecting this. I had thought of some sweeping emotional change, an upsurge of gaiety and irresponsibility, a feeling of law-lessness and escape, accompanied by a little dizziness and perhaps a tendency to giggle out loud. I did not have in mind the ceiling spin-ning like a great plate somebody had thrown at me, nor the pale green blobs of the chairs swelling, converging, disintegrating, play-ing with me a game full of enormous senseless inanimate malice. My head sank back; I closed my eyes. And at once opened them, opened them wide, threw myself out of the chair and down the hall and reached—thank God, thank God!—the Berrymans' bathroom, where I was sick everywhere, everywhere, and dropped like a stone.

From this point on I have no continuous picture of what happened; my memories of the next hour or two are split into vivid and im-probable segments, with nothing but murk and uncertainty between. I do remember lying on the bathroom floor looking sideways at the little six-sided white tiles, which lay together in such an admirable and logical pattern, seeing them with the brief broken gratitude and sanity of one who has just been torn to pieces with vomiting. Then I remember sitting on the stool in front of the hall phone, asking weakly for Joyce's number. Joyce was not home. I was told by her mother (a rather rattlebrained woman, who didn't seem to notice a thing the matter—for which I felt weakly, mechanically grateful) that she was at Kay Stringer's house. I didn't know Kay's number so I just asked the operator; I felt I couldn't risk looking down at the tele-phone book.

Kay Stringer was not a friend of mine but a new friend of Joyce's. She had a vague reputation for wildness and a long switch of hair, very oddly, though naturally, coloured—from soap-yellow to cara-mel-brown. She knew a lot of boys more exciting than Martin Col-lingwood, boys who had quit school or been imported into town to play on the hockey team. She and Joyce rode around in these boys' cars, and sometimes went with them—having lied of course to their mothers—to the Gay-la dance hall on the highway north of town.

I got Joyce on the phone. She was very keyed-up, as she always was with boys around, and she hardly seemed to hear what I was saying.

"Oh, I can't tonight," she said. "Some kids are here. We're going to play cards. You know Bill Kline? He's here. Ross Armour—"

"I'm *sick*," I said trying to speak distinctly; it came out an inhuman croak. "I'm *drunk*. Joyce!" Then I fell off the stool and the receiver dropped out of my hand and banged for a while dismally against the wall.

I had not told Joyce where I was, so after thinking about it for a moment she phoned my mother, and using the elaborate and unnecessary subterfuge that young girls delight in, she found out. She and Kay and the boys—there were three of them—told some story about where they were going to Kay's mother, and got into the car and drove out. They found me still lying on the broadloom carpet in the hall; I had been sick again, and this time I had not made it to the bathroom.

It turned out that Kay Stringer, who arrived on this scene only by accident, was exactly the person I needed. She loved a crisis, particularly one like this, which had a shady and scandalous aspect and which must be kept secret from the adult world. She became excited, aggressive, efficient; that energy which was termed wildness was simply the overflow of a great female instinct to manage, comfort and control. I could hear her voice coming at me from all directions, telling me not to worry, telling Joyce to find the biggest coffeepot they had and make it full of coffee (*strong* coffee, she said), telling the boys to pick me up and carry me to the sofa. Later, in the fog beyond my reach, she was calling for a scrub-brush.

Then I was lying on the sofa, covered with some kind of crocheted throw they had found in the bedroom. I didn't want to lift my head. The house was full of the smell of coffee. Joyce came in, looking very pale; she said that the Berryman kids had wakened up but she had given them a cookie and told them to go back to bed, it was all right; she hadn't let them out of their room and she didn't believe they'd remember. She said that she and Kay had cleaned up the bathroom and the hall though she was afraid there was still a spot on the rug. The coffee was ready. I didn't understand anything very well. The boys had turned on the radio and were going through the Berrymans' record collection; they had it out on the floor. I felt there was something odd about this but I could not think what it was.

Kay brought me a huge breakfast mug full of coffee.

"I don't know if I can," I said. "Thanks."

"Sit up," she said briskly, as if dealing with drunks was an everyday business for her, I had no need to feel myself important. (I met, and recognized, that tone of voice years later, in the maternity ward.) "Now drink," she said. I drank, and at the same time realized that I was wearing only my slip. Joyce and Kay had taken off my blouse and skirt. They had brushed off the skirt and washed out the blouse, since it was nylon; it was hanging in the bathroom. I pulled the throw up under my arms and Kay laughed. She got everybody coffee. Joyce brought in the coffeepot and on Kay's instructions she kept filling my cup whenever I drank from it. Somebody said to me with interest, "You must have really wanted to tie one on."

"No," I said rather sulkily, obediently drinking my coffee. "I only had two drinks."

Kay laughed, "Well it certainly gets to you, I'll say that. What time do you expect *they*'ll be back?" she said.

"Late, After one I think."

"You should be all right by that time. Have some more coffee."

Kay and one of the boys began dancing to the radio. Kay danced very sexily, but her face had the gently superior and indulgent, rather cold look it had when she was lifting me up to drink the coffee. The boy was whispering to her and she was smiling, shaking her head. Joyce said she was hungry, and she went out to the kitchen to see what there was—potato chips or crackers, or something like that, that you could eat without making too noticeable a dint. Bill Kline came over and sat on the sofa beside me and patted my legs through the crocheted throw. He didn't say anything to me, just patted my legs and looked at me with what seemed to me a very stupid, half-sick, absurd and alarming expression. I felt very uncomfortable; I wondered how it had ever got around that Bill Kline was so good looking, with an expression like that. I moved my legs nervously and he gave me a look of contempt, not ceasing to pat me. Then I scrambled off the sofa, pulling the throw around me, with the idea of going to the bathroom to see if my blouse was dry. I lurched a little when I started to walk, and for some reason—probably to show Bill Kline that he had not panicked me—I immediately exaggerated this, and calling out, "Watch me walk a straight line!" I lurched and stumbled, to the accompaniment of everyone's laughter, towards the hall. I was standing in the archway between the hall and the living room when the knob of the front door turned with a small matter-of-fact click and everything became silent behind me except the radio of course and the crocheted throw inspired by some delicate malice of its own slithered down around my feet and there—oh, delicious moment in a well-organized farce!—there stood the Berrymans, Mr. and Mrs., with expressions on their faces as appropriate to the occasion as any old-fashioned director of farces could wish. They must have been preparing those expressions, of course; they could not have produced them in the first moment of shock; with the noise we were making, they had no doubt heard us as soon as they got out of the car; for the same reason, we had not heard them. I don't think I ever knew what brought them home so early—a headache, an argument —and I was not really in a position to ask.

Mr. Berryman drove me home. I don't remember how I got into that car, or how I found my clothes and put them on, or what kind of a good-night, if any, I said to Mrs. Berryman. I don't remember what happened to my friends, though I imagine they gathered up their coats and fled, covering up the ignominy of their departure with a mechanical roar of defiance. I remember Joyce with a box of crackers in her hand, saying that I had become terribly sick from eating—I think she said *sauerkraut*—for supper, and that I had called them for help. (When I asked her later what they made of this she said,"'It wasn't any use. You *reeked*.") I remember also her saying, "Oh, no, Mr. Berryman I beg of you, my mother is a terribly nervous person I don't know what the shock might do to her. I will go down on my knees to you if you like but *you must not phone my mother*." I have no picture of her down on her knees—and she would have done it in a minute—so it seems this threat was not carried out.

Mr. Berryman said to me, "Well I guess you know your behaviour tonight is a pretty serious thing." He made it sound as if I might be charged with criminal negligence or something worse. "It would be very wrong of me to overlook it," he said. I suppose that besides be-ing angry and disgusted with *me*, he was worried about taking me home in this condition to my strait-laced parents, who could always say I got the liquor in his house. Plenty of Temperance people would think that enough to hold him responsible, and the town was full of Temperance people. Good relations with the town were very important to him from a business point of view.

"I have an idea it wasn't the first time," he said. "If it was the first time, would a girl be smart enough to fill three bottles up with water? No. Well in this case, she *was* smart enough, but not smart enough to know I could spot it. What do you say to that?" I opened my mouth to answer and although I was feeling quite sober the only sound that came out was a loud, desolate-sounding giggle. He stopped in front of our house. "Light's on," he said. "Now go in and tell your parents the straight truth. And if you don't, remember I will." He did not mention paying me for my baby-sitting services of the evening and the subject did not occur to me either.

I went into the house and tried to go straight upstairs but my mother called to me. She came into the front hall, where I had not turned on the light, and she must have smelled me at once for she ran forward with a cry of pure amazement, as if she had seen somebody falling, and caught me by the shoulders as I did indeed fall down against the bannister, overwhelmed by my fantastic lucklessness, and I told her everything from the start, not omitting even the name of Martin Collingwood and my flirtation with the aspirin bottle, which was a mistake.

On Monday morning my mother took the bus over to Baileyville and found the liquor store and bought a bottle of Scotch whisky. Then she had to wait for a bus back, and she met some people she knew and she was not quite able to hide the bottle in her bag; she was furious with herself for not bringing a proper shopping-bag. As soon as she got back she walked out to the Berrymans'; she had not even had lunch. Mr. Berryman had not gone back to the factory. My mother went in and had a talk with both of them and made an excellent impression and then Mr. Berryman drove her home. She talked to them in the forthright and unemotional way she had, which was always agreeably surprising to people prepared to deal with a mother, and she told them that although I seemed to do well enough at school I was extremely backward—or perhaps eccentric—in my emotional development. I imagine that this analysis of my behaviour was especially effective with Mrs. Berryman, a great reader of Child

Guidance books. Relations between them warmed to the point
where my mother brought up a specific instance of my difficulties,
and disarmingly related the whole story of Martin Collingwood.

Within a few days it was all over town and the school that I had
tried to commit suicide over Martin Collingwood. But it was already
all over school and the town that the Berrymans had come home on
Saturday night to find me drunk, staggering, wearing nothing but my
slip, in a room with three boys, one of whom was Bill Kline. My
mother had said that I was to pay for the bottle she had taken the
Berrymans out of my baby-sitting earnings, but my clients melted
away like the last April snow, and it would not be paid for yet if new-
comers to town had not moved in across the street in July, and
needed a baby sitter before they talked to any of their neighbours.

My mother also said that it had been a great mistake to let me go
out with boys and that I would not be going out again until well after
my sixteenth birthday, if then. This did not prove to be a concrete
hardship at all, because it was at least that long before anybody
asked me. If you think that news of the Berrymans adventure would
put me in demand for whatever gambols and orgies were going on in
and around that town, you could not be more mistaken. The ex-
traordinary publicity which attended my first debauch may have
made me seem marked for a special kind of ill luck, like the girl
whose illegitimate baby turns out to be triplets: nobody wants to
have anything to do with her. At any rate I had at the same time one
of the most silent telephones and positively the most sinful reputation in the whole High School. I had to put up with this until the next
fall, when a fat blonde girl in Grade Ten ran away with a married man
and was picked up two months later, living in sin—though not with
the same man—in the city of Sault Ste. Marie. Then everybody forgot
about me.

But there was a positive, a splendidly unexpected, result of this affair: I got completely over Martin Collingwood. It was not only that
he at once said, publicly, that he had always thought I was a nut;
where he was concerned I had no pride, and my tender fancy could
have found a way around that, a month, a week, before. What was it
that brought me back into the world again? It was the terrible and
fascinating reality of my disaster; it was *the way things happened.*
Not that I enjoyed it; I was a self-conscious girl and I suffered a good

deal from all this exposure. But the development of events on that Saturday night—that fascinated me; I felt that I had had a glimpse of the shameless, marvellous, shattering absurdity with which the plots of life, though not of fiction, are improvised. I could not take my eyes off it.

And of course Martin Collingwood wrote his Senior Matric that June, and went away to the city to take a course at a school for Morticians, as I think it is called, and when he came back he went into his uncle's undertaking business. We lived in the same town and we would hear most things that happened to each other but I do not think we met face to face or saw one another, except at a distance, for years. I went to a shower for the girl he married, but then everybody went to everybody else's showers. No, I do not think I really saw him again until I came home after I had been married several years, to attend a relative's funeral. Then I saw him; not quite Mr. Darcy but still very nice-looking in those black clothes. And I saw him looking over at me with an expression as close to a reminiscent smile as the occasion would permit, and I knew that he had been surprised by a memory either of my devotion or my little buried catastrophe. I gave him a gentle uncomprehending look in return. I am a grown-up woman now; let him unbury his own catastrophes.

Alice Munro (1931-)
Alice Munro was awarded the Governor General's Award for fiction in 1968 for her first book, a collection of stories entitled Dance of the Happy Shades. *"An Ounce of Cure" is taken from that collection. Since then, she has published her first novel,* Lives of Girls and Women, *and a second collection of stories,* Something I've Been Meaning To Tell You. *Mrs. Munro lives in London, Ontario.*

It is difficult to maintain your dignity
when you are *persistently followed
by pigs*!

tiresome company

Jacques Ferron

I was new to the practice; with an air of self-importance I sought to hide the misgivings I had concerning my person. One day I was called out to St-Yvon, one of the villages in the parish of Cloridorme, in the county of North Gaspe. It was winter; the sea was a vast field of ice, with, here and there, dark and steaming cracks.

In the older counties where the stay-at-home habitant reigns, jealously guarding his land, the only living things ever to be shared with a neighbour are the birds of the air. At St-Yvon it is not the same; here is felt the influence of the sea, which belongs to each and every man. This makes for a less petty way of life and encourages mutual aid and sociability. For example, cats and dogs are everyone's responsibility, and so, alas, are pigs.

These pigs remain out of doors all winter. This is supposed to smarten them up. Impudent and familiar, they wander around the houses in search of scraps. On sunny days they separate into bands of boars and sows, the better to come together; which they then do with great gusto and not the slightest restraint, like real animals. Should a passer-by appear, they will follow along behind him without waiting to be asked. If there is a heavy snowfall, it is they who trace paths in the fresh snow. Such are the pigs of St-Yvon, producers of bacon for all that, like their cousins in the older counties, and squealing their displeasure every bit as loudly when the hour for delivery comes.

I was summoned then to this village. I arrived. The mailman's
snowmobile continued towards Gaspe. I went into the store to make
enquiries about my patient. "Come over here," said the storekeeper;
and from the window he pointed out the house, to the east of the
bay, beside the shore, where the patient was waiting for me. Thus informed, I returned to the counter where I had placed my bag before
going to the window. It was a fine bag, black and shiny, its ears
pricked up. A mere glance would have told you it was new! "By
Jove," said the storekeeper, "fine *portuna* you have there, doctor!" I
was disconcerted: why had he called my bag that? Was he trying to
make fun of me? With a rather inane grin I thanked him, wished him
good day, and at last reached the door, glad indeed to be out of the
store. Then, somewhat heartened by the fresh air, I set off, with my
portuna under my arm, along the path of the trail-blazing pigs.

I soon noticed that my person was arousing some interest; curtains would be drawn discreetly aside in order to watch me pass, or I
would be stared at shamelessly through the glass. This curiosity was
in a sense justified: was I not new to the place? In order to create a
favourable impression I walked slowly, with all the dignity I could
muster. And for a time all went well. Then I heard a grunt. I glanced
behind me and saw the animal. At first I asked myself, amused:
"What on earth can have possessed this pig to follow me?"

My amusement was, alas! short-lived. I remembered that dark,
somewhat truffled corner of my mind, which at the time I felt I was
the only person to possess. Not for the world would I have admitted
it was there. And now, just when I was endeavouring, with the bearing of a funeral horse, to be worthy of my noble profession, this hor-
rid animal, with its infallible snout, was uncovering that secret corner
for an entire village to behold. What to do in such circumstances?
"The best thing," I said to myself, "is to pay no attention." So I kept
on going, but I was not happy. The pig stayed right behind me. I
could hear it grunting at regular intervals. Soon it seemed to me that
these intervals were becoming shorter, and that the grunting noises
were not at all alike. What could this mean? To satisfy my curiosity, I
glanced once more over my shoulder: the *portuna* almost fell from
my grasp: there were four of them! One was bad enough, but four! It
was more than my pride could take. And I very nearly lost my head,
turned on those cursed pigs and booted them in the snout. My sense

of dignity prevailed. Besides, I was not yet ready to admit defeat. "If I stop," I said to myself, "perhaps they will pass me. Then all I will have to do is not follow them."

So I stepped to the side of the path; I lit a cigarette. The pigs had nothing to smoke, but they too stopped, and there was no indication that they might be persuaded to take the lead. So I moved on in the hope that they would remain fixed to the spot; they started off again immediately. My only hope now was to quicken my pace, forcing them to abandon the pursuit. My efforts were in vain. They would not leave me; they trotted along behind me, grunting joyfully. There was nothing else I could do. I was disgraced for ever more. The houses crowded in on me as I passed; the whole village was afforded the spectacle of a doctor of medicine being followed by four pigs.

I had the courage to continue. Besides, I was now approaching my patient's house. I knocked. The door was opened. I was prepared for the worst, prepared, for example, to hear them say: "By all means, doctor, feel free to bring your friends in."

I was received with the utmost courtesy. The pigs remained outside.

Jacques Ferron (1921-)
Jacques Ferron, a Montreal doctor and author, has written novels, plays, stories and tales, and many controversial newspaper articles about the struggle for Quebec independence. In 1962 he was awarded the Governor General's prize for literature.

"Why not take that nice Wanda
Hickey?"—"Aw, come on, Ma. This is
the prom. This is important. You
don't take Wanda Hickey to the
prom."

wanda hickey's night
of golden memories

Jean Shepherd

"Puberty rites in the more primitive tribal societies are almost in-
variably painful and traumatic experiences."

I half dozed in front of my TV set as the speaker droned on in his
high, nasal voice. One night a week, as a form of masochistic self-
discipline, I sentence myself to a minimum of three hours viewing
educational television. Like so many other things in life, educational
TV is a great idea but a miserable reality: murky films of home life in
Kurdistan, jowly English authors being interviewed by jowly English
literary critics, pinched-faced ladies demonstrating Japanese brush
techniques. But I watch all of it religiously—I suppose because it is
there, like Mount Everest.

"A classic example is the Ugga Buggah tribe of lower Micronesia,"
the speaker continued, tapping a pointer on the map behind him.

A shot of an Ugga Buggah teenager appeared on the screen,
eyes rolling in misery, face bathed in sweat. I leaned forward. His expression was strangely familiar.

"When an Ugga Buggah reaches puberty, the rites are rigorous and
unvarying for both sexes. Difficult dances are performed and the
candidate for adulthood must eat a sickening ritual meal during the
post-dance banquet. You will also notice that his costume is as uncomfortable as it is decorative."

Again the Ugga Buggah appeared, clothed in a garment that

seemed to be made of feathers and chain mail, the top grasping his Adam's apple like an iron clamp, his tongue lolling out in pain.

"The adults attend these tribal rituals only as chaperones and observers, and look upon the ceremony with indulgence. Here we see the ritual dance in progress."

A heavy rumble of drums; then a moiling herd of sweating feather-clad dancers of both sexes appeared on screen amid a great cloud of dust.

"Of course, we in more sophisticated societies no longer observe these rites."

Somehow, the scene was too painful for me to continue watching. Something dark and lurking had been awakened in my breast.

"What the hell do you mean we don't observe puberty rites?" I mumbled rhetorically as I got up and switched off the set. Reaching up to the top bookshelf, I took down a leatherette-covered volume. It was my high school class yearbook. I leafed through the pages of photographs: beaming biology teachers, pimply-faced students, lantern-jawed football coaches. Suddenly, there it was—a sharply etched photographic record of a true puberty rite among the primitive tribes of northern Indiana.

The caption read: "The Junior Prom was heartily enjoyed by one and all. The annual event was held this year at the Cherrywood Country Club. Mickey Iseley and his Magic Music Makers provided the romantic rhythms. All agreed that it was an unforgettable evening, the memory of which we will all cherish in the years to come."

True enough. In the gathering gloom of my Manhattan apartment, it all came back.

"You going to the prom?" asked Schwartz, as we chewed on our salami sandwiches under the stands of the football field, where we preferred for some reason to take lunch at that period of our lives.

"Yep, I guess so," I answered as coolly as I could.

"Who ya takin'?" Flick joined the discussion, sucking at a bottle of Nehi orange.

"I don't know. I was thinking of Daphne Bigelow." I had dropped the name of the most spectacular girl in the entire high school, if not in the state of Indiana itself.

"No kidding!" Schwartz reacted in a tone of proper awe and respect, tinged with disbelief.

"Yep. I figure I'd give her a break."

Flick snorted, the gassy orange pop going down the wrong pipe. He coughed and wheezed brokenly for several moments.

I had once dated Daphne Bigelow and, although the occasion, as faithful readers will recall, was not a riotous success, I felt that I was still in the running. Several occasions in the past month had led me to believe that I was making a comeback with Daphne. Twice she had distinctly acknowledged my presence in the halls between classes, once actually speaking to me.

"Oh, hi there, Fred," she had said in that musical voice.

"Uh . . . hi, Daph," I had replied wittily. The fact that my name is not Fred is neither here nor there; she had *spoken* to me. She had remembered my face from somewhere.

"Ya gotta go formal," said Schwartz. "I read on the bulletin board where it said ya gotta wear a summer formal to the prom."

"No kiddin'?" Flick had finished off the orange and was now fully with us. "What's a summer formal?"

"That's where you wear one of those white coats," I explained. I was known as the resident expert in our group on all forms of high life. This was because my mother was a fanatical Fred Astaire fan.

"Ya gotta rent 'em," I said with the finality of an expert.

Two weeks later, each one of us received a prim white envelope containing an engraved invitation.

The Junior Class is proud to invite you to the Junior Prom, to be held at the Cherrywood Country Club beginning eight P.M. June fifth. Dance to the music of Mickey Iseley and his Magic Music Makers.

Summer formal required.

The Committee

It was the first engraved invitation I had ever received. The puberty rites had begun. That night around the supper table, the talk was of nothing else.

"Who ya gonna take?" my old man asked, getting right to the heart of the matter. Who you were taking to the prom was considered a highly significant decision, possibly affecting your whole life, which, in some tragic cases, it did.

"Oh, I don't know. I was thinking of a couple of girls." I replied in an

offhand manner, as though this slight detail didn't concern me at all.
My kid brother, who was taking all this in with sardonic interest,
sneered derisively and went back to shoveling in his red cabbage. He
had not yet discovered girls. My mother paused while slicing the
meat loaf.

"Why not take that nice Wanda Hickey?"

"Aw, come on, Ma. This is the prom. This is important. You don't
take Wanda Hickey to the *prom*."

Wanda Hickey was the only girl who I knew for an absolute fact
liked me. Ever since we had been in third grade, Wanda had been
hanging around the outskirts of my social circle. She laughed at my
jokes and once, when we were 12, actually sent me a valentine. She
was always loitering around the tennis courts, the ball diamonds, the
alleys where on long summer nights we played kick the can or
siphoned gas to keep Flick's Chevy running. In fact, there were times
when I couldn't shake her.

"Nah, I haven't decided who I'm gonna take. I was kind of thinking
of Daphne Bigelow."

The old man set his bottle of Pabst Blue Ribbon down carefully on
the table. Daphne Bigelow was the daughter of one of the larger men
in town. There was, in truth, a street named after her family.

"You're a real glutton for punishment, ain't cha?" The old man
flicked a spot of foam off the table. He was referring to that unforgettable evening I had once spent with Daphne in my callow
youth. "Oh, well, you might as well learn your lesson once and for
all."

He was in one of his philosophical moods. The White Sox had
dropped nine straight, and a losing streak like that usually brought
out his fatalistic side. He leaned back in his chair, blew some smoke
toward the ceiling and went on: "Yep. Too many guys settle for the
first skirt that shows up. And regret it the rest of their lives."

Ignoring the innuendo, my mother set the mashed potatoes down
on the table and said, "Well, I think Wanda is a very nice girl. But
then, what I think doesn't matter."

My mother had the practiced turn of phrase of the veteran martyr,
whose role in life is to suffer as publicly as possible.

"I gotta rent a summer formal," I announced.

"You gonna wear one a' them monkey suits?" the old man chuckled.

He had never, to my knowledge, worn anything more formal than a sports jacket in his entire life.

"I'm going down to that place on Hohman Avenue tomorrow with Schwartz and see about it."

"Oh, boy! La-di-da," said my kid brother with characteristically eloquent understatement. Like father, like son.

The next day, after school, Schwartz and I went downtown to a place we both had passed countless times in our daily meanderings. Hanging out over the street was the cutout of a tall, cream-faced man dressed to the nines in high silk hat, stiff starched shirt, swallow-tailed coat, striped morning trousers and an ivory-headed walking stick held with an easy grace by his dove-gray gloved hand. In red, sputtering neon underneath: AL'S SWANK FORMALWEAR. RENTED BY THE DAY OR HOUR. FREE FITTINGS.

We climbed the narrow, dark wooden steps to the second floor. Within a red arrow painted on the wall were the words SWANK FORMAL—TURN LEFT.

We went past a couple of dentists' offices and a door marked BAIL BONDSMAN—FREEDOM FOR *YOU* DAY OR NIGHT.

"I wonder if Fred Astaire ever comes here," Schwartz said.

"Oh, come on, Schwartz. This is serious!" I could feel excitement rising deep inside me. The prom, the engraved invitation, the summer formal; it was all starting to come together.

Al's Swank Formalwear turned out to be a small room with a yellow light bulb hanging from the ceiling, a couple of tall glass cases containing suits on hangers, a counter and a couple of smudgy full-length mirrors. Schwartz opened negotiations with a swarthy, bald, hawk-eyed, shirt-sleeved man behind the counter. Around his neck hung a yellow measuring tape. He wore a worn vest with a half-dozen chalk pencils sticking out of the pocket.

"Uh . . . we'd like to . . . uh . . ." Schwartz began confidently.

"OK, boys. Ya wanna make it big at the prom, am I right? Ya come to the right place. Ya goin' to that hop out at Cherrywood, right?"

"Uh . . . yeah," I replied.

"And ya wanna summah fawmal, right?"

"HEY, MORTY!" he shouted out. "HERE'S TWO MORE FOR THAT BASH AT CHERRYWOOD. I'D SAY ONE THIRTY-SIX SHAWT, ONE FAWTY REGULAH." His practiced eye had immediately sized us correctly.

"COMIN' UP!" Morty's voice echoed from the bowels of the establishment.

Humming to himself, Al began to pile and unpile boxes like we
weren't even there. I looked around the room at the posters of various smartly turned out men of the world. One in particular, wearing a
summer formal, had a striking resemblance to Cesar Romero, his
distinguished gray sideburns and bronze face contrasting nicely
with the snowy whiteness of his jacket.

There was another picture, of Tony Martin, who was at that time at
the peak of his movie career, usually portraying Arab princes who
disguised themselves as beggars in order to make the scene at the
market place. He was always falling in love with a slave girl who
turned out to be a princess in disguise, played by somebody like
Paulette Goddard. Tony's roguish grin, somewhat flyspecked,
showed that he was about to break into *Desert Song*.

Schwartz was busily inspecting a collection of bow ties displayed
under glass in one of the showcases.

"OK ON THE THIRTY-SIX SHAWT, AL, BUT I'M OUTA
FAWTIES. HOW 'BOUT THAT FAWTY-TWO REGULAH THAT
JUST CAME BACK FROM THAT DAGO WEDDING?" shouted
Morty from the back room.

"CUT THE TALK AN' BRING THE GOODS!" Al shouted back,
straightening up, his face flushed.

"THE FAWTY-TWO AIN'T BEEN CLEANED YET!" came from
the back room.

"BRING IT OUT, AWREADY!" barked Al. He turned to me.

"This suit just come in from anothah job. Don't worry about how it
looks. We'll clean it up an' take it in so's it'll fit good."

Morty emerged, a tall, thin, sad man in a gray smock, even balder
than Al. He carried two suits on hangers, draped them over the counter, gave Al a dirty look and stalked back into the shadows.

"OK now, boys. First you." Al nodded to Schwartz. "Take this and
try it on behind the curtain. It should fit good. It's maybe a little long
at the cuffs, but we'll take 'em up."

Schwartz grabbed the hanger and scurried behind the green curtain. Al held up the other suit. In the middle of a dark reddish-brown
stain that covered the entire breast pocket was a neat little hole right

through the jacket. Al turned the hanger around and stuck his finger through the hole.

"HEY, MORTY!" he shouted.

"WHAT NOW?"

"HOW 'BOUT THIS HOLE INNA FAWTY-TWO? CAN YA FIX IT?"

"WADDAYA WANT, MIRACLES?"

"Don't worry, kid. We can fix this up good as new. You'll never tell it ain't a new coat."

Schwartz emerged from the fitting room shrouded in what looked like a parachute with sleeves.

"Perfick! Couldn' be bettuh!" shouted Al exultantly, darting from behind the counter. He grabbed Schwartz by the shoulders, spun him around and, with a single movement, ran his hand up into Schwartz' crotch, measured the inseam, spun him around again, made two chalk marks on the sleeves—which came almost to his fin-ger tips—yanked up the collar, punched him smartly in the kidney, all the while murmuring in a hoarse stage whisper:

"It's made for you. Just perfick. Couldn' be bettuh. Perfick. Like tailor-made."

Schwartz smiled weakly throughout the ordeal.

"OK, kid, take it off. I'll have it ready for you next week." Obediently, Schwartz disappeared into the fitting room. Al turned to me. "Here, slip on this coat." He held it out invitingly. I plunged my arms into its voluminous folds. I felt his iron grip on my shoulder blades as he yanked me upward and spun me around, his appraising eye darting everywhere.

"Just perfick. Couldn' be bettuh. Fits like a glove. Take it in a little here; pull in the bias here. . . ."

He took out his chalk and made a few marks on my back.

"OK, Slip outa it."

Al again thrust his finger through the hole.

"Reweave it like new. An' doan worry 'bout the stain; we'll get it out. Musta been some party. Here, try on these pants."

He tossed a pair of midnight-blue trousers over the counter at me. Inside the hot little cubicle, as I changed into the pants, I stroked the broad black-velvet stripe that lined the outer seam. I was really in the big time now. They were rumpled, of course, and they smelled strongly of some spilled beverage, but they were truly magnificent. The waist came to just a shade below my armpits. Tossing the curtain aside, I sashayed out like Cary Grant.

"Stand up straight, kid," Al breathed into my ear. An aromatic blast of pastrami and pickled herring made my head reel.

"Ah. Perfick. Just right. Put a little tuck in the waist, so." He grabbed several yards of the seat. "An' a little in here." A sudden thrill of pain as he violently measured the inseam. Then it was all over.

"Now, he said, back behind his counter once again, "how do ya see the shirts? Ya want 'em straight or ruffled? Or pleated, maybe? Very smart." He indicated several shirts on display in his grimy glass case. "I would recommend our Monte Carlo model, a real spiffy numbah."

We both peered down at the shirts. The Monte Carlo number was, indeed, spiffy, its high, stiff, V-cut collar arching over cascading ribbons of razor-sharp pleats.

"Boy, now that's a shirt!" Schwartz breathed excitedly.

"That's what *I* want," I said aloud. No other shirt would do.

"Me, too," Schwartz seconded.

"Fifteen neck, thirty-three sleeve for you, sonny?" he asked Schwartz.

"Uh, yeah," said Schwartz with knitted brow. "But how did you—"

"And fifteen and a half, thirty-four for you, right?"

I nodded, wondering why he bothered to wear a tape measure around his neck.

"OK now," Al continued briskly, "how 'bout studs? Ya got 'em?"

"Uh . . . what?"

He had caught me off guard. I had heard the word "stud" before, but never in a tailor shop.

"OK, I guess not. I'll throw 'em in. Maybe even some matchin' cuff links, too, because you're such high-class customers. Now. I suppose ya wanna go first-class, right?"

Al directed this question at both of us, his face assuming a look of concerned forthrightness.

"Right?" he repeated.

"Yeah." Schwartz answered uncertainly for both of us.

"I knew that the minute you two walked in. Now, I'm gonna show you somepin that is exclusive with Al's Swank Formalwear."

With an air of surreptitious mystery he bent over, slid open a drawer and placed atop the counter an object that unfocused my eyes with its sheer kaleidoscopic brilliance.

"No place else in town can supply you with a genuwine Hollywood paisley cummabund. It's our trademark."

I stared at the magnificent band of glowing, scintillating fabric, already seeing myself a total smash on the dance floor.

"It's only a buck extra. And worth five times the price. Adolphe Menjou always wears this model. How 'bout it, men?"

We both agreed in unison. After all, you only live once.

"Of course, included for only half a dolla more is our fawmal bow tie and matchin' booteneer. I would suggest the maroon."

"Sounds great," I answered.

"Isn't that everything?" asked Schwartz with some concern.

"Is that all! You gotta be kiddin', sonny. How do you expect to trip the light fantastic widout a pair a black patent-leathah dancin' pumps?"

"Dancin' what?" I asked.

"Shoes, shoes," he explained irritably. "An' we throw in the socks for nuttin'. How 'bout it?"

"Well, uh . . ."

"Fine! So that's it, boys I'll have everything all ready the day before the prom. You'll really knock 'em dead."

"As we left, another loud argument broke out between Morty and Al. Their voices accompanied us down the long flight of narrow stairs and out into the street.

Step by step, in the ancient tradition, the tribal ritual was being acted out. The prom, which was now two weeks off, began to occupy our minds most of the waking day. The semester had just about played itself out; our junior year was almost over. The trees and flowers were in blossom, great white clouds drifted across deep-blue skies and baseball practice was in full swing—but somehow, this spring was different from the rest. The prom was something that we had heard about since our earliest days. A kind of golden aura hung over the word itself. Every couple of days, the bulletin board at school announced that the prom committee was meeting or requesting something.

There was only one thing wrong. As each day ticked inexorably by toward that magic night at the Cherrywood Country Club, I still

could not steel myself to actually seek out Daphne Bigelow and ask
her the fatal question. Time and again, I spotted her in the halls,
drifting by on gossamer wings, her radiant complexion casting a
glow on all those around her, her dazzling smile lighting up the corners of the world. But each time, I broke into a fevered sweat and
chickened out at the last instant.

The weekend before the prom was sheer torture. Schwartz, always
efficient and methodical, had already made all his plans. We sat on
the steps of my back porch late Sunday afternoon, watching Lud
Kissel next door struggle vainly to adjust the idling speed on his
time-ravaged carburetor so that the family Nash didn't stall at 35
miles an hour. He had been drinking, of course, so it was quite a
show.

"How ya doin' with Daphne Bigelow?" asked Schwartz sardonically, knowing full well the answer.

"Oh, that. I haven't had time to ask her," I lied.

"Ya better get on the stick. There's only a week left."

"Who *you* got lined up?" I asked, tossing a pebble at old Lud, who
was now asleep under his running board.

"Clara Mae Mattingly." Schwartz replied in a steady, expressionless
voice.

I was surprised. Clara Mae was one of those shadowy, quiet girls
who rarely were mentioned outside of honor rolls and stuff like that.
She wore goldrimmed glasses and still had pigtails.

"Yep," Schwartz added smugly, gratified by my reaction.

"Boy, she sure can spell." It was all I could think of to say that was
good about her, other than the fact that she was female.

"Sure can," Schwartz agreed. He, too, had been quite a speller in
our grade school days; and on more than one occasion, Clara Mae
had demolished him with a brilliant display of virtuosity in a school-
wide spelldown, a form of verbal Indian wrestling now almost extinct
but which at one time was a Waterloo for many of us among the un-
lettered. Clara Mae had actually once gone to the state final and had
lost out to a gangly farm girl from downstate who apparently had
nothing else to do down there but read *Webster's* through the long
winter nights.

"You gonna send her a corsage?" I asked.

"Already ordered it. At the Cupid Florist." Schwartz' self-satisfaction was overflowing.

"An orchid?"

"Yep. Cost eight bucks."

"Holy God! Eight bucks!" I was truly impressed.

"That includes a gold pin for it."

Our conversation trailed off as Lud Kissel rolled out from under the running board, rose heavily to his knees and crawled off down the driveway on all fours, heading for the Bluebird Tavern, which was closed on Sundays. Lud always got restless in the spring.

A few hours later, after supper, I went out gloomily to water the lawn, a job that purportedly went toward earning my allowance, which had reached an all-time high that spring of three dollars a week. Fireflies played about the cottonwoods in the hazy twilight, but I was troubled. One week to go; less, now, because you couldn't count the day of the prom itself. In the drawer where I kept my socks and scout knife, buried deep in the back, were 24 one-dollar bills, which I had saved for the prom. Just as deep in my cowardly soul, I knew I could never ask Daphne Bigelow to be my date.

Refusing to admit it to myself, I whistled moodily as I sprayed the irises and watched a couple of low-flying bats as they skimmed over the lawn and up into the poplars. Mrs. Kissel, next door, creaked back and forth on her porch swing, a copy of *True Romance* open in her lap, as she waited for Lud's return with his usual snootful. My kid brother came out onto the porch and, from sheer habit, I quickly shot a stream of water over him, catching him in mid-air as he leaped high to avoid the stream. It was a superbly executed shot. I had led him just right. He caught it full in the chest, his yellow polo shirt clinging to his ribs wetly, like a second skin. Bawling at the top of his lungs, he disappeared into the house and slammed the screen door behind him. Ordinarily, this small triumph would have cheered me up for hours; but tonight, I tasted nothing but ashes. Suddenly, his face reappeared in the doorway.

"I'M GONNA TELL MA!" he yelled.

Instantly, like a cobra, I struck. Sweeping the stream quickly over the screen door, I got him again. Another scream of rage and he was gone. Again, I sank into my moody sea of reflection. Was I going to boot the prom?

Flick had asked Janie Hutchinson, a tall, funny girl who had been

in our class since kindergarten. And Schwartz was lined up with
Clara Mae; all he had talked about had been that crummy orchid and
how good a dancer he was. Flick had stopped asking me about
Daphne ever since the past Wednesday, when I had gotten mad because he'd been needling me. All week, I had been cleaning up my
Ford for the big night. If there was one thing in my life that went all
the way, my only true and total love, it was my Ford V8, a convertible
that I had personally rebuilt at least 35 times. I knew every valve
spring personally, had honed each valve, burnished every nut and
bolt she carried. Tuesday, I had Simonized her completely; Wednesday, I had repeated the job; and Thursday I had polished the chrome
until my knuckles ached and my back was stiff. I had spent the past
two days minutely cleaning the interior, using a full can of saddle
soap on the worn leather. Everything was set to go, except for one
thing—no girl.

A feeling of helpless rage settled over me as I continued spraying
the lawn. I flushed out a poor, hapless caterpillar from under a bush,
squirting him mercilessly full blast until he washed down the sidewalk and disappeared into the weeds. I felt a twinge of evil satisfaction as he rolled over and over helplessly. It was getting dark. All
that was left of the sun was a long purple-orange streak along the
western horizon. The glow of the steel mills to the north and east began to light up the twilight sky. I had worked my way down to the
edge of our weedy, pock-marked bed of sod when, out of the corner
of my eye, I noticed something white approaching out of the gloom. I
sprinkled on, not knowing that another piece was being fitted into
the intricate mosaic of adolescence. I kicked absent-mindedly at a
passing toad as I soaked down the dandelions.

"What are you doing?"

So deeply was I involved in self-pity that at first my mind wouldn't
focus. Startled, I swung my hose around, spraying the white figure
on the sidewalk ten feet away.

"I'm sorry!" I blurted out, seeing at once that I had washed down a
girl dressed in white tennis clothes.

"Oh, hi, Wanda. I didn't see you there."

She dried herself with a Kleenex.

"What are you doing?" she asked again.

"I'm sprinkling the lawn." The toad hopped past, going the other way now. I squirted him briefly, out of general principles.

"You been playing tennis?" Since she was wearing tennis clothes and was carrying a racket, it seemed the right thing to say.

"Me and Eileen Akers were playing. Down at the park," she answered.

Eileen Akers was a sharp-faced, bespectacled girl I had, inexplicably, been briefly in love with in the third grade. I had come to my senses by the time we got into 4-B. It was a narrow escape. By then, I had begun to dimly perceive that there was more to women than being able to play a good game of run sheep run.

"I'm sure glad school's almost over," she went on, when I couldn't think of anything to say. "I can hardly wait. I never thought I'd be a senior."

"Yeah," I said.

"I'm going to camp this summer. Are you?"

"Yeah," I lied. I had a job already lined up for the summer, working for a surveyor. The next camp I would see would be in the Ozarks, and I'd be carrying an M-1.

Wanda swung her tennis racket at a June bug that flapped by barely above stall speed. She missed. The bug soared angrily up and whirred off into the darkness.

"Are you going to college when you graduate next year?" she asked. For some reason, I didn't like the drift of the conversation.

"Yeah, I guess so, if I don't get drafted."

"My brother's in the Army. He's in the artillery." Her brother, Bud Hickey, was a tall, laconic type four or five years older than both of us.

"Yeah, I heard. Does he like it?"

"Well, he doesn't write much," she said. "But he's gonna get a pass next September, before he goes overseas."

"How come he's in the artillery?" I asked.

"I don't know. They just put him there. I guess because he's tall."

"What's that gotta do with it? Do they have to *throw* the shells, or something?"

"I don't know. They just did it."

Then it happened. Without thinking, without even a shadow of a suspicion of planning. I heard myself asking: "You going to the prom?"

For a long instant she said nothing, just swung her tennis racket at the air.

"I guess so," she finally answered, weakly.

"It's gonna be great," I said, trying to change the subject.

"Uh . . . who are you going with?" She said it as if she really didn't care one way or the other.

"Well, I haven't exactly made up my mind yet." I bent down unconcernedly and pulled a giant milkweed out by the roots.

"Neither have I," she said.

It was then that I realized there was no sense fighting it. Some guys are born to dance forever with the Daphne Bigelows on shining ballroom floors under endless starry skies. Others—well, they do the best they can. I didn't know that yet, but I was beginning to suspect something.

"Wanda?"

"Yes?"

"Wanda. Would you . . . well . . . I mean . . . would you, you see, I was thinking. . . ."

"Yes?"

Here I go, in over the horns: "Wanda, uh . . . how about . . . going to the prom with me?"

She stopped twitching her tennis racket. The crickets cheeped, the spring air was filled with the sound of singing froglets. A soft breeze carried with it the promise of a rich summer and the vibrant aromas of a nearby refinery.

She began softly, "Of course, I've had a lot of invitations, but I didn't say yes to any of them yet. I guess it would be fun to go with you," she ended lamely.

"Yeah, well, naturally, I've had four or five girls who wanted to go with me, but I figured that they were mostly jerks, anyway, and . . . ah . . . I meant to ask you all along."

The die was cast. There was no turning back. It was an ironclad rule. Once a girl was asked to the prom, only a total bounder would even consider ducking out of it. There had been one or two cases in the past, but the perpetrators had become social pariahs, driven from the tribe to fend for themselves in the unfriendly woods. Later that night, hunched over the kitchen table, still somewhat numbed by the unexpected turn of events, I chewed thoughtfully on a peanut-butter-and-jelly sandwich while my mother, hanging over the sink in her rump-sprung Chinese-red chenille bathrobe, droned on monotonously: "You're just going to *have* to stop squirting Randy."

"Yeah," I answered, my mind three light-years away.

"You got his new Flash Gordon T-shirt all wet."

"Sorry," I said automatically. It was a phrase I used often in those days.

"It shrunk. And now he can't wear it."

"Why not?" I asked.

"It comes up around his chest now."

"Well, why can't he stretch it?"

"You just stop squirting him, that's all. You hear me?"

"It's a silly T-shirt, anyway," I said truculently.

"You heard what I said. No more squirting." That ended the conversation.

Later, in bed, I thought briefly of Daphne Bigelow, but was interrupted by a voice from the bed on the other side of the room.

"You rotten crumb. You squirted my T-shirt!"

"Ah, shaddup."

"You wait. I'm gonna get you!"

I laughed raucously. My kid brother wailed in rage.

"SHUT UP, YOU TWO! CUT OUT THE FIGHTING OR I'LL COME IN THERE AND DO SOME HEAD KNOCKING!"

The old man meant what he said and we knew it. I promptly fell asleep. It had been a long and tumultuous day.

I broke the news to Schwartz the next morning, after biology. We were hurrying through the halls between classes on our way to our lockers, which were side by side on the second floor.

"Hey, Schwartz, how about double-dating for the prom?" I asked. I knew he had no car and I needed moral support, anyway.

"Great! I'll help you clean up the car."

"I've already Simonized her. She's all set."

"Are you gonna send Daphne an orchid, or what?"

"Well, no . . ." I said, hoping he'd forget what he asked.

"What do you mean? Ya gotta send a corsage."

"Well, I *am* going to send a corsage."

"I thought you said you weren't."

"I never said I wasn't gonna send a corsage."

"Are you nuts? You just said you weren't gonna."

"I'm not gonna send a corsage to Daphne Bigelow. You asked me if I was gonna send a corsage to Daphne, and I'm not."

"She's gonna think you're a real cheap skate."

It was getting ridiculous. Schwartz was being even more of a numskull than usual.

"Schwartz, I have decided not to ask Daphne Bigelow to the prom."

He looked directly at me, which caused him to slam into two strolling freshman girls. Their books slid across the foor, where they were trampled underfoot by the thundering mob.

"Well, who *are* you taking?" he asked, oblivious to their shrieks of dismay.

"Wanda Hickey."

"*Wanda Hickey!*"

Schwartz was completely thrown by this bit of news. Wanda Hickey had never been what you could call a major star in our Milky Way. We walked on, saying nothing, until finally, as we opened our lockers, Schwartz said: "Well, she sure is good at algebra."

It was true. Wanda was an algebra shark in the same way that Clara Mae was a spelling nut. Maybe we both got what we deserved.

Later that day, in the study hall, after I had polished off a history theme on some stupid thing like the Punic Wars, I got to thinking about Wanda. I could see her sitting way over on the other side of the room, a dusty sunbeam filtering through the window shades and lighting up her straw-colored hair. She was kind of cute. I'd never really noticed it before. Ever since second grade, Wanda had just been there, along with Eileen Akers, Helen Weathers and all the rest of that anonymous throng of girls who formed an erotic backdrop for the theater of my mind. And here I was, at long last, taking Wanda Hickey—*Wanda Hickey*—to the prom, the only junior prom I would ever attend in my life.

As I chewed on the end of my fake-marble Wearever pen, I watched Wanda through half-closed eyes in the dusty sunbeam as she read the *Lady of the Lake.* Ahead of me, Schwartz dozed fitfully, as he always did in study hall, his forehead occasionally thumping the desk. Flick, to my right, struggled sullenly over his chemistry workbook. We both knew it was hopeless. Flick was the only one in our crowd

who consistently flunked everything. In the end, he never even grad-
uated, but we didn't know that then.

The prom was just five days away. This was the last week of
school. Ahead, our long summer in the sun stretched out like a lazy
yellow road. For many of us, it was the last peaceful summer we were
to know.

Mr. Wilson, the study-hall teacher, wandered aimlessly up and
down the aisles, pretending he was interested in what we were pretending to be doing. From somewhere outside drifted the cries of a
girls' volleyball game, while I drew pictures of my Ford on the inside
cover of my three-ring notebook: front view, side view, rear view,
outlining the drawings with ink.

That morning, on my way to school, I had gone down to the Cupid
Florist Shop and ordered an orchid. My 24 dollars were shrinking
fast. The eight-dollar bite for the orchid didn't help. Schwartz and I
were going to split on the gas, which would come to maybe a buck
apiece. After paying for the summer formal, I'd have a fast ten dollars
left for the big night. As I sat in study hall, I calculated, writing the
figures down, adding and subtracting. But it didn't come out to
much, no matter how I figured it.

Schwartz passed a note back to me. I opened it: "How about the
Red Rooster afterward?"

I wrote underneath, "Where else?' and passed it back. The Red
Rooster was part of the tribal ritual. It was *the* place you went after a
big date, if you could afford it.

I glanced over across the room at Wanda and caught her looking
at me. She instantly buried her head in her book. Good old Wanda.

On the way home from school every day that week, of course, all
we talked about was the prom. Flick was double-dating with Jossway
and we were all going to meet afterward at the Rooster and roister
until dawn, drinking deeply of the sweet elixir of the good life.
The only thing that nagged me now was financial. Ten bucks didn't
look as big as it usually did. Ordinarily, ten bucks could have gotten
me through a month of just fooling around, but the prom was the big
time.

Friday night, as I sat in the kitchen before going to bed, knocking
down a liverwurst on whole wheat and drinking a glass of chocolate
milk, the back door squeaked open and in breezed the old man, car-

rying his bowling bag. Friday night was his big night down at the
Pin-Bowl. He was a fanatical bowler, and a good one, too. He slid the
bag across the floor, pretending to lay one down the groove, his
right arm held out in a graceful follow-through, right leg trailing in
the classic bowling stance.

"Right in the pocket," he said with satisfaction.

"How'd you do tonight?" I asked.

"Not bad. Had a two-oh-seven game. Damn near cracked six hundred."

He opened the refrigerator and fished around for a beer, then sat
down heavily, downed two thirds of the bottle in a mighty drag, bur-
ped loudly and said:

"Well, tomorrow's the big day, ain't it?"

"Yep," I answered. "Sure is."

"You takin' Daphne Bigelow?" he asked.

"Nah. Wanda Hickey."

"Oh, yeah? Well, you can't win 'em all. Wanda's old man is some
kind of a foreman at the mill or something, ain't he?"

"I guess so."

"He drives a Studebaker Champion, don't he? The green two-door
with the whitewalls."

The old man had a fine eye for cars. He judged all men by what
they drove. Apparently, a guy who drove a two-door Studebaker was
not absolutely beyond the pale.

"Not a bad car. Except they burn oil after a while," he mused, omitting no aspects of the Studebaker.

"They used to have a weak front end. Bad kingpins." He shook his
head critically, opening another beer and reaching for the rye bread.

I said nothing, lost in my own thoughts. My mother and kid brother
had been in bed for an hour or so. We were, for all practical purposes, alone in the house. Next door, Mrs. Kissel threw out a pan of
dishwater into the back yard with a swoosh. Her screen door
slammed.

"How ya fixed for tomorrow night?" the old man asked suddenly,
swirling his beer bottle around to raise the head.

"What do you mean?"

"I mean, how are ya *fixed?*"

My father never talked money to me. I got my allowance every

Monday and that was that.

"Well, I've got about ten bucks."

"Hm." That was all he said.

After sitting in silence for a minute or so, he said, "You know, I always wished I coulda gone to a prom."

How can you answer something like that? He had barely gotten out of eighth grade when he had to go to work, and he never stopped for the rest of his life.

"Oh, well, what the hell." He finally answered himself.

He cut himself a couple of slices of boiled ham and made a sandwich.

"I was really hot tonight. Got a string of six straight strikes in the second game. The old hook was movin', getting a lot of wood."

He reached into his hip pocket, took out his wallet and said, "Look, don't tell Ma." He handed me a $20 bill.

"I had a couple of bets going on the second game, and I'm a money bowler."

He was that. No doubt of it. In his early teens, he had scrounged out a living as a pool shark, and he had never lost the touch. I took the $20, glommed onto it the way the proverbial drowning man grabs at a straw. I was so astounded at this unprecedented gesture that it never occurred to me to say thanks. He would have been embarrassed if I had. A miracle had come to pass. There was no doubt about it—the prom was going to be an unqualified blast.

The next day dawned bright and sunny, as perfect as a June day can be—in a steel-mill town. Even the blast-furnace dust that drifted aimlessly through the soft air glowed with promise. I was out early, dusting off the car. It was going to be a top-down night. If there is anything more romantic than a convertible with the top down in June going to a prom, I'd like to hear about it. Cleopatra's barge couldn't have been much more seductive.

My kid brother, his diminutive Flash Gordon T-shirt showing a great expanse of knobby backbone and skinny belly, yapped around me as I toiled over the Ford.

"Look what you done to my T-shirt!" he whined, his runny nose atrickle. He was in the midst of his annual spring cold, which would be superseded by his summer cold, which lasted nicely to the whopper he got in the fall, which, of course, was only a prelude to his winter-long *monster* cold.

"Stay away from the fender. You're dripping on it!" I shouted angrily, shoving him away.

"Flash Gordon's only about an inch high now!"

I couldn't help laughing. It was true. Flash had shrunk, along with the shirt, which Randy had earned by doggedly eating three boxes of Wheaties, saving the box tops and mailing them in with 25 cents that he had, by dint of ferocious self-denial, saved from his 30-cent weekly allowance.

"Look, I'll get you another Flash Gordon T-shirt."

"You can't. They're not givin' 'em away no more. They're givin' away Donald Duck beanies with a propeller on top now."

"Well, then, stretch the one you got now, stupid."

"It won't stretch. It keeps getting littler."

He bounced up and down on a clothes pole, joggling the clothesline and my mother's wash. Within three seconds, she was out on the back porch.

"CUT IT OUT WITH THE CLOTHES POLE!"

Sullenly, he slid off onto the ground. I went back to work, until the Ford gleamed like some rare jewel. Then I went into the house to begin the even more laborious process of getting myself in shape for the evening ahead. Locking the bathroom door, I took two showers, wearing a brand-new bar of Lifebuoy down to a nub. I knew what happened to people who didn't use it; every week, little comic strips underneath *Moon Mullins* told endless tales of disastrous proms due to dreaded b.o. It would not happen to me.

I then shaved for the second time that week, using a new Gillette Blue Blade. As usual when an important shave was executed, I nicked myself nastily in several places.

"Son of a bitch," I muttered, plastering the wounds with little pieces of toilet paper.

Carefully, I went over every inch of my face, battling that age-old enemy, the blackhead, and polished off the job with a copious application of stinging Aqua Velva. Next, I attacked my hair, combing and recombing, getting just the right insouciant pitch to my pride and joy, my d.a. cut. Tonight, I would be a truly magnificent specimen of lusty manhood.

Twilight was fast approaching when I emerged from the bathroom, redolent of rare aromas, pink and svelte. But the real battle had not yet begun. Laid out on my bed was my beautiful summer formal. Al was right: The elegant white coat truly gleamed in virginal splendor. Not a trace of the red stain nor the sinister hole could be detected. The coat was ready for another night of celebration, its lapels spotless, its sleeves smooth and uncreased.

Carefully, I undid the pins that festooned my pleated Monte Carlo shirt. It was the damnedest thing I had ever seen, once I got it straightened out: long, trailing, gauzelike shirttails, a crinkly front that thrummed like sheet metal and a collar that seemed to be carved of white rock. I slipped it on. Panic! It had no buttons—just holes.

Rummaging around frantically in the box the tux came in, I found a cellophane bag containing little round black things. Ripping the bag open, I poured them out: there were five of them, two of which immediately darted under the bed. From the looks of the remaining three, they certainly weren't buttons; but they'd have to do. Although I didn't know it at the time, I had observed a classic maneuver executed by at least one stud out of every set ever rented with a tux. Down on my hands and knees, already beginning to lose my Lifebuoy sheen, sweat popping out here and there, I scrambled around for the missing culprits.

The ordeal was well under way. Seven o'clock was approaching with such rapidity as to be almost unbelievable. Schwartz, Clara Mae and Wanda would *already* be waiting for me, and here I was in my drawers, crawling around on my hands and knees. Finally, amid the dust and dead spiders under my bed, I found the two studs cowering together behind a hardball I'd lost three months earlier.

Back before the mirror, I struggled to get them in place between the concrete slits. Sweat was beginning to show under my arms. I got two in over my breastbone and then I tried to get the one at the collar over my Adam's apple. It was impossible! I could feel from deep within me several sobs beginning to form. The more I struggled, the more ham-fisted I became. Oh, no! Two blackish thumb smudges appeared on my snow-white collar.

"MA!" I screamed, "LOOK AT MY SHIRT!"

She rushed in from the kitchen, carrying a paring knife and a pan of apples.

"What's the matter?"

"Look!" I pointed at the telltale prints.

My kid brother cackled in delight when he saw the trouble I was in.

"Don't touch it," she barked, taking control immediately. Dirty collars were her métier. She had fought them all her life. She darted out of the room and returned instantly with an artgum eraser.

"Now, hold still."

I obeyed as she carefully worked the stud in place and then artistically erased the two monstrous thumbprints. Never in my life had I experienced a collar remotely like the one that now clamped its iron grasp around my windpipe. Hard and unyielding, it dug mercilessly into my throat—a mere sample of what was to come.

"Where's your tie?" she asked. I had forgotten about that detail.

"It . . . ack . . . must be . . . in the box," I managed to gasp out. The collar had almost paralyzed my voice box.

She rummaged around and came up with the bow tie. It was black and it had two metal clips. She snapped it onto the wing collar and stood back.

"Now, look at yourself in the mirror." I didn't recognize myself.

She picked up the midnight-blue trousers and held them open, so that I could slip into them without bending over.

True to his word, Al had, indeed, taken in the seat. The pants clamped me in a viselike grip that was to damn near emasculate me before the evening was out. I sucked in my stomach, buttoned the waistband tight, zippered up the fly and stood straight as a ramrod before the mirror. I had no other choice.

"Gimme your foot."

My mother was down on all fours, pulling the silky black socks onto my feet. Then, out of a box on the bed, she removed the gleaming pair of patent-leather dancing pumps, grabbed my right foot and shoved it into one of them, using her finger as a shoehorn. I tromped down. She squealed in pain.

"I can't get my finger out!"

I hobbled around, taking her finger with me.

"STAND STILL!" she screamed.

I stood like a crane, one foot in the air, with her finger jammed deep into the heel.

"RANDY! COME HERE!" she yelled.

My kid brother, who was sulking under the day bed, ran into the room.

"PULL HIS SHOE OFF, RANDY!" She was frantic.

"What for?" he asked sullenly.

"DON'T ASK STUPID QUESTIONS. JUST DO WHAT I SAY!"

I was getting an enormous cramp in my right buttock.

"STAND STILL!" she yelled. "YOU'RE BREAKING MY FINGER!"
Randy looked on impassively, observing a scene that he was later to
weave into a family legend, embroidering it more and more as the
years went by—making himself the hero, of course.

"RANDY! TAKE OFF HIS SHOE!" Her voice quavered with pain and
exasperation.

"He squirted my T-shirt."

"If you don't take off his shoe this instant, you're gonna regret it."
This time, her voice was low and menacing. We both knew the tone.
It was the end of the line.

Randy bent over and tugged off the shoe. My mother toppled
backward in relief, rubbing her index finger, which was already blue.

"Go back under the day bed," she snapped. He scurried out of the
room. I straightened out my leg—the cramp subsiding like a volcano
in the marrow of my bones—and the gleaming pumps were put in
place without further incident. I stood encased as in armor.

"What's this thing?" she asked from behind me. I executed a careful
180-degree turn.

"Oh, that's my cummerbund."

Her face lit up like an Italian sunrise. "A cummerbund!" She had
seen Fred Astaire in many a cummerbund while he spun down marble staircases with Ginger Rogers in his arms, but it was the first ac-
tual specimen she had ever been close to. She picked it up reverently, its paisley brilliance lighting up the room like an iridescent
jewel.

"How does it work?" she asked, examining it closely.

Before I could answer, she said, "Oh, I see. It has snaps on the
back. Hold still."

Around my waist it went. She drew it tight. The snaps clicked into
place. It rode snugly halfway up my chest.

She picked up the snowy coat and held it out. I lowered my arms
into it, straightened up and there I stood—Adonis!

Posing before the full-length mirror on the bathroom door, I noted

the rich accent of my velvet stripes, the gleam of my pumps, the
magnificent dash and sparkle of my high-fashion cummerbund.
What a sight! What a feeling! This is the way life should be. This is
what it's all about.

I heard my mother call out from the next room: "Hey, what's this
thing?" She came out holding a cellophane bag containing a maroon
object.

"Oh, that's my boutonniere."

"Your what?"

"It's a thing for the lapel. Like a fake flower."

It was the work of an instant to install my elegant wool carnation. It
was the crowning touch. I was so overwhelmed that I didn't care
about the fact that it didn't match my black tie, as Al had promised.
With the cummerbund I was wearing, no one would notice, anyway.

Taking my leave as Cary Grant would have done, I sauntered out
the front door, turned to give my mother a jaunty wave—just in time
for her to call me back to pick up Wanda's corsage, which I'd left on
the front-hall table.

Slipping carefully into the front seat with the celluloid-topped box
safely beside me, I leaned forward slightly, to avoid wrinkling the
back of my coat, started the motor up and shoved off into the warm
spring night. A soft June moon hung overhead, and the Ford purred
like a kitten. When I pulled up before Wanda's house, it was lit up
from top to bottom. Even before my brakes had stopped squealing,
she was out on the porch, her mother fluttering about her, her father
lurking in the background, beaming.

With stately tread, I moved up the walk; my pants were so tight that
if I'd taken one false step, God knows what would have happened. In
my sweaty, Aqua Velva-scented palm, I clutched the ritual largess in
its shiny box.

Wanda wore a long turquoise taffeta gown, her milky skin and
golden hair radiating in the glow of the porch light. This was *not* the
old Wanda. For one thing, she didn't have her glasses on, and her
eyes were unnaturally large and liquid, the way the true myopia vic-
tim's always are.

"Gee, thanks for the orchid," she whispered. Her voice sounded
strained. In accordance with the tribal custom, she, too, was being
mercilessly clamped by straps and girdles.

Her mother, an almost exact copy of Wanda, only slightly puffy here and there, said, "You'll take care of her now, won't you?"

"Now, Emily, don't start yapping," her old man muttered in the darkness. "They're not kids anymore."

They stood in the doorway as we drove off through the soft night toward Schwartz' house, our conversation stilted, our excitement almost at the boiling point. Schwartz rushed out of his house, his white coat like a ghost in the blackness, his hair agleam with Brylcreem, and surrounded by a palpable aura of Lifebuoy.

Five minutes later, Clara Mae piled into the back seat beside him carefully holding up her daffodil-yellow skirts, her long slender neck arched. She, too, wasn't wearing her glasses. I had never realized that a good speller could be so pretty. Schwartz, a good half head shorter, laughed nervously as we tooled on toward the Cherrywood Country Club. From all over town, other cars, polished and waxed, carried the rest of the junior class to their great trial by fire.

The club nestled amid the rolling hills, where the Sinclair oil aroma was only barely detectable. Parking the car in the lot, we threaded our way through the starched and crinolined crowd—the girls' girdles creaking in unison—to the grand ballroom. Japanese lanterns danced in the breeze through the open doors to the garden, bathing the dance floor in a fairy-tale glow.

I found myself saying things like, "Why, hello there, Albert, how are you?" And, "Yes, I believe the weather is perfect." Only Flick, the unregenerate Philistine, failed to rise to the occasion. Already rumpled in his summer formal, he made a few tasteless wisecracks as Mickey Iseley and his Magic Music Makers struck up the sultry sounds that had made them famous in every steel-mill town that ringed Lake Michigan. Dark and sensuous, the dance floor engulfed us all. I felt tall, slim and beautiful, not realizing at the time that everybody feels that way wearing a rented white coat and black pants. I could see myself standing on a mysterious balcony, a lonely, elegant figure, looking out over the lights of some exotic city, a scene of sophisticated gaiety behind me.

There was a hushed moment when Mickey Iseley stood in the baby spot, his wavy hair shining, before a microphone shaped like a chromium bullet.

"All right, boys and girls." The metallic ring of feedback framed his

words in an echoing nimbus. "And now, something really romantic.
A request: *When the Swallows Come Back to Capistrano*. We're
going to turn the lights down for this one."

Oh, wow! The lights faded even lower. Only the Japanese lanterns
glowed dimly—red, green, yellow and blue—in the enchanted
darkness. It was unquestionably the high point of my existence.

Wanda and I began to maneuver around the floor. My experience
in dancing had been gained almost entirely from reading Arthur
Murray ads and practicing with a pillow for a partner behind the
locked door of the bathroom. As we shuffled across the floor, I could
see the black footprints before my eyes, marching on a white page:
1-2-3; then the white one that said, "Pause."

Back and forth, up and down, we moved metronomically. My box
step was so square that I went in little right angles for weeks afterward. The wool carnation rode high up on my lapel and was beginning to scratch my cheek, and an insistent itch began to nag at my
right shoulder. There was some kind of wire or horsehair or something in the shoulder pad that was beginning to bore its way into my
flesh.

By now, my dashing concrete collar, far from having wilted, had
set into the consistency of Carborundum, and its incessant abrasive
action had removed a wide strip of skin encircling my neck. As for
my voice—due to the manic strangulation of the collar, it was now
little more than a hoarse croak.

"When the swallows . . . come baaaaaack to Capistraaaaaano . . ."
mooed the drummer, who doubled as the band's romantic vocalist.

I began to notice Wanda's orchid leering up at me from her shoulder. It was the most repulsive flower I had ever seen. At least 14
inches across, it looked like some kind of overgrown Venus-flytrap
waiting for the right moment to strike. Deep purple, with an obscene
yellow tongue that stuck straight out of it, and greenish knobs on the
end, it clashed almost audibly with her turquoise dress. It looked like
it was breathing, and it clung to her shoulder as if with claws.

As I glided back and forth in my graceful box step, my left shoulder began to develop an itch that helped take my mind off of the insane itch in my right shoulder, which was beginning to feel like an
army of hungry soldier ants on the march. The contortions I made to

relieve the agony were camouflaged nicely by a short sneezing fit brought on by the orchid, which was exhaling directly into my face. So was Wanda, with a heady essence of Smith Brothers cough drops and sauerkraut.

"When the deeeep purpullllll fallllllls . . . Over sleeeeepy gaaardennnn wallllls . . ." warbled the vocalist into his microphone, with which he seemed to be dancing the tango. The loud-speakers rattled in three-quarter time as Wanda started to sweat through her taffeta. I felt it running down her back. My own back was already so wet you could read the label on my undershirt right through the dinner jacket.

Back and forth we trudged doggedly across the crowded floor. Another Arthur Murray ad man, Schwartz was doing exactly the same step with Clara Mae directly behind me. We were all in a four-part lock step. As I hit the lower left-hand footprint in my square— the one marked "Pause"—he was hitting the upper right-hand corner of his square. Each time we did that, our elbows dug smartly into each other's ribs.

The jungle fragrance of the orchid was getting riper by the minute and the sweat, which had now saturated my Jockey shorts, was pouring down my legs in rivulets. My soaked cummerbund had turned two shades darker. So that she shouldn't notice, I pulled Wanda closer to me. Sighing, she hugged me back. Wanda was the vaguely chubby type of girl that was so popular at the time. Like Judy Garland, by whom she was heavily influenced, she strongly resembled a pink beach ball—but a *cute* beach ball, soft and rubbery. I felt bumpy things under her taffeta gown, with little hooks and knobs. Schwartz caught me a nasty shot in the rib cage just as I bent over to kiss her lightly on the bridge of her nose. It tasted salty. She looked up at me, her great liquid myopic eyes catching the reflection of the red and green lanterns overhead.

During a brief intermission, Schwartz and I carried paper cups dripping syrupy punch back to the girls, who had just spent some time in the ladies' room struggling unsuccessfully to repair the damage of the first half. As we were sipping, a face from my dim past floated by from out of nowhere—haughty, alabaster, green-eyed, dangerous.

"Hi, Daph," I muttered, spilling a little punch on my gleaming pumps, which had turned during the past hour into a pair of iron maidens.

"Oh, Howard." She spoke in the breathy, sexy way that such girls always have at proms. "I'd like you to meet Budge. Budge Cameron. He's at Princeton." A languid figure, probably born in a summer formal, loomed overhead.

"Budge, this is Howard."

"Hiya, fella." It was the first time I had heard the tight, nasal, swinging-jaw accent of the true Princetonian. It was not to be the last.

They were gone. Funny, I couldn't even remember actually dating her, I reflected, as the lights dimmed once again. We swung back into action. They opened with *Sleepy Lagoon.* 1-2-3-pause . . . 1-2-3-pause.

It was certain now. I had broken out in a raging rash. I felt it spreading like lava across my shoulder blades, lashed on by the sweat. The horsehair, meanwhile, had penetrated my chest cavity and was working its way toward a vital organ. Trying manfully to ignore it, I stared fixedly at the tiny turquoise ribbon that held Wanda's golden ponytail in place. With troubles of her own, she looked with an equally level gaze at my maroon-wool carnation, which by this time had wilted into a clump of lint.

All of a sudden, it was over. The band played *Good Night, Sweetheart* and we were out—into a driving rain. A violent cloudburst had begun just as we reached the door. My poor little car, the pride and joy of my life, was outside in the lot. With the top down.

None of us, of course, had an umbrella. We stood under the canopy as the roaring thunderstorm raged on. It wasn't going to stop.

"You guys stay here. I'll get the car," I said finally. After all, I was in charge.

Plunging into the downpour, I sloshed through the puddles and finally reached the Ford. She must have had at least a foot of water in her already. Hair streaming down over my eyes, soaked to the skin and muddied to the knees, I bailed it out with a coffee can from the trunk, slid behind the wheel and pressed the automatic-top lever. Smooth as silk, it began to lift—and stuck halfway up. As the rain poured down in sheets and the lightning flashed, I pounded on the relays, furiously switched the lever off and on. I could see the country club dimly through the downpour. Finally, the top groaned and flapped into place. I threw down the snaps, rolled up the windows and turned on the ignition; the battery was dead. The strain of hoisting that damn top had drained it dry. I yelled out the window at a passing car. It was Flick in his Chevy.

"GIMME A PUSH! MY BATTERY'S DEAD!"

This had never, to my knowledge, happened to Fred Astaire.

Flick expertly swung his Chevy around and slammed into my trunk as I eased her into gear, and when she started to roll, the Ford shuddered and caught. Flick backed up and was gone, hollering out the window:

"SEE YOU AT THE ROOSTER."

Wanda, Schwartz and Clara Mae piled in on the damp, soggy seats and we took off. Do you know what happens to a maroon-wool carnation on a white-serge lapel in a heavy June downpour in the Midwest, where it rains not water but carbolic acid from the steel-mill fallout? I had a dark, wide, spreading maroon stripe that went all the way down to the bottom of my white coat. My French cuffs were covered with grease from fighting the top, and I had cracked a nail, which was beginning to throb.

Undaunted, we slogged intrepidly through the rain toward the Red Rooster. Wedged against my side, Wanda looked up at me—oblivious to the elements—with luminous love eyes. She was truly an incurable romantic. Schwartz wisecracked in the back seat and Clara giggled from time to time. The savage tribal rite was nearing its final and most vicious phase.

We arrived at the Red Rooster, already crowded with other candidates for adulthood. A giant red neon rooster with a blue neon tail that flicked up and down in the rain set the tone for this glamorous establishment. An aura of undefined sin was always connected with the name Red Rooster. Sly winks, nudgings and adolescent cacklings about what purportedly went on at the Rooster made it the "in" spot for such a momentous revel. Its waiters were rumored really to be secret henchmen of the Mafia. But the only thing we knew for sure about the Rooster was that anybody on the far side of seven years old could procure any known drink without question.

The decor ran heavily to red-checkered-oilcloth table covers and plastic violets, and the musical background was provided by a legendary jukebox that stood a full seven feet high, featuring red and

blue cascading waterfalls that gushed endlessly through its volup-
tuous façade. In full 200-watt operation, it could be *felt,* if not clearly
heard, as far north as Gary and as far south as Kankakee. A triumph
of American aesthetics.

Surging with anticipation, I guided Wanda through the uproarious
throng of my peers. Schwartz and Clara Mae trailed behind, ex-
changing ribald remarks with the gang.

We occupied the only remaining table. Immediately, a beady-eyed
waiter sidled over and hovered like a vulture. Distributing the famous
Red Rooster Ala Carte Deluxe Menu, he stood back, smirking, and
waited for us to impress our dates.

"Can I bring you anything to drink, gentlemen?" he said, heavily ac-
centing the gentlemen.

My first impulse was to order my favorite drink of the period, a bot-
tled chocolate concoction called Kayo, the Wonder Drink; but remembering that better things were expected of me on prom night, I
said, in my deepest voice, "Uh . . . make mine bourbon."

Schwartz grunted in admiration. Wanda ogled me with great,
swimming, lovesick eyes. Bourbon was the only drink that I had actually heard of. My old man ordered it often down at the Bluebird
Tavern. I had always wondered what it tasted like. I was soon to find
out.

"How will you have it, sir?"

"Well, in a glass, I guess." I had failed to grasp the subtlety of his
question, but the waiter snorted in appreciation of my humorous
sally.

"Rocks?" he continued.

Rock? I had heard about getting your rocks, but never in a restaurant. Oh, well, what the hell.

"Sure," I said. "Why not?"

All around me, the merrymaking throng was swinging into high
gear. Carried away by it all, I added a phrase I had heard my old man
use often: "And make it a triple." I had some vague idea that this was
a brand or something.

"A triple? Yes, sir." His eyes snapped wide—in respect, I gathered.
He knew he was in the presence of a serious drinker.

The waiter turned his gaze in Schwartz' direction. "And you, sir?"

"Make it the same." Schwartz had never been a leader.

The die was cast. Pink ladies, at the waiter's suggestion, were ordered for the girls, and we then proceeded to scan the immense menu with feigned disinterest. When the waiter returned with our drinks, I ordered—for reasons that even today I am unable to explain —French lamb chops, turnips, mashed potatoes and gravy, a side dish of the famous Red Rooster Roquefort Italian Cole Slaw and strawberry shortcake. The others wisely decided to stick with their drinks.

Munching bread sticks, Wanda, Clara, Schwartz and I engaged in sophisticated postprom repartee. Moment by moment, I felt my strength and maturity, my dashing bonhomie, my clean-cut handsomeness enveloping my friends in its benevolent warmth. Schwartz, too, seemed to scintillate as never before. Clara giggled and Wanda sighed, overcome by the romance of it all. Even when Flick, sitting three tables away, clipped Schwartz behind the left ear with a poppy-seed roll, our urbanity remained unruffled.

Before me reposed a sparkling tumbler of beautiful amber liquid, ice cubes bobbing merrily on its surface, a swizzle stick sporting an enormous red rooster sticking out at a jaunty angle. Schwartz was similarly equipped. And the fluffy pink ladies looked lovely in the reflected light of the pulsating jukebox.

I had seen my old man deal with just this sort of situation. Raising my beaded glass, I looked around at my companions and said suavely, "Well, here's mud in yer eye." Clara giggled; Wanda sighed dreamily, now totally in love with this man of the world who sat across from her on this, our finest night.

"Yep, Schwartz parried wittily, hoisting his glass high and slopping a little bourbon on his pants as he did so.

Swiftly, I brought the bourbon to my lips, intending to down it in a single devil-may-care draught, the way Gary Cooper used to do in the Silver Dollar Saloon. I did, and Schwartz followed suit. Down it went—a screaming 100-proof rocket searing savagely down my gullet. For an instant, I sat stunned, unable to comprehend what had happened. Eyes watering copiously, I had a brief urge to sneeze, but my throat seemed to be paralyzed. Wanda and Clara Mae swam before my misted vision; and Schwartz seemed to have disappeared under the table. He popped up again—face beet red, eyes bugging, jaw slack, tongue lolling.

"Isn't this romantic? Isn't this the most wonderful night in all our lives? I will forever treasure the memories of this wonderful night." From far off, echoing as from some subterranean tunnel, I heard Wanda speaking.

Deep down in the pit of my stomach, I felt crackling flames licking at my innards. I struggled to reply, to maintain my *elan,* my fabled *savoir-faire.* "Urk . . . urk . . . yeah," I finally managed with superhuman effort.

Wanda swam hazily into focus. She was gazing across the table at me with adoring eyes.

"Another, gents?" The waiter was back still smirking.

Schwartz nodded dumbly. I just sat there, afraid to move. An instant later, two more triple bourbons materialized in front of us.

Clara raised her pink lady high and said reverently, "Let's drink to the happiest night of our lives."

There was no turning back. Another screamer rocketed down the hatch. For an instant, it seemed as though this one wasn't going to be as lethal as the first, but then the room suddenly tilted sideways. I felt torrents of cold sweat pouring from my forehead. Clinging to the edge of the table, I watched as Schwartz gagged across from me. Flick, I noticed, had just chugalugged his third rum and Coke and was eating a cheeseburger.

The conflagration deep inside me was now clearly out of control. My feet were smoking; my diaphragm heaved convulsively, jiggling my cummerbund; and Schwartz began to shrink, his face alternating between purple-red and chalk-white, his eyes black holes staring fixedly at the ketchup bottle. He sat stock-still. Wanda, meanwhile, cooed on ecstatically—but I was beyond understanding what she was saying. Faster and faster, in ever-widening circles, the room, the jukebox, the crowd swirled dizzily about me. In all the excitement of preparations for the prom, I realized that I hadn't eaten a single thing all day.

Out of the maelstrom, a plate mysteriously appeared before me: paper-pantied lamb chops hissing in bubbling grease, piled yellow turnips, gray mashed potatoes awash in rich brown gravy. Maybe this would help, I thought incoherently. Grasping my knife and fork as firmly as I could, I poised to whack off a piece of meat. Suddenly, the landscape listed 45 digrees to starboard and the chop I was about to attack skidded off my plate—plowing a swath through the mashed potatoes—and right into the aisle.

Pretending not to notice, I addressed myself to the remaining chop, which slid around eluding my grasp, until I managed to skewer it with my fork. Hacking off a chunk, I jammed it fiercely mouthward, missing my target completely. Still impaled on my fork, the chop slithered over my cheekbone, spraying gravy as it went, all over my white lapels. On the next try, I had better luck and finally I managed to get the whole chop down.

To my surprise, I didn't feel any better. Maybe the turnips will help, I thought. Lowering my head to within an inch of the plate, to prevent embarrassing mishaps, I shoveled them in—but the flames within only fanned higher and higher. I tried the potatoes and gravy. My legs began to turn cold. I wolfed down the Red Rooster Roquefort Italian Cole Slaw. My stomach began to rise like a helium balloon, bobbing slowly up the alimentary canal.

My nose low over the heaping dish of strawberry shortcake, piled high with whipped cream and running with juice, I knew at last for a dead certainty what I had to do before it happened right there in front of everybody. I struggled to my feet. A strange rubbery numbness had struck my extremities. I tottered from chair to chair, grasping for the wall.

Twenty seconds later, I was on my knees, gripping the bowl of the john like a life preserver in pitching seas. Schwartz, imitating me as usual, lay almost prostrate on the tiles beside me, his body wracked with heaving sobs. Lamb chop, bourbon, turnips, mashed potatoes, cole slaw—all of it came rushing out of me in a great roaring torrent, out of my mouth, my nose, my ears, my very soul. Then Schwartz opened up, and we took turns retching and shuddering. A head thrust itself between us directly into the pot. It was Flick, moaning wretchedly. Up came the cheeseburger, the rum and Cokes, pretzels, potato chips, punch, gumdrops, a corned-beef sandwich, a fingernail or two—everything he'd eaten for the past week. For long minutes, the three of us lay there limp and quivering, smelling to high heaven, too weak to get up. It was the absolute high point of the junior prom; the rest was anticlimax.

Finally, we returned to the table, ashen-faced and shaking. Schwartz, his coat stained and rumpled, sat zombilike across from

me. The girls didn't say much. Pink ladies just aren't straight bourbon.

But our little group played the scene out bravely to the end. My
dinner jacket was now even more redolent and disreputable than
when I'd first seen it on the hanger at Al's. And my bow tie, which
had hung for a while by one clip, had somehow disappeared completely, perhaps flushed into eternity with all the rest. But as time
wore on, my hearing and eyesight began slowly to return, my legs
began to lose their rubberiness and the room slowly resumed its
even keel—at least even enough to consider getting up and leaving.
The waiter seemed to know. He returned as if on cue, bearing a slip
of paper.

"The damages, gentlemen."

Taking the old man's $20 out of my wallet, I handed it to him with
as much of a flourish as I could muster. There wouldn't have been
any point in looking over the check; I wouldn't have been able to
read it, anyway. In one last attempt to recoup my cosmopolitan
image, I said offhandedly, "Keep the change." Wanda beamed in un-
concealed ecstasy.

The drive home in the damp car was not quite the same as the one
that had begun the evening so many weeks earlier. Our rapidly fer-
menting coats made the enclosed air rich and gamy, and Schwartz,
who had stopped belching, sat with head pulled low between his
shoulder blades, staring straight ahead. Only the girls preserved the
joyousness of the occasion. Women always survive.

In a daze, I dropped off Schwartz and Clara Mae and drove in silence toward Wanda's home, the faint light of dawn beginning to
show in the east.

We stood on her porch for the last ritual encounter. A chill dawn
wind rustled the lilac bushes.

"This was the most wonderful, wonderful night of my whole life. I
always dreamed the prom would be like this," breathed Wanda,
gazing passionately up into my watering eyes.

"Me, too," was all I could manage.

I knew what was expected of me now. Her eyes closed dreamily.
Swaying slightly, I leaned forward—and the faint odor of sauerkraut
from her parted lips coiled slowly up to my nostrils. This was not in
the script. I knew I had better get off that porch fast, or else. Back-

pedaling desperately down the stairs, I blurted, "Bye!" and—fighting down my rising gorge—clamped my mouth tight, leaped into the Ford, burned rubber and tore off into the dawn. Two blocks away, I squealed to a stop alongside a vacant lot containing only a huge Sherwin-Williams paint sign. We Cover The Earth, it aptly read. In the blessed darkness behind the sign, concealed from prying eyes, I completed the final rite of the tribal ceremony.

The sun was just rising as I swung the car up the driveway and eased myself quietly into the kitchen. The old man, who was going fishing that morning, sat at the enamel table sipping black coffee. He looked up as I came in.

"You look like you had a hell of a prom," was all he said.

"I sure did."

The yellow kitchen light glared harshly on my muddy pants, my maroon-streaked, vomit-stained white coat, my cracked fingernail, my greasy shirt.

"You want anything to eat?" he asked sardonically.

At the word "eat," my stomach heaved convulsively. I shook my head numbly.

"That's what I thought," he said. "Get some sleep. You'll feel better in a couple of days, when your head stops banging."

He went back to reading his paper. I staggered into my bedroom, dropping bits of clothing as I went. My soggy Hollywood paisley cummerbund, the veteran of another gala night, was flung beneath my dresser as I toppled into bed. My brother muttered in his sleep across the room. He was still a kid. But his time would come.

Jean Shepherd (1929-)
An American writer, Jean Shepherd published his first delightful account of teen-age life in a story for Playboy *magazine. Since then his stories have been in constant demand. A number of them have recently been collected in the book,* Wanda Hickey's Night of Golden Memories, & Other Disasters *(1971).*

anguish

"I keep seeing the ghosts of the men
I've killed. And the worst part of it is
they don't know they're dead."

What sort of person do you imagine
saying this? A troubled man? a dis-
appointed child? or both?

the gunfighter
Alden Nowlan

I come out of the Lord Wellington Hotel, where I have interviewed a
famous politician who told me that the Jews were out to get him, but
that he would sue *The Clarion* if I quoted him. "Those fellows are still
trying to rub the blood off their hands," the politician had said. "But
I'm not dead yet. I'm going to save this Canada of ours despite the
Jews and the Frenchmen. By the way, did you ever hear why the
States has the Darkies and Canada has the Frenchmen?" Here the
honourable gentleman paused and smiled benignly. "It's because
the States had first choice."

It is about ten o'clock on a crisp December night and the square is
a kaleidoscope of Christmas lights. In Princess Park a spotlight illu-
minates Samuel de Champlain, his marble hand outstretched toward
Europe, his back turned on North America. As I walk past the Monte
Carlo Restaurant, the glass door opens and a swarm of laughing
adolescents rushes by me. For a moment the air smells of french

fries, hamburgers and pizzas. In the window of the Air Canada ticket office, there are signs urging me to vacation in Bermuda, Jamaica and Spain.

"Hey, Kevin! Kevin O'Brien!"

The Wichita Kid is hailing me from across the street. He stands in front of Tony's Mag and Fag Shop, a baroque figure in a black gaucho hat laced under his chin, a black and red neckerchief, an imitation buckskin jacket, black levis and high-heeled boots. Two Buntline Specials hang low on his hips, their imitation-silver-plated holsters strapped to his thighs.

I cross the street, dodging cars, almost losing my footing on a patch of ice.

"Hello, Wichita. I haven't seen you for a thousand years. What's new with the fastest gun east of Montreal?"

Wichita looks old at nineteen, and will look young at fifty. He has felt joy and sadness, but neither has left its mark on his face. His lips are full, his eyes blue-grey, his cheeks red from the cold.

He punches my shoulder and laughs.

"Been away," he says. "Been out in Missouri. You know. Across the wide Missouri." He laughs again. Passers-by glance our way and grin. Several of them nod or wave to Wichita, who is given the mock-obeisance the ancients gave their sacrificial kings. One day, perhaps, the Mayor will proclaim a holiday, and Wichita, smiling happily, will be offered up to the waning moon or the setting sun.

"Missouri, eh? What have you been doing out there?" Tony's show window contains cigars twelve inches long, pepper-flavoured chewing gum, trick beer glasses that won't pour, "physical culture" magazines, the covers of which show young boys naked except for jockstraps. I think of the Bizarro World in one of my son's comic books, in which everything on earth is reversed, a world in which, I suppose, men are born old and become younger and younger until at last they die of youth.

Wichita's mouth is close to my ear. "I been riding with Dingus and Buck," he confides.

"Dingus and Buck. Oh, I remember. Those were their nicknames. Jesse and Frank James."

"Sure. Dingus and Frank. I was with 'em at Liberty and Lexington and Richmond ____"

"And I suppose you helped rob the Gallatin bank and the Glendale train. Isn't that what the song says?

Oh, it was Jess and Frank
Who robbed the Gallatin bank,
Held up the Glendale train;
With the agent on his knees,
He delivered up the keys
To those outlaws, Frank and Jesse James."

"Don't talk crazy," Wichita says, "the Gallatin robbery hasn't happened yet. It won't happen until 1869. Don't you even know what year this is? This is only 1867."

"I guess I didn't stop to think, Wichita. Sorry."

The televised head and shoulders of the famous politician appear in the window of Bill's TV Sales and Service. He is smiling like a madman enjoying a secret joke: it is a Vincent Price kind of smile. I can't hear him through the plate glass but earlier in the hotel he gave me an advance copy of his speech, so I know he is saying that this Canada of ours is a mosaic and not a melting pot and that all men of goodwill must put their shoulders to the wheel to create a country in which brotherhood is not just a word but a way of life.

"What's that you say, Wichita? I'm sorry. I'm afraid I wasn't listening."

"I said, do you know how many notches I have on my sixguns now?"

"I haven't any idea, Wichita. Tell me."

"Make a guess."

"No, really, I couldn't. Tell me."

"You won't believe me."

"I'll believe almost anything, Wichita. Come on, tell me."

"Forty-two!"

"Forty-two."

"Yep. Billy the Kid, he only had twenty-one. I've gunned down more men than Billy the Kid, Wild Bill Hickok, Jesse James and John Wesley Harden put together."

"By Gad, sir, I do admire you."

"You making fun of me or something?"

"I wouldn't think of it, Wichita."

"Here. Look." He removes his pistols from their holsters and shows me their butts. I don't count the notches, but there are many of them, chipped into the plastic. Suddenly I feel as sad and guilty as I felt once after I absent-mindedly pushed in front of an old woman waiting at the check-out counter in a supermarket and she whimpered "I'm sorry," she was that used to begging forgiveness. At that moment I felt as if I were responsible for creating the old woman who apologized when other people were rude to her.

Now I feel that I have created Wichita.

"I'd better be on my way," I tell him. "Do you have a place to sleep? It's getting colder all the time." I rub my ears and clap my hands together, as though to convince him.

"I don't sleep much," he says. "Later, when everybody goes home, maybe I'll ride my horse down Trafalgar Street. I do that, sometimes, when I feel like it."

"Sure, Wichita, sure. But you'd better take this anyway." I press a dollar bill into his hand. "Put that in your pocket where you won't lose it. It will buy you some soup and coffee, or maybe a hot sandwich, something hot anyway." I put two quarters in his other hand. "Put those in your other pocket, and don't lose them, either. They'll pay for a bed at the Salvation Army. Do you understand me, Wichita?"

On second thought, I take the money from his hands and put it in the pockets of his jacket. "Don't forget where it is, Wichita. Okay?"

He grabs the sleeve of my topcoat.

"Ghosts," he says, "Ghosts!"

"Huh?"

"I keep seeing the ghosts of the men I've killed. And the worst part of it is they don't know that they're dead. That fellow that went past a second ago, did you see him? The guy in the UNB jacket ___"

"Easy now, Kid. Easy now."

"___Young punk with a smirk on his kisser. Smirking little bastard. I killed him a week ago, and he doesn't know. What do you think of that, huh? What do you think of that?"

"Maybe it's better that way, Kid. What they don't know won't hurt them."

He releases my arm, steps back, draws his sixguns and shoots. One pistol is pointed at my head, the other at my belly. At this distance, he can't miss. *Bang! Bang!* He empties both guns.

I laugh, nervously. "Well, so long, Kid. I'll be seeing you around. Don't forget about your money." I turn away and walk rapidly down the street toward the parking lot.

Wichita screams after me. "You see what I mean?" he yells. "You see what I mean?"

Alden Nowlan (1933-)
Perhaps better known as a poet, Nova Scotia-born Alden Nowlan has also published a fine collection of short stories, Miracle at Indian River *(1968), and a novel,* Various Persons Named Kevin O'Brien *(1973). Nowlan lives in Fredericton, New Brunswick.*

"You heathens, you savages," he
shouted. "I'm going to get out of
here someday! I am going to get
away!" The Crow people listened respectfully. In the Crow tongue he
shouted, "Horse! I am Horse!" and
they nodded.

This man must adapt or die. If he
lives he will be forever changed, and
if he dies who will care?

a man called horse

Dorothy Johnson

He was a young man of good family, as the phrase went in the New
England of a hundred-odd years ago, and the reasons for his bitter
discontent were unclear, even to himself. He grew up in the gracious
old Boston home under his grandmother's care, for his mother had
died in giving him birth; and all his life he had known every comfort
and privilege his father's wealth could provide.

But still there was the discontent, which puzzled him because he
could not even define it. He wanted to live among his equals—people
who were no better than he and no worse either. That was as close as
he could come to describing the source of his unhappiness in
Boston and his restless desire to go somewhere else.

In the year 1845, he left home and went out West, far beyond the
country's creeping frontier, where he hoped to find his equals. He
had the idea that in Indian country, where there was danger, all white
men were kings, and he wanted to be one of them. But he found, in
the West as in Boston, that the men he respected were still his supe-
riors, even if they could not read, and those he did not respect
weren't worth talking to.

He did have money, however, and he could hire the men he respected. He hired four of them, to cook and hunt and guide and be
his companions, but he found them not friendly.

They were apart from him and he was still alone. He still brooded about his status in the world, longing for his equals.

On a day in June, he learned what it was to have no status at all. He became a captive of a small raiding party of Crow Indians.

He heard gunfire and the brief shouts of his companions around the bend of the creek just before they died, but he never saw their bodies. He had no chance to fight, because he was naked and unarmed, bathing in the creek, when a Crow warrior seized and held him.

His captor let him go at last, let him run. Then the lot of them rode him down for sport, striking him with their coup sticks. They carried the dripping scalps of his companions, and one had skinned off Baptiste's black beard as well, for a trophy.

They took him along in a matter-of-fact way, as they took the captured horses. He was unshod and naked as the horses were, and like them he had a rawhide thong around his neck. So long as he didn't fall down, the Crows ignored him.

On the second day they gave him his breeches. His feet were too swollen for his boots, but one of the Indians threw him a pair of moccasins that had belonged to the halfbreed, Henri, who was dead back at the creek. The captive wore the moccasins gratefully. The third day they let him ride one of the spare horses so the party could move faster, and on that day they came in sight of their camp.

He thought of trying to escape, hoping he might be killed in flight rather than by slow torture in the camp, but he never had a chance to try. They were more familiar with escape than he was and, knowing what to expect, they forestalled it. The only other time he had tried to escape from anyone, he had succeeded. When he had left his home in Boston, his father had raged and his grandmother had cried, but they could not talk him out of his intention.

The men of the Crow raiding party didn't bother with talk.

Before riding into camp they stopped and dressed in their regalia, and in parts of their victims' clothing; they painted their faces black. Then, leading the white man by the rawhide around his neck as though he were a horse, they rode down toward the tepee circle, shouting and singing, brandishing their weapons. He was unconscious when they got there; he fell and was dragged.

He lay dazed and battered near a tepee while the noisy, busy life of the camp swarmed around him and Indians came to stare. Thirst consumed him, and when it rained he lapped rain water from the ground like a dog. A scrawny, shrieking, eternally busy old woman with ragged graying hair threw a chunk of meat on the grass, and he fought the dogs for it.

When his head cleared, he was angry, although anger was an emotion he knew he could not afford.

It was better when I was a horse, he thought—when they led me by the rawhide around my neck. I won't be a dog, no matter what!

The hag gave him stinking, rancid grease and let him figure out what it was for. He applied it gingerly to his bruised and sun-seared body.

Now, he thought, I smell like the rest of them.

While he was healing, he considered coldly the advantages of being a horse. A man would be humiliated, and sooner or later he would strike back and that would be the end of him. But a horse had only to be docile. Very well, he would learn to do without pride.

He understood that he was the property of the screaming old woman, a fine gift from her son, one that she liked to show off. She did more yelling at him than at anyone else, probably to impress the neighbors so they would not forget what a great and generous man her son was. She was bossy and proud, a dreadful sag of skin and bones, and she was a devilish hard worker.

The white man, who now thought of himself as a horse, forgot sometimes to worry about his danger. He kept making mental notes of things to tell his own people in Boston about this hideous adventure. He would go back a hero, and he would say, "Grandmother, let me fetch your shawl. I've been accustomed to doing little errands for another lady about your age."

Two girls lived in the tepee with the old hag and her warrior son. One of them, the white man concluded, was his captor's wife and the other was his little sister. The daughter-in-law was smug and spoiled. Being beloved, she did not have to be useful. The younger girl had bright, wandering eyes. Often enough they wandered to the white man who was pretending to be a horse.

The two girls worked when the old woman put them at it, but they were always running off to do something they enjoyed more. There were games and noisy contests, and there was much laughter. But not for the white man. He was finding out what loneliness could be.

That was a rich summer on the plains, with plenty of buffalo for
meat and clothing and the making of tepees. The Crows were
wealthy in horses, prosperous and contented. If their men had not
been so avid for glory, the white man thought, there would have
been a lot more of them. But they went out of their way to court
death, and when one of them met it, the whole camp mourned ex-
travagantly and cried to their God for vengeance.

The captive was a horse all summer, a docile bearer of burdens,
careful and patient. He kept reminding himself that he had to be bet-
ter-natured than other horses, because he could not lash out with
hoofs or teeth. Helping the old woman load up the horses for travel,
he yanked at a pack and said, "Whoa, brother. It goes easier when
you don't fight."

The horse gave him a big-eyed stare as if it understood his language—a comforting thought, because nobody else did. But even
among the horses he felt unequal. They were able to look out for
themselves if they escaped. He would simply starve. He was envious
still, even among the horses.

Humbly he fetched and carried. Sometimes he even offered to
help, but he had not the skill for the endless work of the women, and
he was not trusted to hunt with the men, the providers.

When the camp moved, he carried a pack trudging with the
women. Even the dogs worked then, pulling small burdens on travois
of sticks.

The Indian who had captured him lived like a lord, as he had a
right to do. He hunted with his peers, attended long ceremonial
meetings with much chanting and dancing, and lounged in the
shade with his smug bride. He had only two responsibilities: to kill
buffalo and to gain glory. The white man was so far beneath him in
status that the Indian did not even think of envy.

One day several things happened that made the captive think he
might sometime become a man again. That was the day when he began to understand their language. For four months he had heard it,
day and night, the joy and the mourning, the ritual chanting and
sung prayers, the squabbles and the deliberations. None of it meant
anything to him at all.

But on that important day in early fall the two young women set out for the river, and one of them called over her shoulder to the old woman. The white man was startled. She had said she was going to bathe. His understanding was so sudden that he felt as if his ears had come unstopped. Listening to the racket of the camp, he heard fragments of meaning instead of gabble.

On that same important day the old woman brought a pair of new moccasins out of the tepee and tossed them on the ground before him. He could not believe she would do anything for him because of kindness, but giving him moccasins was one way of looking after her property.

In thanking her, he dared greatly. He picked a little handful of fading fall flowers and took them to her as she squatted in front of her tepee, scraping a buffalo hide with a tool made from a piece of iron tied to a bone. Her hands were hideous—most of the fingers had the first joint missing. He bowed solemnly and offered the flowers.

She glared at him from beneath the short, ragged tangle of her hair. She stared at the flowers, knocked them out of his hand and went running to the next tepee, squalling the story. He heard her and the other women screaming with laughter.

The white man squared his shoulders and walked boldly over to watch three small boys shooting arrows at a target. He said in English, "Show me how to do that, will you?"

They frowned, but he held out his hand as if there could be no doubt. One of them gave him a bow and one arrow, and they snickered when he missed.

The people were easily amused, except when they were angry. They were amused, at him, playing with the little boys. A few days later he asked the hag, with gestures, for a bow that her son had just discarded, a man-size bow of horn. He scavenged for old arrows. The old woman cackled at his marksmanship and called her neighbors to enjoy the fun.

When he could understand words, he could identify his people by their names. The old woman was Greasy Hand, and her daughter was Pretty Calf. The other young woman's name was not clear to him, for the words were not in his vocabulary. The man who had captured him was Yellow Robe.

Once he could understand, he could begin to talk a little, and then he was less lonely. Nobody had been able to see any reason for talking to him, since he would not understand anyway. He asked the old woman, "What is my name?" Until he knew it, he was incomplete. She shrugged to let him know he had none.

He told her in the Crow language, "My name is Horse." He repeated it, and she nodded. After that they called him Horse when they called him anything. Nobody cared except the white man himself.

They trusted him enough to let him stray out of camp, so that he might have got away and, by unimaginable good luck, might have reached a trading post or a fort, but winter was too close. He did not dare leave without a horse; he needed clothing and a better hunting weapon than he had, and more certain skill in using it. He did not dare steal, for then they would surely have pursued him, and just as certainly they would have caught him. Remembering the warmth of the home that was waiting in Boston, he settled down for the winter.

On a cold night he crept into the tepee after the others had gone to bed. Even a horse might try to find shelter from the wind. The old woman grumbled, but without conviction. She did not put him out.

They tolerated him, back in the shadows, so long as he did not get in the way.

He began to understand how the family that owned him differed from the others. Fate had been cruel to them. In a short, sharp argument among the old women, one of them derided Greasy Hand by sneering, "You have no relatives!" and Greasy Hand raved for minutes of the deeds of her father and uncles and brothers. And she had had four sons, she reminded her detractor—who answered with scorn, "Where are they?"

Later the white man found her moaning and whimpering to herself, rocking back and forth on her haunches, staring at her mutilated hands. By that time he understood. A mourner often chopped off a finger joint. Old Greasy Hand had mourned often. For the first time he felt a twinge of pity, but he put it aside as another emotion, like anger, that he could not afford. He thought: What tales I will tell when I get home!

He wrinkled his nose in disdain. The camp stank of animals and meat and rancid grease. He looked down at his naked, shivering legs and was startled, remembering that he was still only a horse.

He could not trust the old woman. She fed him only because a starved slave would die and not be worth boasting about. Just how fitful her temper was he saw on the day when she got tired of stumbling over one of the hundred dogs that infested the camp. This was one of her own dogs, a large, strong one that pulled a baggage travois when the tribe moved camp.

Countless times he had seen her kick at the beast as it lay sleeping in front of the tepee, in her way. The dog always moved, with a yelp, but it always got in the way again. One day she gave the dog its usual kick and then stood scolding at it while the animal rolled its eyes sleepily. The old woman suddenly picked up her axe and cut the dog's head off with one blow. Looking well satisfied with herself, she beckoned her slave to remove the body.

It could have been me, he though, if I were a dog. But I'm a horse.

His hope of life lay with the girl, Pretty Calf. He set about courting her, realizing how desperately poor he was both in property and honor. He owned no horse, no weapon but the old bow and the battered arrows. He had nothing to give away, and he needed gifts, because he did not dare seduce the girl.

One of the customs of courtship involved sending a gift of horses to a girl's older brother and bestowing much buffalo meat upon her mother. The white man could not wait for some far-off time when he might have either horses or meat to give away. And his courtship had to be secret. It was not for him to stroll past the groups of watchful girls, blowing a flute made of an eagle's wing bone, as the flirtatious young bucks did.

He could not ride past Pretty Calf's tepee, painted and bedizened; he had no horse, no finery.

Back home, he remembered, I could marry just about any girl I'd want to. But he wasted little time thinking about that. A future was something to be earned.

The most he dared do was wink at Pretty Calf now and then, or state his admiration while she giggled and hid her face. The least he dared do to win his bride was to elope with her, but he had to give her a horse to put the seal of tribal approval on that. And he had no horse until he killed a man to get one. . . .

His opportunity came in early spring. He was casually accepted by that time. He did not belong, but he was amusing to the Crows, like a strange pet, or they would not have fed him through the winter.

His chance came when he was hunting small game with three young boys who were his guards as well as his scornful companions. Rabbits and birds were of no account in a camp well fed on buffalo meat, but they made good targets.

His party walked far that day. All of them at once saw the two horses in a sheltered coulee. The boys and the man crawled forward on their bellies, and then they saw an Indian who lay on the ground, moaning, a lone traveler. From the way the boys inched eagerly forward, Horse knew the man was fair prey—a member of some enemy tribe.

This is the way the captive white man acquired wealth and honor to win a bride and save his life: He shot an arrow into the sick man, a split second ahead of one of his small companions, and dashed forward to strike the still-groaning man with his bow, to count first coup. Then he seized the hobbled horses.

By the time he had the horses secure, and with them his hope for freedom, the boys had followed, counting coup with gestures and shrieks they had practiced since boyhood, and one of them had the scalp. The white man was grimly amused to see the boy double up with sudden nausea when he had the thing in his hand. . . .

There was a hubbub in the camp when they rode in that evening, two of them on each horse. The captive was noticed. Indians who had ignored him as a slave stared at the brave man who had struck first coup and had stolen horses.

The hubbub lasted all night, as fathers boasted loudly of their young sons' exploits. The white man was called upon to settle an argument between two fierce boys as to which of them had struck second coup and which must be satisfied with third. After much talk that went over his head, he solemnly pointed at the nearest boy. He didn't know which boy it was and didn't care, but the boy did.

The white man had watched warriors in their triumph. He knew what to do. Modesty about achievements had no place among the Crow people. When a man did something big, he told about it.

The white man smeared his face with grease and charcoal. He walked inside the tepee circle, chanting and singing. He used his own language.

"You heathens, you savages," he shouted. "I'm going to get out of here someday! I am going to get away!" The Crow people listened respectfully. In the Crow tongue he shouted, "Horse! I am Horse!" and they nodded.

He had a right to boast, and he had two horses. Before dawn, the white man and his bride were sheltered beyond a far hill, and he was telling her, "I love you, little lady. I love you."

She looked at him with her great dark eyes, and he thought she understood his English words—or as much as she needed to understand.

"You are my treasure," he said, "more precious than jewels, better than fine gold. I am going to call you Freedom."

When they returned to camp two days later, he was bold but worried. His ace, he suspected, might not be high enough in the game he was playing without being sure of the rules. But it served.

Old Greasy Hand raged—but not at him. She complained loudly that her daughter had let herself go too cheap. But the marriage was as good as any Crow marriage. He had paid a horse.

He learned the language faster after that, from Pretty Calf, whom he sometimes called Freedom. He learned that his attentive, adoring bride was fourteen years old.

One thing he had not guessed was the difference that being Pretty Calf's husband would make in his relationship to her mother and brother. He had hoped only to make his position a little safer, but he had not expected to be treated with dignity. Greasy Hand no longer spoke to him at all. When the white man spoke to her, his bride murmured in dismay, explaining at great length that he must never do that. There could be no conversation between a man and his mother-in-law. He could not even mention a word that was part of her name.

Having improved his status so magnificently, he felt no need for hurry in getting away. Now that he had a woman, he had as good a chance to be rich as any man. Pretty Calf waited on him; she seldom ran off to play games with other young girls, but took pride in learning from her mother the many women's skills of tanning hides and making clothing and preparing food.

He was no more a horse but a kind of man, a half-Indian, still poor and unskilled but laden with honors, clinging to the buckskin fringes of Crow society.

Escape could wait until he could manage it in comfort, with fit clothing and a good horse, with hunting weapons. Escape could wait until the camp moved near some trading post. He did not plan how he would get home. He dreamed of being there all at once, and of telling stories nobody would believe. There was no hurry.

Pretty Calf delighted in educating him. He began to understand tribal arrangements, customs and why things were as they were. They were that way because they had always been so. His young wife giggled when she told him, in his ignorance, things she had always known. But she did not laugh when her brother's wife was taken by another warrior. She explained that solemnly with words and signs.

Yellow Robe belonged to a society called the Big Dogs. The wife stealer, Cut Neck, belonged to the Foxes. They were fellow tribesmen; they hunted together and fought side by side, but men of one society could take away wives from the other society if they wished, subject to certain limitations.

When Cut Neck rode up to the tepee, laughing and singing, and called to Yellow Robe's wife, "Come out! Come out!" she did as ordered, looking smug as usual, meek and entirely willing. Thereafter she rode beside him in ceremonial processions and carried his coup stick, while his other wife pretended not to care.

"But why?" the white man demanded of his wife, his Freedom. "Why did our brother let his woman go? He sits and smokes and does not speak."

Pretty Calf was shocked at the suggestion. Her brother could not possibly reclaim his woman, she explained. He could not even let her come back if she wanted to—and she probably would want to when Cut Neck tired of her. Yellow Robe could not even admit that his heart was sick. That was the way things were. Deviation meant dishonor.

The woman could have hidden from Cut Neck, she said. She could even have refused to go with him if she had been *ba-wurokee* —a really virtuous woman. But she had been his woman before, for a little while on a berrying expedition, and he had a right to claim her.

There was no sense in it, the white man insisted. He glared at his young wife. "If you go, I will bring you back!" he promised.

She laughed and buried her head against his shoulder. "I will not have to go," she said. "Horse is my first man. There is no hole in my moccasin."

He stroked her hair and said, *"Ba-wurokee."*

With great daring, she murmured, *"Hayha,"* and when he did not answer, because he did not know what she meant, she drew away, hurt.

"A woman calls her man that if she thinks he will not leave her. Am I wrong?"

The white man held her closer and lied, "Pretty Calf is not wrong. Horse will not leave her. Horse will not take another woman, either." No, he certainly would not. Parting from this one was going to be harder than getting her had been. *"Hayha,"* he murmured. "Freedom."

His conscience irked him, but not very much. Pretty Calf could get another man easily enough when he was gone, and a better provider. His hunting skill was improving, but he was still awkward.

There was no hurry about leaving. He was used to most of the Crow ways and could stand the rest. He was becoming prosperous. He owned five horses. His place in the life of the tribe was secure, such as it was. Three or four young women, including the one who had belonged to Yellow Robe, made advances to him. Pretty Calf took pride in the fact that her man was so attractive.

By the time he had what he needed for a secret journey, the grass grew yellow on the plains and the long cold was close. He was enslaved by the girl he called Freedom and, before the winter ended, by the knowledge that she was carrying his child. . . .

The Big Dog society held a long ceremony in the spring. The white man strolled with his woman along the creek bank, thinking: When I get home I will tell them about the chants and the drumming. Sometime. Sometime.

Pretty Calf would not go to bed when they went back to the tepee.

"Wait and find out about my brother," she urged. "Something may happen."

So far as Horse could figure out, the Big Dogs were having some kind of election. He pampered his wife by staying up with her by the fire. Even the old woman, who was a great one for getting sleep when she was not working, prowled around restlessly.

The white man was yawning by the time the noise of the ceremony

died down. When Yellow Robe strode in, garish and heathen in his
paint and feathers and furs, the women cried out. There was conversation, too fast for Horse to follow, and the old woman wailed
once, but her son silenced her with a gruff command.

When the white man went to sleep, he thought his wife was weeping beside him.

The next morning she explained.

"He wears the bearskin belt. Now he can never retreat in battle. He
will always be in danger. He will die."

Maybe he wouldn't, the white man tried to convince her. Pretty
Calf recalled that some few men had been honored by the bearskin
belt, vowed to the highest daring, and had not died. If they lived
through the summer, then they were free of it.

"My brother wants to die," she mourned. "His heart is bitter."

Yellow Robe lived through half a dozen clashes with small parties
of raiders from hostile tribes. His honors were many. He captured
horses in an enemy camp, led two successful raids, counted first
coup and snatched a gun from the hand of an enemy tribesman. He
wore wolf tails on his moccasins and ermine skins on his shirt, and
he fringed his leggings with scalps in token of his glory.

When his mother ventured to suggest, as she did many times, "My
son should take a new wife, I need another woman to help me," he
ignored her. He spent much time in prayer, alone in the hills or in
conference with a medicine man. He fasted and made vows and kept
them. And before he could be free of the heavy honor of the bearskin
belt, he went on his last raid.

The warriors were returning from the north just as the white man
and two other hunters approached from the south, with buffalo and
elk meat dripping from the bloody hides tied on their restive ponies.
One of the hunters grunted, and they stopped to watch a rider on the
hill north of the tepee circle.

The rider dismounted, held up a blanket and dropped it. He repeated the gesture.

The hunters murmured dismay. "Two! Two men dead!" They rode
fast into the camp, where there was already wailing.

A messenger came down from the war party on the hill. The rest of
the party delayed to paint their faces for mourning and for victory.
One of the two dead men was Yellow Robe. They had put his body in

a cave and walled it in with rocks. The other man died later, and his body was in a tree.

There was blood on the ground before the tepee to which Yellow Robe would return no more. His mother, with her hair chopped short, sat in the doorway, rocking back and forth on her haunches, wailing her heartbreak. She cradled one mutilated hand in the other. She had cut off another finger joint.

Pretty Calf had cut off chunks of her long hair and was crying as she gashed her arms with a knife. The white man tried to take the knife away, but she protested so piteously that he let her do as she wished. He was sickened with the lot of them.

Savages! he thought. Now I will go back! I'll go hunting alone, and I'll keep on going.

But he did not go just yet, because he was the only hunter in the lodge of the two grieving women, one of them old and the other pregnant with his child.

In their mourning, they made him a pauper again. Everything that meant comfort, wealth and safety they sacrificed to the spirits because of the death of Yellow Robe. The tepee, made of seventeen fine buffalo hides, the furs that should have kept them warm, the white deerskin dress, trimmed with elk teeth, that Pretty Calf loved so well, even their tools and Yellow Robe's weapons—everything but his sacred medicine objects—they left there on the prairies, and the whole camp moved away. Two of his best horses were killed as a sacrifice, and the women gave away the rest.

They had no shelter. They would have no tepee of their own for two months at least of mourning, and then the women would have to tan hides to make it. Meanwhile they could live in temporary huts made of willows, covered with skins given them in pity by their friends. They could have lived with relatives, but Yellow Robe's women had no relatives.

The white man had not realized until then how terrible a thing it was for a Crow to have no kinfolk. No wonder old Greasy Hand had only stumps for fingers. She had mourned, from one year to the next, for everyone she had ever loved. She had no one left but her daughter, Pretty Calf.

Horse was furious at their foolishness. It had been bad enough for him, a captive, to be naked as a horse and poor as a slave, but that was because his captors had stripped him. These women had voluntarily given up everything they needed.

He was too angry at them to sleep in the willow hut. He lay under a sheltering tree. And on the third night of the mourning he made his plans. He had a knife and a bow. He would go after meat, taking two horses. And he would not come back. There were, he realized, many things he was not going to tell when he got back home.

In the willow hut, Pretty Calf cried out. He heard rustling there, and the old woman's querulous voice.

Some twenty hours later his son was born, two months early, in the tepee of a skilled medicine woman. The child was born without breath, and the mother died before the sun went down.

The white man was too shocked to think whether he should mourn, or how he should mourn. The old woman screamed until she was voiceless. Piteously she approached him, bent and trembling, blind with grief. She held out her knife and he took it.

She spread out her hands and shook her head. If she cut off any more finger joints, she could no more work. She could not afford any more lasting signs of grief.

The white man said, "All right! All right!" between his teeth. He hacked his arms with the knife and stood watching the blood run down. It was little enough to do for Pretty Calf, for little Freedom.

Now there is nothing to keep me, he realized. When I get home, I must not let them see the scars.

He looked at Greasy Hand, hideous in her grief-burdened age, and thought: I really am free now! When a wife dies, her husband has no more duty toward her family. Pretty Calf had told him so, long ago, when he wondered why a certain man moved out of one tepee and into another.

The old woman, of course, would be a scavenger. There was one other with the tribe, an ancient crone who had no relatives, toward whom no one felt any responsibility. She lived on food thrown away by the more fortunate. She slept in shelters that she built with her own knotted hands. She plodded wearily at the end of the procession when the camp moved. When she stumbled, nobody cared. When she died, nobody would miss her.

Tomorrow morning, the white man decided, I will go.

His mother-in-law's sunken mouth quivered. She said one word, questioningly. She said, *"Eero-oshay?"* She said, "Son?"

Blinking, he remembered. When a wife died, her husband was free. But her mother, who had ignored him with dignity, might if she wished ask him to stay. She invited him by calling him Son, and he accepted by answering Mother.

Greasy Hand stood before him, bowed with years, withered with unceasing labor, loveless and childless, scarred with grief. But with all her burdens, she still loved life enough to beg it from him, the only person she had any right to ask. She was stripping herself of all she had left, her pride.

He looked eastward across the prairie. Two thousand miles away was home. The old woman would not live forever. He could afford to wait, for he was young. He could afford to be magnanimous, for he knew he was a man. He gave her the answer. *"Eegya,"* he said. "Mother."

He went home three years later. He explained no more than to say, "I lived with Crows for a while. It was some time before I could leave. They called me Horse."

He did not find it necessary either to apologize or to boast, because he was the equal of any man on earth.

Dorothy M. Johnson (1905-)
Iowa-born Dorothy Johnson has written a number of award-winning novels and stories about American Indians. Some of her stories have been anthologized and adapted for radio, television and film, including "The Hanging Tree" and "A Man Called Horse". An honorary member of a Montana Blackfeet tribe, her Indian name is "Kills-both-places".

A small boy awakens in a forest to
find himself in the aftermath of battle. What is he to do? He takes his
wooden sword and leads the bleeding army of losers.

chickamauga
Ambrose Bierce

One sunny autumn afternoon a child strayed away from its rude
home in a small field and entered a forest unobserved. It was happy
in a new sense of freedom from control—happy in the opportunity of
exploration and adventure; for this child's spirit, in bodies of its ancestors, had for many thousands of years been trained to memorable
feats of discovery and conquest—victories in battles whose critical
moments were centuries, whose victors' camps were cities of hewn
stone. From the cradle of its race it had conquered its way through two
continents, and, passing a great sea, had penetrated a third, there to
be born to war and dominance as a heritage.

The child was a boy, aged about six years, the son of a poor
planter. In his younger manhood the father had been a soldier, had
fought against naked savages, and followed the flag of his country
into the capital of a civilised race to the far South. In the peaceful life
of a planter the warrior-fire survived; once kindled it is never ex-
tinguished. The man loved military books and pictures, and the boy
had understood enough to make himself a wooden sword, though
even the eye of his father would hardly have known it for what it was.
This weapon he now bore bravely, as became the son of an heroic
race, and, pausing now and again in the sunny spaces of the forest,
assumed, with some exaggeration, the postures of aggression and
defence that he had been taught by the engraver's art. Made reckless

by the ease with which he overcame invisible foes attempting to stay
his advance, he committed the common enough military error of
pushing the pursuit to a dangerous extreme, until he found himself
upon the margin of a wide but shallow brook, whose rapid waters
barred his direct advance against the flying foe who had crossed
with illogical ease. But the intrepid victor was not to be baffled; the
spirit of the race which had passed the great sea burned uncon-
querable in that small breast and would not be denied. Finding a
place where some boulders in the bed of the stream lay but a step or
a leap apart, he made his way across and fell again upon the rear
guard of his imaginary foe, putting all to the sword.

Now that the battle had been won, prudence required that he with-
draw to his base of operations. Alas! like many a mightier conqueror,
and like one, the mightiest, he could not

> Curb the lusts for war,
> Nor learn that tempted Fate will leave the loftiest star.

Advancing from the bank of the creek, he suddenly found himself
confronted with a new and more formidable enemy; in the path that
he was following, bolt upright, with ears erect and paws suspended
before it, sat a rabbit. With a startled cry the child turned and fled, he
knew not in what direction, calling with inarticulate cries for his
mother, weeping, stumbling, his tender skin cruelly torn by
brambles, his little heart beating hard with terror—breathless, blind
with tears—lost in the forest! Then, for more than an hour, he wandered with erring feet through the tangled undergrowth, till at last,
overcome with fatigue, he lay down in a narrow space between two
rocks, within a few yards of the stream, and, still grasping his toy
sword, no longer a weapon but a companion, sobbed himself to
sleep. The wood birds sang merrily above his head; the squirrels,
whisking their bravery of tail, ran barking from tree to tree, unconscious of the pity of it, and somewhere far away was a strange, muf-
fled thunder, as if the partridges were drumming in celebration of
nature's victory over the son of her immemorial enslavers. And back
at the little plantation, where white men and black were hastily
searching the fields and hedgerows in alarm, a mother's heart was
breaking for her missing child.

Hours passed, and then the little sleeper rose to his feet. The chill of the evening was in his limbs, the fear of the gloom in his heart. But he had rested, and he no longer wept. With some blind instinct which impelled to action, he struggled through the undergrowth about him and came to a more open ground—on his right the brook, to the left a gentle acclivity studded with infrequent trees, over all the gathering gloom of twilight. A thin ghostly mist rose along the water. It frightened and repelled him; instead of recrossing, in the direction whence he had come, he turned his back upon it and went forward toward the dark inclosing wood. Suddenly he saw before him a strange moving object which he took to be some large animal—a dog, a pig—he could not name it; perhaps it was a bear. He had seen pictures of bears, but knew of nothing to their discredit, and had vaguely wished to meet one. But something in the awkwardness of its approach—told him that it was not a bear, and curiosity was stayed by fear. He stood still, and as it came slowly on, gained courage every moment, for he saw that at least it had not the long, menacing ears of the rabbit. Possibly his impressionable mind was half conscious of something familiar in its shambling, awkward gait. Before it had approached near enough to resolve his doubts, he saw that it was followed by another and another. To right and to left were many more; the whole open space about him was alive with them—all moving forward toward the brook.

They were men. They crept upon their hands and knees. They used their hands only, dragging their legs. They used their knees only, their arms hanging useless at their sides. They strove to rise to their feet, but fell prone in the attempt. They did nothing naturally, and nothing alike, save only to advance foot by foot in the same direction. Singly, in pairs, and in little groups, they came on through the gloom, some halting now and again while others crept slowly past them, then resuming their movement. They came by dozens and by hundreds; as far on either hand as one could see in the deepening gloom they extended, and the black wood behind them appeared to be inexhaustible. The very ground seemed in motion toward the creek. Occasionally one who had paused did not again go on, but lay motionless. He was dead. Some, pausing, made strange gestures with their hands, erected their arms and lowered them again, clasped their heads; spread their palms upward, as men are sometimes seen to do in public prayer.

Not all of this did the child note; it is what would have been noted by an older observer; he saw little but that these were men, yet crept like babes. Being men, they were not terrible, though some of them were unfamiliarly clad. He moved among them freely, going from one to another and peering into their faces with childish curiosity. All their faces were singularly white and many were streaked and gouted with red. Something in this—something too, perhaps, in their grotesque attitudes and movements—reminded him of the painted clown whom he had seen last summer in the circus, and he laughed as he watched them. But on and ever on they crept, these maimed and bleeding men, as heedless as he of the dramatic contrast between his laughter and their own ghastly gravity. To him it was a merry spectacle. He had seen his father's negroes creep upon their hands and knees for his amusement—had ridden them so, 'making believe' they were his horses. He now approached one of these crawling figures from behind and with an agile movement mounted it astride. The man sank upon his breast, recovered, flung the small boy fiercely to the ground as an unbroken colt might have done, then turned upon him a face that lacked a lower jaw—from the upper teeth to the throat was a great red gap fringed with hanging shreds of flesh and splinters of bone. The unnatural prominence of nose, the absence of chin, the fierce eyes, gave this man the appearance of a great bird of prey crimsoned in throat and breast by the blood of its quarry. The man rose to his knees, the child to his feet. The man shook his fist at the child; the child, terrified at last, ran to a tree near by, got upon the farther side of it, and took a more serious view of the situation. And so the uncanny multitude dragged itself slowly and painfully along in hideous pantomime—moved forward down the slope like a swarm of great black beetles, with never a sound of going—in silence profound, absolute.

Instead of darkening, the haunted landscape began to brighten. Through the belt of trees beyond the brook shone a strange red light, the trunks and branches of the trees making a black lacework against it. It struck the creeping figures and gave them monstrous shadows, which caricatured their movements on the lit grass. It fell upon their faces, touching their whiteness with a ruddy tinge, accentuating the stains with which so many of them were freaked and maculated. It sparkled on buttons and bits of metal in their clothing. Instinctively the child turned toward the growing splendour and moved down the slope with his horrible companions; in a few moments had passed the foremost of the throng—not much of a feat, considering his advantages. He placed himself in the lead, his wooden sword still in hand, and solemnly directed the march, conforming his pace to theirs and occasionally turning as if to see that his forces did not straggle. Surely such a leader never before had such a following.

Scattered about upon the ground now slowly narrowing by the encroachment of this awful march to water, were certain articles to which, in the leader's mind, were coupled no significant associations; an occasional blanket, tightly rolled lengthwise, doubled, and the ends bound together with a string; a heavy knapsack here, and there a broken musket—such things, in short, as are found in the rear of retreating troops, the 'spoor' of men flying from their hunters. Everywhere near the creek, which here had a margin of lowland, the earth was trodden into mud by the feet of men and horses. An observer of better experience in the use of his eyes would have noticed that these footprints pointed in both directions; the ground had been twice passed over—in advance and in retreat. A few hours before, these desperate, stricken men, with their more fortunate and now distant comrades, had penetrated the forest in thousands. Their successive battalions, breaking into swarms and reforming in lines, had passed the child on every side—had almost trodden on him as he slept. The rustle and murmur of their march had not awakened him. Almost within a stone's throw of where he lay they had fought a battle; but all unheard by him were the roar of the musketry, the shock of the cannon, 'the thunder of the captains and the shouting.' He had slept through it all, grasping his little wooden sword with perhaps a tighter clutch in unconscious sympathy with his martial environment, but as heedless of the grandeur of the struggle as the dead who died to make the glory.

The fire beyond the belt of woods on the farther side of the creek, reflected to earth from the canopy of its own smoke, was now suffusing the whole landscape. It transformed the sinuous line of mist to the vapour of gold. The water gleamed with dashes of red, and red, too, were many of the stones protruding above the surface. But that was blood; the less desperately wounded had stained them in crossing. On them, too, the child now crossed with eager steps; he was going to the fire. As he stood upon the farther bank, he turned about to look at the companions of his march. The advance was arriving at the creek. The stronger had already drawn themselves to the brink and plunged their faces in the flood. Three or four who lay without motion appeared to have no heads. At this the child's eyes expanded with wonder; even his hospitable understanding could not accept a phenomenon implying such vitality as that. After slaking their thirst these men had not the strength to back away from the water, nor to keep their heads above it. They were drowned. In rear of these the open spaces of the forest showed the leader as many formless figures of his grim command as at first; but not nearly so many were in motion. He waved his cap for their encouragement and smilingly pointed with his weapon in the direction of the guiding light—a pillar of fire to this strange exodus.

Confident of the fidelity of his forces, he now entered the belt of woods, passed through it easily in the red illumination, climbed a fence, ran across a field, turning now and again to coquette with his responsive shadow, and so approached the blazing ruin of a dwelling. Desolation everywhere. In all the wide glare not a living thing was visible. He cared nothing for that; the spectacle pleased, and he danced with glee in imitation of the wavering flames. He ran about collecting fuel, but every object that he found was too heavy for him to cast in from the distance to which the heat limited his approach. In despair he flung in his sword—a surrender to the superior forces of nature. His military career was at an end. Shifting his position, his eyes fell upon some out-buildings which had an oddly familiar appearance, as if he had dreamed of them. He stood considering them with wonder, when suddenly the entire plantation, with its inclosing forest, seemed to turn as if upon a pivot. His little world swung half around; the points of the compass were reversed. He recognised the blazing building as his own home!

For a moment he stood stupefied by the power of the revelation, then ran with stumbling feet, making a half circuit of the ruin. There, conspicuous in the light of the conflagration, lay the dead body of a woman—the white face turned upward, the hands thrown out and clutched full of grass, the clothing deranged, the long dark hair in tangles and full of clotted blood. The greater part of the forehead was torn away, and from the jagged hole the brain protruded, overflowing the temple, a frothy mass of grey, crowned with clusters of crimson bubbles—the work of a shell!

The child moved his little hands, making wild, uncertain gestures. He uttered a series of inarticulate and indescribable cries—something between the chattering of an ape and the gobbling of a turkey —a startling, soulless, unholy sound, the language of a devil. The child was a deaf mute.

Then he stood motionless, with quivering lips, looking down upon the wreck.

Ambrose Bierce (1842-1914?)
A renowned American master of the horror story, Ambrose Bierce disappeared in Mexico in 1914. He worked as a newspaperman, but it is for his stories that he is best remembered. A distinctive use of suspense, the macabre, and the surprise or shock ending have made many Bierce stories famous.

"He put the harmonica to his mouth
and tore the first note loose from it,
his eyes sinking closed with the
weight of his joy."

out of the rain
Ted Wood

The afternoon light had dimmed to a sulphurous yellow and a sudden frightened wind had sprung up, spinning the roadside maples. Dust eddied along the shoulder of the road and a cloud of fragments tore loose from the load of straw to fly over George's head and away down the long concession that stretched in front of his tractor.

Then the rain began to fall, each drop hard and flat. Within seconds George was soaked, his shirt and work pants black with water. His hair darkened too, clinging close to his round, small head. He drove on uncaring, knowing the straw would stay dry under the tarpaulin his father and brother Walt had tied over it. He stopped where the concession crossed the highway and waited, looking both ways with an earnest ticking motion of his head until the road was clear. Then he pulled across and put the tractor into third gear again as he started up the slow hill that led past Murdoch's pasture.

He became aware that the tractor was labouring at the throttle setting he had given it, the setting he always gave it on this stretch of the road home.

He reached down and pulled the lever a little farther back—not too far, mustn't let her rattle. Dad said it shouldn't rattle, not ever.

The labouring did not improve. George narrowed his eyes again and thought about it. He had a hundred and seventeen bales on the wagon but it was straw. This tractor would draw that many *hay* bales without going slow like this. His hand strayed to the throttle again but he did not open it farther and presently the motor died.

He switched off the ignition as he had been instructed and put the brake on, tapping it into the lock with the toe of his boot. Then, leaving the engine in gear, he stepped down and took a slow walk around the wagon. The rain still spouted down, bouncing knee-high as every drop exploded on the warm tarred surface of the road. And then he saw the trouble. The back tire was flat, torn half off the rim with a frill of tattered inner tube protruding like a black tongue sticking out at his discomfiture. George looked at it and rubbed his head. His Dad would be mad about that. His shallow memory prompted him with cues of a message he had been given. His Dad had said to watch something. Watch the tire. Now he remembered the whole warning—watch the tire, it's blistered, don't keep going on it and tear it all up.

Behind him, over the steady hiss of the rain, he heard laughter. It came and went in little puffs of sound as whoever was laughing ran towards him.

He turned and looked. Two boys his own age and a girl were running down the road from the direction of the camp ground that Mrs. Dickson had opened up alongside her sugarbush by the crick.

One of the boys was black. George couldn't remember seeing a black boy up close before and he stared at him as the three of them ran towards him.

They reached his wagon and the girl shouted, "C'mon under here." The boys laughed and the black boy said, "Hey, yeah," and the three of them dropped to their knees and crept under the wagon bed out of the rain.

The girl looked out at George, laughing from a wide, happy mouth. "Why don't you come out of the rain?" she asked.

"Huh?" George said and the girl began again, "I said why don't you. . . . "

The white boy interrupted her. "Ackwards-bay," he said slowly, mouthing the syllables with a wide movement of his jaws, as if the sounds were hot.

The girl stopped and looked at him for a moment, then nodded, and stopped laughing.

"I didn't realize," she said.

The boy waved at George. "Hey, man, c'mon."

Obediently, George crouched down and came in under the wagon. He was still wet and the road was streaming but it felt better not to have the water beating on his head.

He stared at the girl. She was pretty, like a girl in a commercial. Her hair was wet and so was her shirt. George could see her nipples jutting through the thin material and he stared at them. He couldn't remember ever seeing a girl's nipples before.

He realized the white boy was talking to him. "Your tire's flat, d'you know that?"

George nodded. "It tore all up," he said.

"All to Heeeeeeell," the black boy said and the three of them started laughing. George looked at each of them in turn, trying to see why they were laughing so hard. There was nothing funny anywhere. It was raining and his tire was all tore up and they were sitting on wet road. There was nothing funny. He looked at the bundles they were carrying. Each of them had a haversack and the white boy had a funny-shaped box with a handle. Maybe that was what made them laugh.

He said, "What you got inside there?"

The boy laughed. "Direct little devil, aren't you," he said.

George smiled because they all smiled. "Wha's inside?" he repeated finally.

The girl said, "It's a guitar." She spoke kindly, the way Miss Roberts at school used to. The other boys stopped laughing when she spoke and the white one said, "There's music inside there."

"Yeah?" George felt himself grinning. He knew they were funning him.

"Yeah," the boy said. "You wanna see?"

"All right," George said.

The boy took the case on his knees and moved farther under the wagon, farther away from the hissing rain. There was even less headroom under the center of the wagon and he had to lie almost flat on his back, his head pillowed on his pack as he opened the case and took out the guitar.

It was dark and shiny. George looked at it and knew he mustn't touch it.

The boy handed the box aside and the girl took it, closing it carefully and keeping it in her arms away from the wetness of the road beneath them.

"Play something," she said and George could hardly hear her for the beating of the rain. "Play me a blues for a rainy day."

The boy with the guitar didn't answer. He lay for a moment, then he wiped his hand on the comparatively dry part of his shirt under his other arm, a quick dipping motion that George thought was going to make the music.

And then he started to play. And George felt the little hairs on the back of his head growling up straight as he listened. He felt his belly muscles tighten and his heart swell up in his chest until he could hardly breathe. His head would not stay still, it weaved back and forth to the music, carrying his short neck and wide strong shoulders back and forth, in and out of the sound of the music, in and out of the sound of the rain.

He heard the black boy say, "Hey, man, you got yourself a real live fan."

Then the music stopped.

George said, "Wha'd'ya stop for?"

"Had to, man, there ain't no more," the boy told him. He was smiling, fingers ready to play more, head comfortable against the pack, back flat on the warm, wet road. The black boy was kneeling next to him, head bent under the lowness of the wagon bed. "Here, let a soul brother play," he said and the boy handed him the guitar as freely as if it were a bottle or something else of no consequence.

George watched as the black fingers with their pink undersides stung a spurt of sound from the strings. And then the music had hold of him again, carrying him away as surely as rainwater was carrying away the dross of summer from the shoulder of the road. He sat and rocked and slapped his legs with his hands and as he did so he felt the bump in the pocket and he remembered that he could make music too. He interrupted his rocking and swaying long enough to push his hands deep into his pocket and take out the fifty-cent harmonica he had found on the school bus last year when he still went to school.

He took it in his hands and looked into it, at the damp dust that clogged the holes in it. He could see the boys and girls looking at one another with the look the kids on the bus had worn, not quite laughing but the corners of their mouths tucked down tight so they wouldn't.

He didn't care. The music had him like a horse has a rider.

He raised the harmonica to his lips, and in the moment before he closed his eyes he saw the girl cover her ears with her hands, laughing unashamedly.

George didn't care. He took the tiny instrument between his lips and tore from it the gasping snorts of joy that had soothed him so many times when nothing else could still the mumblings in his head. He swayed and rocked but now his own sounds rode with the guitar sounds, lifting him like some huge bird that could carry him and the wagon and the tractor and the hundred and seventeen bales of straw as if they were nothing, could float them up and through the other side of the sky.

He heard the boy saying, "Can you believe that? An honest to God blues." And the black boy echoing the surprise, "Believe it man, this dude is gooood."

Then the guitar stopped and George stopped with it, wrapping up the sky and the wind and the rainclouds into one big note that felt good down through his teeth and into his chest.

He opened his eyes and found the girl clapping her hands. "You play great," she said.

George shook his head. "No. You wanna hear Walt play. He can play Red River Valley an ever'thing."

The white boy said, "That good, eh?"

George said, "Yes," and wondered why they were laughing again. They were funny people—the one boy's hair was as long as the girl's and the black boy was dressed in a red shirt and pants that were purple where they weren't soaked through.

George looked at the girl again. She was laughing less than the boys, just a big smile really. She had set down the guitar case across her knees and taken hold of the front of her shirt with both forefingers and thumbs and was holding it away from herself so that he couldn't see her nipples any more, drying her shirt.

She said, "Can you play tunes?"

George did not raise his eyes from her fingers and she repeated the question. "Hello in there," she said. "I say can you play tunes?"

George looked at her face again. "No. I can't play tunes. I can't play it, Walt says."

The girl was beginning to say something, not smiling now but serious. And then George cut her off, finding words to explain what he felt. "I can't play it," he said. "But I can make it sing."

The white boy gave a sudden excited whistle and sat up so quickly he almost hit his head on the underside of the wagon. "Man, that's beautiful"—he waved his hand at the other two—"like, that's really beautiful."

George wondered why he was so excited, and why the black boy had lowered his head over the guitar and was shaking it slowly back and forth, squeezing his eyes together as if he was going to cry. But he did not. Instead he struck another ring from the guitar. "Make it sing again," he said softly.

George could not have disobeyed.

He put the harmonica to his mouth and tore the first note loose from it, his eyes sinking closed with the weight of his joy. He could hear the girl singing, a low song with no words, and he could feel the guitar striking fire from his bones and the warm rags of sound from his own harmonica wrapping all of them in happiness.

He played until his mouth was sore at the corners and the little pain had started biting his lips. And then the music stopped. First the singing, then the guitar, and then his own music withered and stopped as he opened his eyes and stared out from under the wagon at the sunlit, steaming roadway.

The white boy was lying on his side, staring out over the top of his pack, forward, past the tractor wheels. "Someone's stopped," he said.

The black boy reached out towards the girl. "Gimme that box," he said. "Let's git."

The girl handed the guitar case to him. "I don't want to. I dig this," she said.

The white boy said, "Yeah, some big dude. He's coming back."

The black boy tumbled the guitar into the case. "Let's git," he said again. "I don't dig some cat' can play Red River Valley, kickin' my black ass."

The three of them began to scramble their way out from under the wagon. George came after them, puzzling why the boy had said "ass" in front of the girl. His father had said he mustn't say "ass" in front of girls.

The harmonica was still in his hand and it tapped on the wet roadway as he came out on hands and knees to find himself facing

Walter's boots and the legs of Walter's green pants.

"Hi, Walter," he said. And Walter told him, "Get up."

The two boys and the girl were putting their packs on. They were standing by the back of the wagon but Walter went over to them. "What's going on?" he asked them, his red face angry under the peaked green cap he had bought at the Co-op.

The black boy said nothing. The white boy shook his head so the shoulder-length hair fell straight to dry in the sun. "Just sheltering from the rain, brother," he said.

Walt was mad. George knew it. He could tell by the jumpiness in his own throat. Walt was mad.

"You're not my brother. You're a long haired hippy and you been messing with this boy." The white boy and the girl both said "No we haven't," together, but the black boy said nothing.

Walter said. "I ought to call the p'lice. Lookit his mouth. His mouth's cut."

George put his fingers up to his mouth and looked at them. There was a little pinkness on them. He wondered why.

"Lookit. He's bleeding," Walter said. "Somebody hit him." Walter looked at George, holding his chin and tilting his face so he could see the tiny cuts on the corners of the mouth. "What happened?" he asked in a voice that made George shivery.

"We sat under the wagon," George said. He wished Walter would let go of his chin, it made talking difficult. Walter said nothing and did not release his face, but stared into it angrily as if it were a mirror and he were practising his angry face. "Out of the rain," George said finally.

He could see that his three friends were going to leave him and he wanted them to stay, he wanted the music to go on some more.

Walter let go of his chin suddenly, almost throwing his face aside as he turned to the three young people. "You ought to be ashamed, picking on a boy that don't know what's going on," he said. He was blazing angry. "Making fun of him, laughing at him while he makes a damn fool of himself with that there mouth organ." He turned to George and whipped the harmonica from his hand and threw it away over the fence into the Murdoch's pasture. George wailed "Walter . . ." but stood still, not knowing what made his brother so mad.

And then the girl was angry too. She stepped up in front of Walter and shouted into his face. "You're sick. You know that. You're a stupid ignorant bully."

And then everyone was shouting. Walter was shouting and the two boys were shouting, standing one pace away from him, either side of him so that he had to swing his head from one to the other as he shouted down their expressions of contempt and hatred.

The black boy kept saying, "He's a natural musician, man, a natural blues musician," and it was this that made Walter angriest of all. 'You think that's funny, eh? Him honking away making a monkey of himself while you laugh at him, you bastards. Get away from here, get the hell away."

And as George watched, they left, first the white boy, then the black and finally the girl, pausing only to spit at Walter's feet. The three of them walked away, shoulders hunched, down the steaming road while Walter stood, his hands in his belt, looking after them.

George watched until they had reached the county road and had swung around limply to hang their thumbs against the city-bound traffic. Then he turned to find Walter walking away to the flat tire of the wagon. He felt his earlier nervousness come back as he walked to join his brother who was stooping, hands on his knees, staring at the ruin of the tire. "It bust," he explained.

Walter straightened up, easing his shoulders as if some load had just been taken from them. "Yeah, I can see that," he said, kindly. He reached out his hand and ruffled George's short, crisp hair. "You're crazy as a hoot owl George, y'know that?" he said.

He turned away to the pickup, calling over his shoulder, "Come on now, gimme a hand with this jack. We got work to do, not like some folks."

And George could feel his back and arms growing eager at the thought of working on the wheel and he laughed, once, a shred of the same sound he had made earlier with his harmonica.

Ted Wood (1931-)
Born in England, Ted Wood moved to Canada in 1954. He has worked as a policeman and an advertising copywriter. His first book of stories, Somebody Else's Summer, *was published in 1973.*

of the heart

"Suddenly he caught sight of Mrs.
Ramsay's face. It was so white that
she looked as though she were
about to faint."

A wager over a string of pearls terri-
fies this woman. Her fear is the final
proof that Mr. Know-All *really does
know all.*

mr. know-all
W. Somerset Maugham

I was prepared to dislike Max Kelada even before I knew him. The
war had just finished and the passenger traffic in the ocean-going
lines was heavy. Accommodation was very hard to get and you had
to put up with whatever the agents chose to offer you. You could not
hope for a cabin to yourself and I was thankful to be given one in
which there were only two berths. But when I was told the name of
my companion my heart sank. It suggested closed port-holes and
the night air rigidly excluded. It was bad enough to share a cabin for
fourteen days with anyone (I was going from San Francisco to
Yokohama), but I should have looked upon it with less dismay if my
fellow-passenger's name had been Smith or Brown.

When I went on board I found Mr. Kelada's luggage already below.
I did not like the look of it; there were too many labels on the suitcases, and the wardrobe trunk was too big. He had unpacked his toilet things, and I observed that he was a patron of the excellent Monsieur Coty; for I saw on the washing-stand his scent, his hair-wash

and his brilliantine. Mr. Kelada's brushes, ebony with his monogram in gold, would have been all the better for a scrub. I did not at all like Mr. Kelada. I made my way into the smoking-room. I called for a pack of cards and began to play patience. I had scarcely started before a man came up to me and asked me if he was right in thinking my name was so-and-so.

"I am Mr. Kelada," he added, with a smile that showed a row of flashing teeth, and sat down.

"Oh, yes, we're sharing a cabin, I think."

"Bit of luck, I call it. You never know who you're going to be put in with. I was jolly glad when I heard you were English. I'm all for us English sticking together when we're abroad, if you understand what I mean."

I blinked.

"Are you English?" I asked, perhaps tactlessly.

"Rather. You don't think I look like an American, do you? British to the backbone, that's what I am."

To prove it, Mr. Kelada took out of his pocket a passport and airily waved it under my nose.

King George has many strange subjects. Mr. Kelada was short and of a sturdy build, clean-shaven and dark-skinned, with a fleshy, hooked nose and very large, lustrous and liquid eyes. His long black hair was sleek and curly. He spoke with a fluency in which there was nothing English and his gestures were exuberant. I felt pretty sure that a closer inspection of that British passport would have betrayed the fact that Mr. Kelada was born under a bluer sky than is generally seen in England.

"What will you have?" he asked me.

I looked at him doubtfully. Prohibition was in force and to all appearances the ship was bone-dry. When I am not thirsty I do not know which I dislike more, ginger-ale or lemon-squash. But Mr. Kelada flashed an oriental smile at me.

"Whiskey and soda or a dry Martini, you have only to say the word."

From each of his hip-pockets he fished a flask and laid them on the table before me. I chose the Martini, and calling the steward he ordered a tumbler of ice and a couple of glasses.

"A very good cocktail," I said.

"Well, there are plenty more where that came from, and if you've got any friends on board, you tell them you've got a pal who's got all the liquor in the world."

Mr. Kelada was chatty. He talked of New York and of San Francisco. He discussed plays, pictures, and politics. He was patriotic. The Union Jack is an impressive piece of drapery, but when it is flourished by a gentleman from Alexandria or Beirut, I cannot but feel that it loses somewhat in dignity. Mr. Kelada was familiar. I do not wish to put on airs, but I cannot help feeling that it is seemly in a total stranger to put mister before my name when he addresses me. Mr. Kelada, doubtless to set me at my ease, used no such formality. I did not like Mr. Kelada. I had put aside the cards when he sat down, but now, thinking that for this first occasion our conversation had lasted long enough, I went on with my game.

"The three on the four," said Mr. Kelada.

There is nothing more exasperating when you are playing patience than to be told where to put the card you have turned up before you have had a chance to look for yourself.

"It's coming out, it's coming out," he cried. "The ten on the knave."

With rage and hatred in my heart I finished. Then he seized the pack.

"Do you like card tricks?"

"No, I hate card tricks," I answered.

"Well, I'll just show you this one."

He showed me three. Then I said I would go down to the dining-room and get my seat at table.

"Oh, that's all right," he said. "I've already taken a seat for you. I thought that as we were in the same state-room we might just as well sit at the same table."

I did not like Mr. Kelada.

I not only shared a cabin with him and ate three meals a day at the same table, but I could not walk round the deck without his joining me. It was impossible to snub him. It never occurred to him that he was not wanted. He was certain that you were as glad to see him as he was to see you. In your own house you might have kicked him downstairs and slammed the door in his face without the suspicion dawning on him that he was not a welcome visitor. He was a good mixer, and in three days knew everyone on board. He ran everything. He managed the sweeps, conducted the auctions, collected money for prizes at the sports, got up quoit and golf matches, organised the concert and arranged the fancy dress ball. He was everywhere and always. He was certainly the best-hated man in the ship. We called him Mr. Know-All, even to his face. He took it as a compliment. But it was at meal times that he was most intolerable. For the better part of an hour then he had us at his mercy. He was hearty, jovial, loquacious and argumentative. He knew everything better than anybody else, and it was an affront to his over-weening vanity that you should disagree with him. He would not drop a subject, however unimportant, till he had brought you round to his way of thinking. The possibility that he could be mistaken never occurred to him. He was the chap who knew. We sat at the doctor's table. Mr. Kelada would certainly have had it all his own way, for the doctor was lazy and I was frigidly indifferent, except for a man called Ramsay who sat there also. He was as dogmatic as Mr. Kelada and resented bitterly the Levantine's cocksureness. The discussions they had were acrimonious and interminable.

Ramsay was in the American Consular Service, and was stationed at Kobe. He was a great heavy fellow from the Middle West, with loose fat under a tight skin, and he bulged out of his ready-made clothes. He was on his way back to resume his post, having been on a flying visit to New York to fetch his wife, who had been spending a year at home. Mrs. Ramsay was a very pretty little thing, with pleasant manners and a sense of humour. The Consular Service is ill paid, and she was dressed always very simply; but she knew how to wear her clothes. She achieved an effect of quiet distinction. I should not have paid any particular attention to her but that she possessed a quality that may be common enough in women, but nowadays is not obvious in their demeanour. You could not look at her without being struck by her modesty. It shone in her like a flower on a coat.

One evening at dinner the conversation by chance drifted to the subject of pearls. There had been in the papers a good deal of talk about the culture pearls which the cunning Japanese were making, and the doctor remarked that they must inevitably diminish the value of real ones. They were very good already; they would soon be perfect. Mr. Kelada, as was his habit, rushed the new topic. He told us all that was to be known about pearls. I do not believe Ramsay knew anything about them at all, but he could not resist the opportunity to have a fling at the Levantine, and in five minutes we were in the middle of a heated argument. I had seen Mr. Kelada vehement and voluble before, but never so voluble and vehement as now. At last something that Ramsay said stung him, for he thumped the table and shouted:

"Well, I ought to know what I am talking about. I'm going to Japan just to look into this Japanese pearl business. I'm in the trade and there's not a man in it who won't tell you that what I say about pearls goes. I know all the best pearls in the world and what I don't know about pearls isn't worth knowing."

Here was news for us, for Mr. Kelada, with all his loquacity, had never told anyone what his business was. We only knew vaguely that he was going to Japan on some commercial errand. He looked round the table triumphantly.

"They'll never be able to get a culture pearl that an expert like me can't tell with half an eye." He pointed to a chain that Mrs. Ramsay wore. "You take my word for it, Mrs. Ramsay, that chain you're wearing will never be worth a cent less than it is now."

Mrs. Ramsay in her modest way flushed a little and slipped the chain inside her dress. Ramsay leaned forward. He gave us all a look and a smile flickered in his eyes.

"That's a pretty chain of Mrs. Ramsay's, isn't it?"

"I noticed it at once," answered Mr. Kelada. "Gee, I said to myself, those are pearls all right."

"I didn't buy it myself, of course. I'd be interested to know how much you think it cost."

"Oh, in the trade somewhere round fifteen thousand dollars. But if it was bought on Fifth Avenue I shouldn't be surprised to hear that anything up to thirty thousand was paid for it."

Ramsay smiled grimly.

"You'll be surprised to hear that Mrs. Ramsay bought that string at a department store the day before we left New York, for eighteen dollars."

Mr. Kelada flushed.

"Rot. It's not only real, but it's as fine a string for its size as I've ever seen."

"Will you bet on it? I'll bet you a hundred dollars it's imitation."

"Done."

"Oh, Elmer, you can't bet on a certainty," said Mrs. Ramsay.

She had a little smile on her lips and her tone was gently depre-
cating.

"Can't I? If I get a chance of easy money like that I should be all
sorts of a fool not to take it."

"But how can it be proved?" she continued. "It's only my word
against Mr. Kelada's."

"Let me look at the chain, and if it's imitation I'll tell you quickly
enough. I can afford to lose a hundred dollars," said Mr. Kelada.

"Take it off, dear. Let the gentleman look at it as much as he wants."

Mrs. Ramsay hesitated a moment. She put her hands to the clasp.

"I can't undo it," she said. "Mr. Kelada will just have to take my word
for it."

I had a sudden suspicion that something unfortunate was about to
occur, but I could think of nothing to say.

Ramsay jumped up.

"I'll undo it."

He handed the chain to Mr. Kelada. The Levantine took a mag-
nifying glass from his pocket and closely examined it. A smile of triumph spread over his smooth and swarthy face. He handed back the
chain. He was about to speak. Suddenly he caught sight of Mrs.
Ramsay's face. It was so white that she looked as though she were
about to faint. She was staring at him with wide and terrified eyes.
They held a desperate appeal; it was so clear that I wondered why
her husband did not see it.

Mr. Kelada stopped with his mouth open. He flushed deeply. You
could almost *see* the effort he was making over himself.

"I was mistaken," he said. "It's a very good imitation, but of course
as soon as I looked through my glass I saw that it wasn't real. I think
eighteen dollars is just about as much as the damned thing's worth."

He took out his pocket-book and from it a hundred-dollar note. He
handed it to Ramsay without a word.

"Perhaps that'll teach you not to be so cocksure another time, my
young friend," said Ramsay as he took the note.

I noticed that Mr. Kelada's hands were trembling.

The story spread over the ship as stories do, and he had to put up
with a good deal of chaff that evening. It was a fine joke that Mr.
Know-All had been caught out. But Mrs. Ramsay retired to her state-

room with a headache.

Next morning I got up and began to shave. Mr. Kelada lay on his bed smoking a cigarette. Suddenly there was a small scraping sound and I saw a letter pushed under the door. I opened the door and looked out. There was nobody there. I picked up the letter and saw that it was addressed to Max Kelada. The name was written in block letters. I handed it to him.

"Who's this from?" He opened it. "Oh!"

He took out of the envelope, not a letter, but a hundred-dollar note. He looked at me and again he reddened. He tore the envelope into little bits and gave them to me.

"Do you mind just throwing them out of the port-hole?"

I did as he asked, and then I looked at him with a smile.

"No one likes being made to look a perfect damned fool," he said.

"Were the pearls real?"

"If I had a pretty little wife I shouldn't let her spend a year in New York while I stayed at Kobe," said he.

At that moment I did not entirely dislike Mr. Kelada. He reached out for his pocket-book and carefully put in it the hundred-dollar note.

W. Somerset Maugham (1874-1965)
This English writer's stories are among the best loved and most anthologized of this century. Maugham was also a widely-respected novelist, and his novel Of Human Bondage *is considered a classic in English literature.*

"Father," I said, feeling I might as well
get it over while I had him in good
humor, "I had it all arranged to kill
my grandmother."

Here is a fellow who has never con-
fessed his sins. He is burdened with
"the crimes of a lifetime".

first confession
Frank O'Connor

All the trouble began when my grandfather died and my grandmother—my father's mother—came to live with us. Relations in the
one house are a strain at the best of times, but, to make matters
worse, my grandmother was a real old countrywoman and quite un-
suited to the life in town. She had a fat, wrinkled old face, and, to
Mother's great indignation, went round the house in bare feet—the
boots had her crippled, she said. For dinner she had a jug of porter
and a pot of potatoes with—sometimes—a bit of salt fish, and she
poured out the potatoes on the table and ate them slowly, with great
relish, using her fingers by way of a fork.

Now, girls are supposed to be fastidious, but I was the one who
suffered most from this. Nora, my sister, just sucked up to the old
woman for the penny she got every Friday out of the old-age pension, a thing I could not do. I was too honest, that was my trouble;
and when I was playing with Bill Connell, the sergeant major's son,
and saw my grandmother steering up the path with the jug of porter
sticking out from beneath her shawl I was mortified. I made excuses
not to let him come into the house, because I could never be sure
what she would be up to when we went in.

When Mother was at work and my grandmother made the dinner I wouldn't touch it. Nora once tried to make me, but I hid under the table from her and took the bread knife with me for protection. Nora let on to be very indignant (she wasn't, of course, but she knew Mother saw through her, so she sided with Gran) and came after me. I lashed out at her with the bread knife, and after that she left me alone. I stayed there till Mother came in from work and made my dinner, but when Father came in later Nora said in a shocked voice: "Oh, Dadda, do you know what Jackie did at dinnertime?" Then, of course, it all came out; Father gave me a flaking; Mother interfered, and for days after that he didn't speak to me and Mother barely spoke to Nora. And all because of that old woman! God knows, I was heart-scalded.

Then, to crown my misfortunes, I had to make my first confession and communion. It was an old woman called Ryan who prepared us for these. She was about the one age with Gran; she was well-to-do, lived in a big house on Montenotte, wore a black cloak and bonnet, and came every day to school at three o'clock when we should have been going home, and talked to us of hell. She may have mentioned the other place as well, but that could only have been by accident, for hell had the first place in her heart.

She lit a candle, took out a new half crown, and offered it to the first boy who would hold one finger—only one finger!—in the flame for five minutes by the school clock. Being always very ambitious I was tempted to volunteer, but I thought it might look greedy. Then she asked were we afraid of holding one finger—only one finger!—in a little candle flame for five minutes and not afraid of burning all over in roasting hot furnaces for all eternity. "All eternity! Just think of that! A whole lifetime goes by and it's nothing, not even a drop in the ocean of your sufferings." The woman was really interesting about hell, but my attention was all fixed on the half crown. At the end of the lesson she put it back in her purse. It was a great disappointment; a religious woman like that, you wouldn't think she'd bother about a thing like a half crown.

Another day she said she knew a priest who woke one night to find a fellow he didn't recognize leaning over the end of his bed. The priest was a bit frightened—naturally enough—but he asked the fellow what he wanted, and the fellow said in a deep, husky voice that he wanted to go to confession. The priest said it was an awkward time and wouldn't it do in the morning, but the fellow said that last time he went to confession, there was one sin he kept back, being ashamed to mention it, and now it was always on his mind. Then the priest knew it was a bad case, because the fellow was after making a bad confession and committing a mortal sin. He got up to dress, and just then the cock crew in the yard outside, and—lo and behold!— when the priest looked round there was no sign of the fellow, only a smell of burning timber, and when the priest looked at his bed didn't he see the print of two hands burned in it? That was because the fellow had made a bad confession. This story made a shocking impression on me.

But the worst of all was when she showed us how to examine our conscience. Did we take the name of the Lord, our God, in vain? Did we honor our father and our mother? (I asked her did this include grandmothers and she said it did.) Did we love our neighbors as ourselves? Did we covet our neighbor's goods? (I thought of the way I felt about the penny that Nora got every Friday.) I decided that, between one thing and another, I must have broken the whole ten commandments, all on account of that old woman, and so far as I could see, so long as she remained in the house I had no hope of ever doing anything else.

I was scared to death of confession. The day the whole class went I let on to have a toothache, hoping my absence wouldn't be noticed; but at three o'clock, just as I was feeling safe, along comes a chap with a message from Mrs. Ryan that I was to go to confession myself on Saturday and be at the chapel for communion with the rest. To make it worse, Mother couldn't come with me and sent Nora instead.

Now, that girl had ways of tormenting me that Mother never knew of. She held my hand as we went down the hill, smiling sadly and saying how sorry she was for me, as if she were bringing me to the hospital for an operation.

"Oh, God help us!" she moaned. "Isn't it a terrible pity you weren't a good boy? Oh, Jackie, my heart bleeds for you! How will you ever think of all your sins? Don't forget you have to tell him about the time you kicked Gran on the shin."

"Lemme go!" I said, trying to drag myself free of her. "I don't want to go to confession at all."

"But sure, you'll have to go to confession, Jackie," she replied in the same regretful tone. "Sure, if you didn't the parish priest would be up to the house, looking for you. 'Tisn't, God knows, that I'm not sorry for you. Do you remember the time you tried to kill me with the bread knife under the table? And the language you used to me? I don't know what he'll do with you at all, Jackie. He might have to send you up to the bishop."

I remember thinking bitterly that she didn't know the half of what I had to tell—if I told it. I knew I couldn't tell it, and understood perfectly why the fellow in Mrs. Ryan's story made a bad confession; it seemed to me a great shame that people wouldn't stop criticizing him. I remember that steep hill down to the church, and the sunlit hillsides beyond the valley of the river, which I saw in the gaps between the houses like Adam's last glimpse of Paradise.

Then, when she had maneuvered me down the long flight of steps to the chapel yard, Nora suddenly changed her tone. She became the raging malicious devil she really was.

" There you are!" she said with a yelp of triumph, hurling me through the church door. "And I hope he'll give you the penitential psalms, you dirty little caffler."

I knew then I was lost, given up to eternal justice. The door with the colored-glass panels swung shut behind me, the sunlight went out and gave place to deep shadow, and the wind whistled outside so that the silence within seemed to crackle like ice under my feet. Nora sat in front of me by the confession box. There were a couple of old women ahead of her, and then a miserable-looking poor devil came and wedged me in at the other side, so that I couldn't escape even if I had the courage. He joined his hands and rolled his eyes in the direction of the roof, muttering aspirations in an anguished tone, and I wondered had he a grandmother too. Only a grandmother could account for a fellow behaving in that heartbroken way, but he was better off than I, for he at least could go and confess his sins; while I would make a bad confession and then die in the night and be continually coming back and burning people's furniture.

Nora's turn came, and I heard the sound of something slamming, and then her voice as if butter wouldn't melt in her mouth, and then another slam, and out she came. God, the hypocrisy of women. Her eyes were lowered, her head was bowed, and her hands were joined very low down on her stomach, and she walked up the aisle to the side altar looking like a saint. You never saw such an exhibition of devotion; and I remembered the devilish malice with which she had tormented me all the way from our door, and wondered were all religious people like that, really. It was my turn now. With the fear of damnation in my soul I went in, and the confessional door closed of itself behind me.

It was pitch dark and I couldn't see priest or anything else. Then I really began to be frightened. In the darkness it was a matter between God and me, and He had all the odds. He knew what my intentions were before I even started; I had no chance. All I had ever been told about confession got mixed up in my mind, and I knelt to one wall and said: "Bless me, father, for I have sinned; this is my first confession." I waited for a few minutes, but nothing happened, so I tried it on the other wall. Nothing happened there either. He had me spotted all right.

It must have been then that I noticed the shelf at about one height with my head. It was really a place for grown-up people to rest their elbows, but in my distracted state I thought it was probably the place you were supposed to kneel. Of course, it was on the high side and not very deep, but I was always good at climbing and managed to get up all right. Staying up was the trouble. There was room only for my knees, and nothing you could get a grip on but a sort of wooden molding a bit above it. I held on to the molding and repeated the words a little louder, and this time something happened all right. A slide was slammed back; a little light entered the box, and a man's voice said: 'Who's there?"

"'Tis me, father," I said for fear he mightn't see me and go away again. I couldn't see him at all. The place the voice came from was under the molding, about level with my knees, so I took a good grip of the molding and swung myself down till I saw the astonished face of a young priest looking up at me. He had to put his head on one side to see me, and I had to put mine on one side to see him, so we were more or less talking to one another upside-down. It struck me as a queer way of hearing confessions, but I didn't feel it my place to criticize.

"Bless me, father, for I have sinned; this is my first confession," I rattled off all in one breath, and swung myself down the least shade more to make it easier for him.

"What are you doing up there?" he shouted in an angry voice, and the strain the politeness was putting on my hold of the molding, and the shock of being addressed in such an uncivil tone, were too much for me. I lost my grip, tumbled, and hit the door an unmerciful wallop before I found myself flat on my back in the middle of the aisle. The people who had been waiting stood up with their mouths open. The priest opened the door of the middle box and came out, pushing his biretta back from his forehead; he looked something terrible. Then Nora came scampering down the aisle.

"Oh, you dirty little caffler!" she said. "I might have known you'd do it. I might have known you'd disgrace me. I can't leave you out of my sight for one minute."

Before I could even get to my feet to defend myself she bent down and gave me a clip across the ear. This reminded me that I was so stunned I had even forgotten to cry, so that people might think I wasn't hurt at all, when in fact I was probably maimed for life. I gave a roar out of me.

"What's all this about?" the priest hissed, getting angrier than ever and pushing Nora off me. "How dare you hit the child like that, you little vixen?"

"But I can't do my penance with him, father," Nora cried, cocking an outraged eye up at him.

"Well, go and do it, or I'll give you some more to do," he said, giving me a hand up. "Was it coming to confession you were, my poor man?" he asked me.

"'Twas, father," said I with a sob.

"Oh," he said respectfully, "a big hefty fellow like you must have terrible sins. Is this your first?"

"'Tis, father," said I.

"Worse and worse," he said gloomily. "The crimes of a lifetime. I don't know will I get rid of you at all today. You'd better wait now till I'm finished with these old ones. You can see by the looks of them they haven't much to tell."

"I will, father," I said with something approaching joy.

The relief of it was really enormous. Nora stuck out her tongue at me from behind his back, but I couldn't even be bothered retorting. I knew from the very moment that man opened his mouth that he was intelligent above the ordinary. When I had time to think, I saw how right I was. It only stood to reason that a fellow confessing after seven years would have more to tell than people that went every week. The crimes of a lifetime, exactly as he said. It was only what he expected, and the rest was the cackle of old women and girls with their talk of hell, the bishop, and the penitential psalms. That was all they knew. I started to make my examination of conscience, and barring the one bad business of my grandmother it didn't seem so bad.

The next time, the priest steered me into the confesssion box himself and left the shutter back the way I could see him get in and sit down at the further side of the grille from me.

"Well, now," he said, "what do they call you?"

"Jackie, father," said I.

"And what's a-trouble to you, Jackie?"

"Father," I said, feeling I might as well get it over while I had him in good humor, "I had it all arranged to kill my grandmother."

He seemed a bit shaken by that, all right, because he said nothing for quite a while.

"My goodness," he said at last, "that'd be a shocking thing to do. What put that into your head?"

"Father," I said, feeling very sorry for myself, "she's an awful woman."

"Is she?" he asked. "What way is she awful?"

"She takes porter, father," I said, knowing well from the way Mother talked of it that this was a mortal sin, and hoping it would make the priest take a more favorable view of my case.

"Oh, my!" he said, and I could see he was impressed.

"And snuff, father," said I.

"That's a bad case, sure enough, Jackie," he said.

"And she goes round in her bare feet, father," I went on in a rush of self-pity, "and she knows I don't like her, and she gives pennies to Nora and none to me, and my dad sides with her and flakes me, and one night I was so heart-scalded I made up my mind I'd have to kill her."

"And what would you do with the body?" he asked with great interest.

"I was thinking I could chop that up and carry it away in a barrow I have," I said.

"Begor, Jackie," he said, "do you know you're a terrible child?"

"I know, father," I said, for I was just thinking the same thing myself. "I tried to kill Nora too with a bread knife under the table, only I missed her."

"Is that the little girl that was beating you just now?" he asked.

"'Tis, father."

"Someone will go for her with a bread knife one day, and he won't miss her," he said rather cryptically. "You must have great courage. Between ourselves, there's a lot of people I'd like to do the same to but I'd never have the nerve. Hanging is an awful death."

"Is it, father?" I asked with the deeper interest—I was always very keen on hanging. "Did you ever see a fellow hanged?"

"Dozens of them," he said solemnly. "And they all died roaring."

"Jay!" I said.

"Oh, a horrible death!" he said with great satisfaction. "Lots of the fellows I saw killed their grandmothers too, but they all said 'twas never worth it."

He had me there for a full ten minutes talking, and then walked out the chapel yard with me. I was genuinely sorry to part with him, because he was the most entertaining character I'd ever met in the religious line. Outside, after the shadow of the church, the sunlight was like the roaring of waves on a beach; it dazzled me; and when the frozen silence melted and I heard the screech of trams on the road my heart soared. I knew now I wouldn't die in the night and come back, leaving marks on my mother's furniture. It would be a great worry to her, and the poor soul had enough.

Nora was sitting on the railing, waiting for me, and she put on a very sour puss when she saw the priest with me. She was mad jealous because a priest had never come out of the church with her.

"Well," she asked coldly, after he left me, "what did he give you?"

"Three Hail Marys," I said.

"Three Hail Marys," she repeated incredulously. "You mustn't have told him anything."

"I told him everything," I said confidently.

"About Gran and all?"

"About Gran and all."

(All she wanted was to be able to go home and say I'd made a bad confession.)

"Did you tell him you went for me with the bread knife?" she asked with a frown.

"I did to be sure."

"And he only gave you three Hail Marys?"

"That's all."

She slowly got down from the railing with a baffled air. Clearly, this was beyond her. As we mounted the steps back to the main road she looked at me suspiciously.

"What are you sucking?" she asked.

"Bullseyes."

"Was it the priest gave them to you?"

"'Twas."

"Lord God," she wailed bitterly, "some people have all the luck! 'Tis no advantage to anybody trying to be good. I might just as well be a sinner like you."

Frank O'Connor (1903-1966)
Frank O'Connor is perhaps the best known of all Irish story writers, his stories having appeared in anthologies around the world. Few writers have employed the first person narrative approach more successfully than O'Connor.

"When the night of the blizzard came
and he hadn't showed up at his
usual time, she got worried,
very worried."

snow

Gwendolyn MacEwen

She, of course, was used to it. Twenty-five years of parkas, furlined snowboots, mittens, scarves and crunching, slushing, sliding through it on the way to work or school. It was a Thing that covered the country four or five months a year, not unlike that billowy white corpuscle or whatever it was that went mad and smothered the villain of the film *Incredible Journey*. But for *him,* fresh from the Mediterranean, it was a kind of heavenly confetti, ambrosia or manna, and he rushed out half-mad at the first snowfall and lost himself in the sweet salt cold. He even dreamed of snow and he had a weird talent for predicting the next snowfall. He'd sleep and see tiny people coming down from the sky in parachutes that were snowflakes, a rain of infinitesimally small doves, ejaculations of white blossoms—the sperm of the great sleeping sky tree.

All through September and October his blood rose in anticipation of the cold, while all around him people lost their summer energy and grew weary and irritable as they thought of the long white siege ahead.

In December he trudged around frozen and delirious with joy in his soft Italian leather shoes with the pointed European toes, while she, bundled up to the chin with countless nameless pieces of wool and fur, hardly able to turn her head to see him, wondered how he could stand having to take his pants to the cleaner's twice a week to get the slush and wintry crud cleaned off of the cuffs. He made snowballs with his *bare hands,* if you can imagine, and when the tips of his ears turned a ghastly white from the cold, it never occurred to him to buy a hat. Coming indoors after an hour or two of strolling through a blizzard he would be *laughing* and freezing as if the winter were a great white clown someone had created solely for his amusement. She meanwhile, huddled in front of the oven or even the toaster, would try to unnerve him with horrendous tales of winter in Winnipeg. 'If you think *this* is something,' she would gasp, 'you should see what it's like out *west!'* and go on to describe how as a child she used to walk to school in the morning through shoulder-high snowbanks and by the time she got to the schoolyard there would be icicles in her nose and all round her mouth and her lips were so frozen she couldn't speak, and all the kids would be trying to laugh with their wooden lips. But he laughed too when he heard the story, and told her he wished he'd been with her out there, because, he explained, what thrilled him wasn't feeling the cold but letting the cold feel *him.*

Actually, she was quite a good sport with him that first winter he was in Kanada. At midnight after a heavy snowfall, they'd go into a little park where the swings and slides stood like skeletons in the blackness, and he, trembling with exitement, would put his foot into a fresh snowscape and examine the footprint of man marring the virgin whiteness. 'A giant step for mankind,' she'd say, as if the park were a moonscape, and slowly slowly they would walk forward pretending they were astronauts, clumsy and weightless in the midnight park, pouncing with glee on a swing or a slide or a water-fountain and radioing back to Earth that they had found evidence of an intelligent civilization. She would pick up a boulder—which turned out once to be somebody's frozen bowling shoe—and he, zooming in with his invisible TV camera, would relay the image to the millions of viewers in Tokyo and New York and Paris and London and Montreal. Then they would take imaginary pictures of each other standing triumphantly in front of the swings, or gazing rapturously at a gleaming slide, which seemed to be giving off inter-galactic signals, like the rectangular slab in *Space Odyssey.*

For the first half hour or so she found it fun; they made cryptic triangles and squares in the snow and she even taught him how to

make an 'angel' by lying on his back in the snow and swinging his
arms up and down on both sides. But he was always wanting to pro-
long the excursions long after the cold had crept into her bones and
she, wet through and shivering horribly, would have to wait for him
to finish his angels—sometimes five, six, even seven of them all done
in a neat circle around the water-fountain with their wings facing
many points of the compass.

Gradually they became quite serious about what they should
make of each fresh snowscape. They would stand on the brink of the
park sometimes for five or ten whole minutes debating what they
should inscribe there with their feet or hands, not wanting to waste
the cleanness, the newness of the snow on trivial ventures. Moon-
scapes and angels started to pall on them, so one night they decided
to do a series of gigantic initials, which seemed easy but was actually quite difficult because they had to make tremendous Nureyev-
like leaps between the bottom of an 'O' and the top of an 'R.' So he
fell down flat in the middle of his name and got up protesting that it
all came of not knowing how to write English well.

Another night they made a magic circle with segments bearing
Cabbalistic Hebrew letters, and they both leapt into the centre of the
circle and stood there under the stars and made secret wishes that
are not our business to know.

Another night they were tired and spent the time throwing snowballs at tree trunks, which left hazy white circles like the fist-marks of
avenging angels.

Another night they did Fantastic Footprints and Imaginary Beast
tracks, trying to make the park look as if it had been the battleground
between three-footed humans and hideous monsters who walked
sideways like crabs. It took two hours to finish and though she had
serious doubts as to whether it had been worth the effort, he was
swollen with pride. You'd think he'd just completed a painting or a
novel.

He was forever thinking up new things to be done with the snow.
He considered (seriously) painting it, even flavouring it with sacks
full of lime or lemon powder, and would have gone ahead with his
plan had she not discouraged him by informing him you couldn't
buy lime or lemon powder by the sack. So they made snowmen and
snowwomen and snowchildren and snowanimals and snowstars. (A

snowstar is a big ball of snow with long icicles—if you can find them —protruding out of the sides.) They made snowstars until her hands hurt. They made snow-trenches—where they lay in wait for the invisible army of abominable snowmen to come—until she thought she'd go mad, screaming mad. They made white fairy castles, they made white futuristic city-scapes, and they made footprints, footprints, footprints.

So I suppose what developed was, after all, to be expected. Which is not to say that she herself expected it in the least. When the night of the blizzard came and he hadn't showed up at his usual time, she got worried, very worried. And so she put on her fur-lined boots and her parka and her scarf and her mittens and went trudging out in the direction of the park. The snowfall that night was like a rapid descent of stars; they came down obliquely, razor-sharp, and her face stung and reddened and burned. *Snowfire,* she thought. Another word.

And she *was* surprised, though not totally, to find Grigori lying there at the bottom of the slide that gave off signals like the metal slab in *Space Odyssey,* with his Mediterranean hair all aflurry from the wind and his absolutely naked stone dead body wedged some-how into the snowdrift, and his arms outstretched at his sides as if he'd been making his last *angel.*

But what really got her was the smile on his face. He never did feel the cold.

Gwendolyn MacEwen (1941-)
Toronto-born Gwendolyn MacEwen's rich imagination comes alive in her poetry, novels and short stories. "Snow" is taken from her col- lection, Noman, *which was published in 1972. Her book of poetry,* The Shadow Maker, *won a Governor General's Award in 1969.*

This story was written in 1935. However, in 1968 William Saroyan wrote, "If such a thing as a Bible of life in the twentieth century were to be brought together out of the writings of all contemporary writers, this story would deserve a place in that book."

the man with the heart in the highlands

William Saroyan

In 1914, when I was not quite six years old, an old man came down San Benito Avenue playing a solo on a bugle and stopped in front of our house. I ran out of the yard and stood at the curb waiting for him to start playing again, but he wouldn't do it. I said, I sure would like to hear you play another tune, and he said, Young man, could you get a glass of water for an old man whose heart is not here, but in the highlands?

What highlands? I said.

The Scotch highlands, said the old man. Could you?

What's your heart doing in the Scotch highlands? I said.

My heart is grieving there, said the old man. Could you bring me a glass of cool water?

Where's your mother? I said.

My mother's in Tulsa, Oklahoma, said the old man, but her heart isn't.

Where *is* her heart? I said.

In the Scotch highlands, said the old man. I am very thirsty, young man.

How come the members of your family are always leaving their hearts in the highlands? I said.

That's the way we are, said the old man. Here today and gone to-morrow.

Here today and gone tomorrow? I said. How do you figure?

Alive one minute and dead the next, said the old man.

Where is your mother's *mother?* I said.

She's up in Vermont, in a little town called White River, but her heart isn't, said the old man.

Is her poor old withered heart in the highlands too? I said.

Right smack in the highlands, said the old man. Son, I'm dying of thirst.

My father came out on the porch and roared like a lion that has just awakened from evil dreams.

Johnny, he roared, get the hell away from that poor old man. Get him a pitcher of water before he falls down and dies. Where in hell are your manners?

Can't a fellow try to find out something from a traveler once in a while? I said.

Get the old gentleman some water, said my father. Damn it, don't stand there like a dummy. Get him a drink before he falls down and dies.

You get him a drink, I said. You ain't doing nothing.

Ain't doing nothing? said my father. Why, Johnny, you know damn well I'm getting a new poem arranged in my mind.

How do you figure I know? I said. You're just standing there on the porch with your sleeves rolled up. How do you figure I know?

Well, you ought to know, said my father.

Good afternoon, said the old man to my father. Your son has been telling me how clear and cool the climate is in these parts.

(I never did tell this old man anything about the climate, I said. Where's he getting that stuff from?)

Good afternoon, said my father. Won't you come in for a little rest? We should be honored to have you at our table for a bit of lunch.

Sir, said the old man, I am starving. I shall come right in.

Can you play "Drink to Me Only with Thine Eyes"? I said to the old man. I sure would like to hear you play that song on the bugle. That song is my favorite. I guess I like that song better than any other song in the world.

Son, said the old man, when you get to be my age you'll know songs aren't important, bread is the thing.

Anyway, I said, I sure would like to hear you play that song.

The old man went up on the porch and shook hands with my father.

My name is Jasper MacGregor, he said. I am an actor.

I am mighty glad to make your acquaintance, said my father. Johnny, get Mr. MacGregor a pitcher of water.

I went around to the well and poured some cool water into a pitcher and took it to the old man. He drank the whole pitcherful in one long swig. Then he looked around at the landscape and up at the sky and away up San Benito Avenue where the evening sun was beginning to go down.

I reckon I'm five thousand miles from home, he said. Do you think we could eat a little bread and cheese to keep my body and spirit together?

Johnny, said my father, run down to the grocer's, and get a loaf of French bread and a pound of cheese.

Give me the money, I said.

Tell Mr. Kosak to give us credit, said my father. I ain't got a penny, Johnny.

He won't give us credit, I said. Mr. Kosak is tired of giving us credit. He's sore at us. He says we don't work and never pay our bills. We owe him forty cents.

Go on down there and argue it out with him, said my father. You know that's your job.

He won't listen to reason, I said. Mr. Kosak says he doesn't know anything about anything, all he wants is the forty cents.

Go on down there and make him give you a loaf of bread and a pound of cheese, said my father. You can do it, Johnny.

Go on down there, said the old man, and tell Mr. Kosak to give you a loaf of bread and a pound of cheese, son.

Go ahead, Johnny, said my father. You haven't yet failed to leave that store with provender, and you'll be back here in ten minutes with food fit for a king.

I don't know, I said. Mr. Kosak says we are trying to give him the merry run around. He wants to know what kind of work you are doing.

Well, go ahead and tell him, said my father. I have nothing to conceal. I am writing poetry night and day.

Well, all right, I said, but I don't think he'll be much impressed. He says you never go out like other unemployed men and look for work. He says you're lazy and no good.

You go on down there and tell him he's crazy, Johnny, said my father. You go on down there and tell that fellow your father is one of the greatest unknown poets living.

He might not care, I said, but I'll go. I'll do my best. Ain't we got nothing in the house?

Only popcorn, said my father. We been eating popcorn four days in a row now, Johnny. You got to get bread and cheese if you expect me to finish that long poem.

I'll do my best, I said.

Don't take too long, said Mr. MacGregor. I'm five thousand miles from home.

I'll run all the way, I said.

If you find any money on the way, said my father, remember we go fifty-fifty.

All right, I said.

I ran all the way to Mr. Kosak's store, but I didn't find any money on the way, not even a penny.

I went into the store and Mr. Kosak opened his eyes.

Mr. Kosak, I said, if you were in China and didn't have a friend in the world and no money, you'd expect some Christian over there to give you a pound of rice, wouldn't you?

What do you want? said Mr. Kosak.

I just want to talk a little, I said. You'd expect some member of the Aryan race to help you out a little, wouldn't you, Mr. Kosak?

How much money you got? said Mr. Kosak.

It ain't a question of money, Mr. Kosak, I said. I'm talking about being in China and needing the help of the white race.

I don't know nothing about nothing, said Mr. Kosak.

How would you feel in China that way? I said.

I don't know, said Mr. Kosak. What would I be doing in China?

Well, I said, you'd be visiting there, and you'd be hungry, and not a friend in the world. You wouldn't expect a good Christian to turn you away without even a pound of rice, would you, Mr. Kosak?

I guess not, said Mr. Kosak, but you ain't in China, Johnny, and neither is your pa. You or your pa's got to go out and work sometime in your lives, so you might as well start now. I ain't going to give you no more groceries on credit because I know you won't pay me.

Mr. Kosak, I said, you misunderstand me: I'm not talking about a few groceries. I'm talking about all them heathen people round you in China, and you hungry and dying.

This ain't China, said Mr. Kosak. You got to go out and make your living in this country. Everybody works in America.

Mr. Kosak, I said, suppose it was a loaf of French bread and a pound of cheese you needed to keep you alive in the world, would you hesitate to ask a Christian missionary for these things?

Yes, I would, said Mr. Kosak. I would be ashamed to ask.

Even if you knew you would give him back two loaves of bread and two pounds of cheese? I said. Even then?

Even then, said Mr. Kosak.

Don't be that way, Mr. Kosak, I said. That's defeatist talk, and you know it. Why, the only thing that would happen to you would be death. You would die out there in China, Mr. Kosak.

I wouldn't care if I would, said Mr. Kosak, you and your pa have got to pay for bread and cheese. Why don't your pa go out and get a job?

Mr. Kosak, I said, how are you, anyway?

I'm fine, Johnny, said Mr. Kosak. How are you?

Couldn't be better, Mr. Kosak, I said. How are the children?

Fine, said Mr. Kosak. Stepan is beginning to walk now.

That's great, I said, How is Angela?

Angela is beginning to sing, said Mr. Kosak. How is your grandmother?

She's feeling fine, I said. She's beginning to sing too. She says she would rather be an opera star than queen. How's Marta, your wife, Mr. Kosak?

Oh, swell, said Mr. Kosak.

I cannot tell you how glad I am to hear that all is well at your house, I said. I know Stepan is going to be a great man some day.

I hope so, said Mr. Kosak. I am going to send him straight through high school and see that he gets every chance I didn't get. I don't want him to open a grocery store.

I have great faith in Stepan, I said.

What do you want, Johnny? said Mr. Kosak. And how much

money you got?

Mr. Kosak, I said, you know I didn't come here to buy anything. You know I enjoy a quiet philosophical chat with you every now and then. Let me have a loaf of French bread and a pound of cheese.

You got to pay cash, Johnny, said Mr. Kosak.

And Esther, I said. How is your beautiful daughter Esther?

Esther is all right, Johnny, said Mr. Kosak, but you got to pay cash. You and your Pa are the worst citizens in this whole country.

I'm glad Esther is all right, Mr. Kosak, I said. Jasper MacGregor is visiting our house. He is a great actor.

I never heard of him, said Mr. Kosak.

And a bottle of beer for Mr. MacGregor, I said.

I can't give you a bottle of beer, said Mr. Kosak.

Certainly you can, I said.

I can't, said Mr. Kosak. I'll let you have one loaf of stale bread, and one pound of cheese, but that's all. What kind of work does your pa do when he works, Johnny?

My father writes poetry, Mr. Kosak, I said. That's the only work my father does. He is one of the greatest writers of poetry in the world.

When does he get any money? said Mr. Kosak.

He never gets any money, I said. You can't have your cake and eat it.

I don't like that kind of a job, said Mr. Kosak. Why doesn't your pa work like everybody else, Johnny?

He works harder than everybody else, I said. My father works twice as hard as the average man.

Well, that's fifty-five cents you owe me, Johnny, said Mr. Kosak. I'll let you have some stuff this time, but never again.

Tell Esther I love her, I said.

All right, said Mr. Kosak.

Goodbye, Mr. Kosak, I said.

Goodbye, Johnny, said Mr. Kosak.

I ran back to the house with the loaf of French bread and the pound of cheese.

My father and Mr. MacGregor were in the street waiting to see if I would come back with food. They ran half a block toward me and when they saw that it was food, they waved back to the house, where my grandmother was waiting. She ran into the house to set the table.

I knew you'd do it, said my father.

So did I, said Mr. MacGregor.

He says we got to pay him fifty-five cents, I said. He says he ain't going to give us no more stuff on credit.

That's his opinion, said my father. What did you talk about, Johnny?

First I talked about being hungry and at death's door in China, I said, and then I inquired about the family.

How is everyone? said my father.

Fine, I said.

So we all went inside and ate the loaf of bread and the pound of cheese, and each of us drank two or three quarts of water, and after every crumb of bread had disappeared, Mr. MacGregor began to look around the kitchen to see if there wasn't something else to eat.

That green can up there, he said. What's in there, Johnny?

Marbles, I said.

That cupboard, he said. Anything edible in there, Johnny?

Crickets, I said.

That big jar in the corner there, Johnny, he said. What's good in there?

I got a gopher snake in that jar, I said.

Well, said Mr. MacGregor, I could go for a bit of boiled gopher snake in a big way, Johnny.

You can't have that snake, I said.

Why not, Johnny? said Mr. MacGregor. Why the hell not, son? I hear of fine Borneo natives eating snakes and grasshoppers. You ain't got half a dozen fat grasshoppers around, have you, Johnny?

Only four, I said.

Well, trot them out, Johnny, said Mr. MacGregor, and after we have had our fill, I'll play "Drink to Me Only with Thine Eyes" on the bugle for you. I'm mighty hungry, Johnny.

So am I, I said, but you ain't going to kill that snake.

My father sat at the table with his head in his hands, dreaming. My grandmother paced through the house, singing arias from Puccini. As through the streets I wander, she roared in Italian.

How about a little music? said my father. I think the boy would be delighted.

I sure would, Mr. MacGregor, I said.

All right, Johnny, said Mr. MacGregor.

So he got up and began to blow into the bugle and he blew louder than any man ever blew into a bugle and people for miles around heard him and got excited. Eighteen neighbors gathered in front of our house and applauded when Mr. MacGregor finished the solo. My father led Mr. MacGregor out on the porch and said, Good neighbors and friends, I want you to meet Jasper MacGregor, the greatest Shakespearian actor of our day.

The good neighbors and friends said nothing and Mr. MacGregor said, I remember my first appearance in London in 1867 as if it was yesterday, and he went on with the story of his career. Rufe Apley the carpenter said, How about some more music, Mr. MacGregor? and Mr. MacGregor said, Have you got an egg at your house?

I sure have, said Rufe. I got a dozen eggs at my house.

Would it be convenient for you to go and get one of them dozen eggs? said Mr. MacGregor. When you return, I'll play a song that will make your heart leap with joy and grief.

I'm on my way already, said Rufe, and he went home to get an egg.

Mr. MacGregor asked Tom Baker if he had a bit of sausage at his house and Tom said he did, and Mr. MacGregor asked Tom if it would be convenient for Tom to go and get that little bit of sausage and come back with it and when Tom returned Mr. MacGregor would play a song on the bugle that would change the whole history of Tom's life. And Tom went home for the sausage, and Mr. Mac-Gregor asked each of the eighteen good neighbors and friends if he had something small and nice to eat at his home and each man said he did, and each man went to his home to get the small and nice thing to eat, so Mr. MacGregor would play the song he said would be so wonderful to hear, and when all the good neighbors and friends had returned to our house with all the small and nice things to eat, Mr. MacGregor lifted the bugle to his lips and played "My Heart's in the Highlands, My Heart Is not Here," and each of the good neighbors and friends wept and returned to his home, and Mr. MacGregor took all the good things into the kitchen and our family feasted and drank and was merry: an egg, a sausage, a dozen green onions, two kinds of cheese, butter, two kinds of bread, boiled potatoes, fresh to-matoes, a melon, tea, and many other good things to eat, and we ate and our bellies tightened, and Mr. MacGregor said, Sir, if it is all the same to you I should like to dwell in your house for some days to come, and my father said, Sir, my house is your house, and Mr. Mac-Gregor stayed at our house seventeen days and seventeen nights, and on the afternoon of the eighteenth day a man from the Old People's Home came to our house and said, I am looking for Jasper MacGregor, the actor, and my father said, What do you want?

I am from the Old People's Home, said the young man, and I want Mr. MacGregor to come back to our place because we are putting on our annual show in two weeks and need an actor.

Mr. MacGregor got up from the floor where he had been dreaming and went away with the young man, and the following afternoon, when he was very hungry, my father said, Johnny, go down to Mr. Kosak's store and get a little something to eat. I know you can do it, Johnny. Get anything you can.

Mr. Kosak wants fifty-five cents, I said. He won't give us anything more without money.

Go on down there, Johnny, said my father. You know you can get that fine Slovak gentleman to give you a bit of something to eat.

So I went down to Mr. Kosak's store and took up the Chinese problem where I had dropped it, and it was quite a job for me to go away from the store with a box of bird seed and half a can of maple syrup, but I did it, and my father said, Johnny, this sort of fare is going to be dangerous for the old lady, and sure enough in the morning we heard my grandmother singing like a canary, and my father said, How the hell can I write great poetry on bird seed?

William Saroyan (1908-)
William Saroyan's unconventional style makes him a distinctive playwright, novelist and storyteller. Born in California of Armenian parents, he has lived there most of his life, his family and Armenian-American friends furnishing him with material for many delightful stories. My Name is Aram *is one of his best known collections.*

and beyond

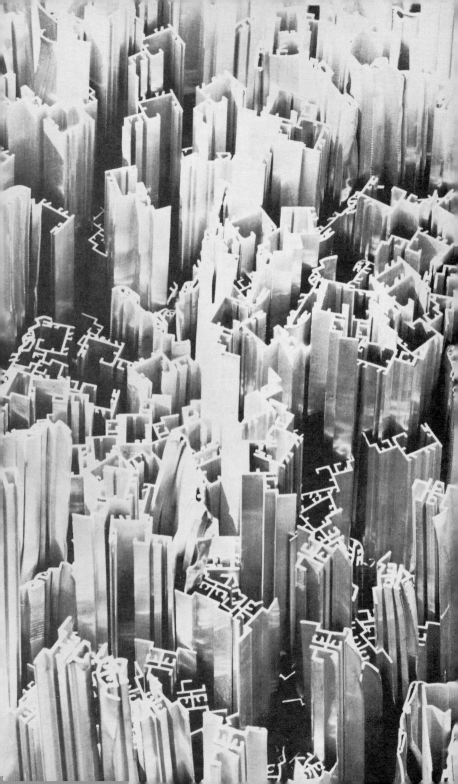

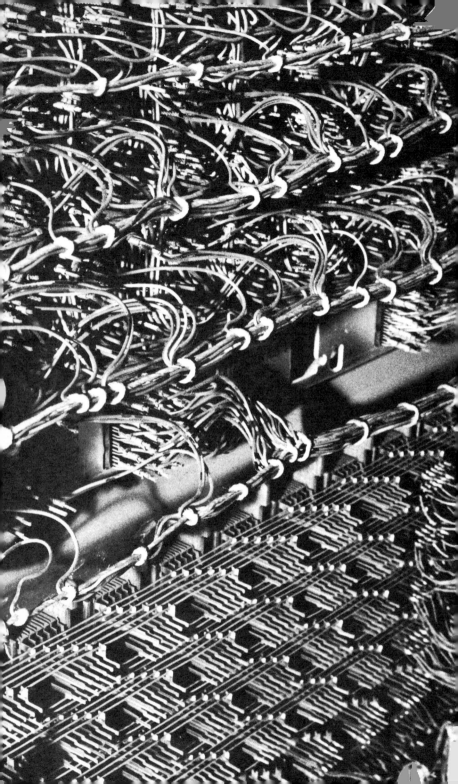

When the man arrives at New York's
Kennedy Airport he is Mr. Derringer,
but before he leaves he becomes
Mr. Dorrengor and on arrival in
Mexico he will be Mr. Farronga. '

And then who will he be?

the connection
Andreas Schroeder

1.

"This is your air ticket and this, as you see, your health certificate. Car reservations have been made for you at your destination, and of course hotel arrangements as well." The secretary speaks in a brisk, confident voice, laying various documents on the desk before one Mr. Derringer, recently-hired employee of a well-established oil company in the Northwest. Derringer murmurs his thanks, double-checks several items on his itinerary, picks up his briefcase and departs.

When the plane touches down at New York's Kennedy Airport, Derringer gathers his belongings, shrugs on his overcoat and prepares to meet the public relations man who is to fill him in on missing details. As he picks his way down the ramp stairs, a stewardess calls his name.

"Mr. Derringe!" "Mr. Derringe of Chicago!" Derringer makes himself known. "Derringer," he corrects. "Derringer with an *r.*" The stewardess glances at a piece of paper in her hand and shrugs. "A message for you Mr. Derringe," she monotones. "Please check with the Passenger Information counter on the Departures level."

Derringer frowns as he rises up the escalator to Departures. There is supposed to be a company man here. At Passenger Information a young girl searches through her files. "Mr. Derring? That's you? Yes, I have a message here that you're to fly on to Florida. A change in plans." She holds out an air ticket for him to sign. "The name's spelled wrong," Derringer notes. "My name ends in *er.*"

"Oh dear, I'd better check this," the girl worries, re-thumbing through her files. "Ah here we are; Mr. Dorrengor right?" "Not quite," Derringer replies. "*er* you know; *e* as in elphinstone, *r* as in rape." The girl lays both tickets on the counter; the second is for Mexico.

"I'd suggest you better decide which refers to you Mr. Dorrengor," she says. "The plane for Mexico leaves in ten minutes, and the one for Florida in twenty-seven. We've got to reroute your luggage, you know." She sounds somehow reproachful.

Derringer feels annoyed and undecided. He has no idea whom he might phone for help; it is now Sunday and no one would be reachable anyway. He chooses Dorrengor, signs the ticket and has the tags on his suitcase changed. In a short time he is on his way to Torreon, Mexico.

2.

A stewardess in Torreon is expecting him. "Mr. Farronga?" she asks politely as he steps from the plane. "Your car is waiting for you on Level 5." "You've got the name wrong again," Dorrengor informs her, tired and irritated. "Then this doesn't apply to you?" the stewardess queries apologetically. "I'm so sorry." The flight passengers disperse, the stewardess circulating among them inquiring "Farronga?" of every man she sees. No one answers to the name. When all the passengers have departed, Dorrengor and the stewardess are left behind. "I suppose that message is for me," he decides, and has his luggage brought to Level 5.

3.

"You're Mr. Fatronca?" the rental agent asks. "Sign here, please." Farronga signs. The agent hesitates. "The signature doesn't match the name," he points out. "I can't possibly let a car go out with a discrepancy like that."

Farronga reflects. He has a choice of bogging down at this point or ploughing on, possibly saving a lot of time. "It's spelled differently in different countries, of course," he snaps at the agent. "Here; if it's so important to you, I'll spell it your way."

The agent looks relieved and checks the papers again. "You can simply leave it at the Sao Santos Airport when you arrive there, Mr. Fatronca," he offers. "We'll send a man to pick it up. The guy who rented the car for you didn't say when your flight was due to leave, but they generally depart in the afternoon there." Fatronca thanks him with a wave of his hand and enters the elevator for the carpark.

4.

The airport is relatively small, serving less than half a dozen airlines, many of them local. Farronga checks with each ticket counter but no one recognizes his name. Eventually, hungry and frustrated, he heads for a coffee bar for breakfast. Suddenly the P.A. system pages a Mr. Garroncton, flying to Peru.

Fatronca mulls over the name; there is a possibility, he thinks. He walks to the airline counter in question and answers the page. The airline agent agrees that the name is certainly not the same, but produces a photograph he has been given to identify the expected passenger. Though the similarity with Fatronca is doubtful, there is enough resemblance for the agent to ignore the dissimilarities. He hands Garroncton his ticket and wishes him a comfortable flight.

5.

The aircraft is a rattling old DC-3, a 37 passenger capacity propellor plane with only a handful of people on board. Garroncton suddenly realizes he doesn't even know his specific destination and rings for a stewardess to ask. He is informed the aircraft is flying to Sicuani, Peru, expecting to land there in about five hours time. Garroncton settles back in his seat and waits.

The service is poor, passengers are served only a cup of coffee and two plastic-wrapped cookies during the entire flight, and it seems to Garroncton the service has been becoming increasingly unsatisfactory since his departure from Chicago some days ago. His complaint merely produces two more plastic-wrapped cookies, however, and he gives up the fight. Nobody else seems to care in any case; most other passengers are either asleep or lazily browsing through magazines.

They land at Sicuani Airport in the thick fog of early morning, the aircraft bumping uncomfortably along the badly patched runway to a cluster of miserable little buildings on the northeast corner of the airfield. The half-dozen passengers quickly disperse and Garroncton is left standing helplessly in the middle of the building, quite at a loss as to how to proceed. A check of the two ticket offices produces nothing; no one appears to be expecting anyone by a name even faintly resembling his own. The cafeteria is closed, an old cleaning woman pushes her mop up and down the floor, the clatter of her wash-pail echoing emptily in the deserted hall.

6.

Garroncton sits on his suitcase in the middle of the floor and tries to take stock of the situation. He thinks of one possibility, then another, but every thought seems to end in the feeling that he's got to get out of here, keep moving toward where he's expected, where a company man can fill him in on the missing details. Maybe this is some sort of test of his stamina, his imagination, his inventiveness. Besides, he thinks he remembers the company man who interviewed him saying they had interests in Peruvian oil.

His reverie is interrupted by the slam of a swinging door. Garroncton looks up to see a leather-clad, heavily bearded man standing in the doorway, looking up and down the hall. He swings a pair of goggles absent-mindedly from his left wrist. There being no one else in the hall, the man approaches Garroncton.

7.

"Your name Garotta by any chance?" he asks Garroncton in broken English. Garroncton hesitates. If he admits to the discrepancy in the name he might end up stuck in this crumbling hole for days. Besides, the name isn't that far off. He nods at the bearded man. "Yeah, that's me I guess. What've you got for me?"

The man in the leather jacket shrugs. "Supposed to take you to Cocama, far as I know," he says. "That sound right to you?" Garotta tries to look informed. "Sounds like the place," he returns. "Here's my suitcase and grip."

They walk out to a peeling, oil-streaked Aztec standing like a forlorn insect on the far end of the runway. The pilot looks at the suitcase critically. " 'M afraid we're gonna have to leave that here," he informs Garotta, shrugging his shoulders with a grimace. "Not enough room in this old heap for us and that thing too. Somebody else gonna have to bring it later." Garotta says nothing. The engines spit and wheeze for some seconds, then splutter into life, the little plane shaking as if it had suddenly contacted Parkinson's Disease. The pilot pulls back on the throttle.

Once airborne, they clamber shakily to 3000 feet, the aircraft dipping and slewing like an uncertain dragonfly. The pilot shouts something which Garotta fails to understand over the noise, then both concentrate on looking ahead at the eery cloud forest through which the aircraft navigates.

As they break clear of the clouds an hour later, Garotta sees a sparse sprinkling of glittering buildings far below, tucked in at the foot of the mountain range dead ahead. The pilot sets the plane about in a steep bank, plummeting down between two peaks toward the valley where Garotta now makes out the faint X pattern of the runway. Five minutes later they bounce down on the close-shorn grass of the tiny airstrip and roll the plane to a halt. There is no sign of life anywhere.

A small herd of goats stampede from the side of the strip as Garotta jumps off the wing of the Aztec and looks around. "I'll get someone to deliver your bag eventually," the pilot shouts, not leaving his seat. "It may take a while." "Hold on!" Garotta commands, somewhat alarmed. "Where's the company man who's supposed to meet me here? The guy who's supposed to fill me in on missing details." "Company man," the pilot shouts back. "Never heard of a company man. Nobody ever meets anyone here. Not on my flights anyway." The last words are almost drowned out by the increased roar of the engines. The pilot shouts something else which Garotta can no longer hear, guns the engine and taxis down the strip. A few moments later he is only a receding speck in the vast, blue sky.

8.
Garotta sits down on the grass, almost dazed; around him, strange birds warble and chirp like bursting bubbles or electronic static. The buildings at the corner of the field are abandoned; he can't find a soul anywhere. Two days later finds him eating berries from bushes

182

around the airstrip to keep alive, waiting for the Aztec to return.

9.
The following day a dusty, haggard-looking native creaks onto the
field in a dilapidated donkey cart. "You Senor Tarotina?" he quavers,
squinting at Garotta in the sun. Tarotina nods and climbs into the
cart. "We are going . . ." the native explains and cracks his long,
frayed whip.

Andreas Schroeder (1946-)
Andreas Schroeder was born in Germany and emigrated to Canada
in 1951 where he has since become established as a poet, storyteller,
critic, columnist and film-maker. He lives in British Columbia and his
collection of short stories, The Late Man, *was published in 1972.*

Daydreamers exist in all countries,
in all ages, in all shapes and sizes.
Some dream of the stars; others
dream of the tantalizing aroma of
fresh-baked bread!
And time and space alter all things.

heav'n, heav'n

Eric Frank Russell

He swung wide the cast-iron doors, peered into the fire-clay tunnel,
and drew a deep breath. It was like looking into the business end of a
spaceship. The doors should have opened upon heat and thunder
and beyond the tunnel the stars. A shuddering in the floor. Silver
buttons upon his jacket, little silver comets on his collar and shoul-
derstraps.

"So!" rasped a voice. "Always you open the doors then pose like
one paralyzed. What is dumbfounding about an oven?"

The uniform with its buttons and comets faded away, leaving him
dressed in soiled white overalls. The floor was creaky but firm. The
stars had gone as if they had never been.

"Nothing, Monsieur Trabaud."

"Attention then! Prepare the heat as you have been shown."

"Yes, Monsieur Trabaud."

Taking an armful of fragrant pine branches from the nearby stack,
he shoved them between the doors, used a long iron rake to poke
them to the back of the tunnel. Then another bundle and another. He
picked from the floor a dozen small, sticky pinecones, tossed them
one by one in among the packed branches. Then he contemplated
the result. A rocket primed with cones and needles. But how absurd.

"Jules!"

"Yes, Monsieur Trabaud."

Snatching hurriedly at pine branches, twigs and tiny logs, he stuffed them between the doors until the tunnel was full. That was done. Everything was ready.

The ship required only the starting spark. Eagle eyes high in the bow must watch for the ground staff to scurry clear of the coming blast. Then the touch of a skilled, experienced finger upon a crimson button. After that a howl from below, a gigantic trembling, a slow upward climb becoming faster, faster, faster.

"Name of a dog! Now he is transfixed yet again. That I should be afflicted with such a dreamer."

Brushing past him, Trabaud thrust a flambeau of blazing paper into the filled oven, slammed shut the doors. He turned upon the other, his heavy black eyebrows frowning. "Jules Rioux, you are of the age sixteen. Yes?"

"Yes, Monsieur Trabaud."

"Therefore you are old enough to know that to bake bread there must be hotness within this sacred oven. And for that we must have fire; and to have fire we must apply a flame. Is that not so?"

"Yes, Monsieur Trabaud," he agreed shamefacedly.

"Then why should I have to tell you these things again and again and again?"

"I am an imbecile, Monsieur."

"If that were so, I could understand; I could forgive you. The good God makes fools in order to create pity." Seating himself on a dusty and bulging sack, Trabaud put forth a hairy arm, drew the other to him, went on in confidential tones. "Your brain wanders like a rejected lover in a strange country. Tell me, my little, who is this girl?"

"Girl?"

"This woman, this divine creature who fills your mind."

"There is no woman, Monsieur."

"No woman?" Trabaud was frankly astonished. "You sicken with desire and yet there is no woman?"

"No, Monsieur."

"Then of what do you dream?"

"Of the stars, Monsieur."

"A thousand thunders!" Trabaud spread hands in mute appeal and gazed prayerfully at the ceiling. "An apprentice baker. Of what does he dream? Of the stars!"

"I cannot help myself, Monsieur."

"Of course you cannot; you are but sixteen." He gave an expressive shrug. "I will ask you two things. How can there be people if no man makes bread? And how can anyone go among the stars if there are no people?"

"I do not know, Monsieur."

"There are ships flying between the stars," continued Trabaud, "for one reason only—because here we have life." Leaning to one side he picked up a yard-long loaf, yeasty and golden-crusted. "And this sustains life."

"Yes, Monsieur."

"Do you think that I would not like to adventure among the stars?" asked Trabaud.

"*You*, Monsieur?" Jules stared at him wide-eyed.

"Of a certainty. But I am old and gray-haired and I have risen to different eminence. There are many things I cannot do, shall never do. But I have become a great artist; I make beautiful bread."

"Yes, Monsieur."

"Not," emphasized Trabaud, wagging an admonitory finger, "*not* the machine-excreted pap of the electric bakery at Besançon, but real hand-made bread prepared to perfection. I make it with care, and with love; that is the secret. Upon each batch I bestow a little of my soul. It is the artist in me. You understand?"

"I understand, Monsieur."

"So, Jules, the citizens do not attend merely to buy bread. True, it reads above my window: *Pierre Trabaud—Boulanger*, but that is no more than becoming modesty. The characteristic of the great artist is that he is modest."

"Yes, Monsieur Trabaud."

"I will tell you, Jules, why the citizens bring their baskets the moment the scent of my opened oven goes down the road. It is because they are of the taste discerning; they are revolted by the crudities of the electric bakery. They come here to purchase my masterpieces. Is that not so, Jules?"

"Yes, Monsieur."

"Then be content. In due time you, too, will be an artist. Meanwhile let us forget the stars; they are for others."

With that, Trabaud left his sack and commenced spreading a thin layer of flour over a zinc-topped table.

Jules stood silently watching the oven doors from behind which came cracks and splits and hissing sounds. An odor of burning pine filled the bakery and invaded the street. After a while he opened the doors and a great blast of heat came out, full and fierce like the flame trail of a rocket.

Heav'n, heav'n, gonna walk all over God's heav'n.

Colonel Pinet's monocle glittered as he leaned over the counter, pointed to the supposedly hidden tray and said, "One of those also, if you please."

"They are not for sale, M. le Colonel," declared Trabaud.

"Why are they not?"

"They are the errors of Jules; one more minute and they would have been charcoal. I do not sell blunders. Who wishes to eat charcoal?"

"I do," Pinet informed. "That is the unresolved difference between myself and my wife. She cooks lightly. I am never served with a well-scorched tidbit. Permit me to enjoy one of Jules' mistakes."

"Monsieur—"

"I insist."

"Madame would never accept such a miserable loaf."

"Madame has an appointment with her hairdresser, and has commissioned me to do the shopping," Colonel Pinet told him. "I propose to do it in my own way. You will perceive, my dear Trabaud, that I am an opportunist. Will you be good enough to serve me with an appetizing cinder, or must I seek one from the electric bakery?"

Trabaud flinched, glowered, selected the least scorched loaf from the tray, wrapped it to hide it from other eyes, handed it over with bad grace. "The good God preserve me. This Jules gains me one customer but then he will lose me a hundred."

"He causes you to suffer?" inquired Pinet.

"It is perpetual agony, M. le Colonel. I am compelled to watch him all the time. I have but to turn my back—so," —he turned his back to demonstrate—"and, *pouf!* his mind is off his work and floating among the stars like a runaway balloon."

"The stars, you say?"

"Yes, M. le Colonel. He is a space conqueror chained to earth by unfortunate circumstances. Of that material I must make a baker."

"And what are these circumstances of which you speak?"

"His mother said to him, 'Trabaud requires an apprentice; this is your chance. You will leave school and become a baker.' So he came to me. He is obedient, you understand—so long as he happens to be with us upon this world."

"Mothers," said Pinet. He polished his monocle, screwed it back into his eye. "My mother wished me to be a beautifier of poodles. She said it was a genteel occupation; there was money in it. Her society friends would rush to me with their pet lapdogs." His long, slender fingers made clipping and curling motions while his face registered acute disdain. "I asked myself: what am I that I should manicure a dog? I enlisted in the Terraforce and was drafted to Mars. My mother was prostrated by the news."

"Alas," said Trabaud, all sympathy.

"Today she brags that her son is an officer of the four-comet rank. Such are mothers. They have no logic."

"It is perhaps as well," Trabaud suggested. "Else some of us might never have been born."

"You will show me this star-gazer," ordered Pinet.

"Jules!" bawled Trabaud, cupping hands around mouth and aiming toward the bakery at back. "Jules, come here."

No reply.

"You see?" Trabaud made a gesture of defeat. "The problem is formidable." He went into the bakery. His voice rang out, loud, impatient. "I called you; why did you not answer? M. le Colonel wishes to see you at once. Brush back your hair and make haste."

Jules appeared, his manner reluctant, his hands and hair white with flour. His gray eyes were clear and steady as he looked at the inquisitive Colonel Pinet.

"So!" commented Pinet, examining him with interest. "You hunger for the stars. *Why?*"

"Why does one desire anything?" said Jules. He gave a deep shrug. "It is my nature."

"An excellent answer," approved Pinet. "It is of one's nature. A thousand people entrust themselves hourly to a single pilot's hands. They are safe. Why? Because what he does is of his nature." He studied Jules slowly from head to feet. "Yet you bake bread."

"Someone must bake it," put in Trabaud. "We cannot all be star-roamers."

"Silence!" commanded Pinet. "You conspire with a woman to slaughter a soul; therefore you are an assassin. That is to be expected. You come from the Côtes du Rhône where assassins swarm like flies."

"M. le Colonel, I resent—"

"You are willing to continue to serve this murderer?" Pinet demanded of Jules.

"Monsieur Trabaud has been kind. You will pardon me—"

"Of course he has been kind," interjected Pinet. "He is a sly one. All the Trabauds are sly ones." He threw a broad wink at Trabaud but Jules caught it and felt vastly relieved. "One thing is demanded of all recruits," continued Pinet, more seriously. "Do you have any idea what that may be?"

"Intelligence, M. le Colonel," suggested Jules.

"Yes, of course; but it is not sufficient. It is required that a recruit should hunger and thirst for the Space Service."

"Which is as it should be," offered Trabaud. "One works hardest and best at the things for which one has some enthusiasm. If I were to care nothing about bread, I would now be a dirty-handed tobacco-spitter at the electric bakery."

"Every year ten thousand aspirants arrive at the Space College," Pinet informed Jules. "Of these, more than eight thousand fail to pass through. Their enthusiasm is not enough to support four years of intensive study and single-minded concentration. So they fail. It is disgusting, do you agree?"

"Yes, M. le Colonel, it is disgusting," confirmed Jules, frowning.

"Hah!" said Pinet, showing satisfaction. "Then let us deprive this vulture Trabaud of his prey. We shall find for him another one who is of the nature to bake."

"Monsieur—?"

"I will recommend you to the college; I ask of you only one thing in return."

"Jules went momentarily breathless. "Oh, M. le Colonel! What do you wish?"

"I ask you, Jules, not to disgust me."

He sat in the cabin, his eyes sunken and red-rimmed, while the

Fantome whistled through space. In twenty tough, hectic years he had builded a ladder and climbed it to a captaincy. His present reputation was that of being one of the most conscientious commanders in the service. It was firmly founded upon a motto that had sustained him through all his most trying times.

"I ask you, Jules, not to disgust me."

His mother and Colonel Pinet had both died proud; and he was a captain.

As navigator, copilot and pilot he had served in the bow, where he'd always wanted to be, visibly plunging into the vast starfield that he loved so much. There had been regular hours of sleep, rest and work, the latter filled with the constant, never-ending thrill of things that could be seen, watched, studied.

Now he'd exchanged all that for imprisonment amidships, nothing around him but dull titanium alloy walls, little before him save a desk smothered with papers.

All his waking hours, all his resting hours and part of his sleeping time, he answered questions, made decisions, wrote entries in official books, filled a thousand and one official forms. *Beaucomp de papierasserie* in the idiom of France-Sud.

One hour after supper, "Your pardon, Captain. The fat man from Dusseldorf is mad drunk again. He has injured a steward who tried to restrain him. Permission requested to lock him in the brig."

"Granted."

Or in the middle of a nervy, restless sleep an imperative shake of his shoulder followed by, "Your pardon, Captain. Tubes ten and eleven have cracked their linings. Permission requested to cut off power for two hours while repairs are carried out."

"Granted. Have the duty navigator bring me the current coordinates immediately you're ready to resume progress."

Two hours later another shoulder shake. "Apologies for disturbing you, Captain. Repairs have been completed. Here are our present coordinates."

Questions.

Form-filling.

Requests, reports, demands, crises, decisions, answers, orders, commands. Continual harassment.

More paperwork.

"Your pardon, Captain. Two passengers, William Archer and Marion White, wish to be married. When would it be convenient for you to conduct the service?"

"Have they passed the medical examiner?"

"Yes, Captain."

"Has the groom a ring?"

"No, Captain."

"Ascertain the correct size and supply him from the ship's store at the standard charge of twenty dollars."

"And the service, Captain?"

"At four bells. Let me know whether that time suits them."

Paper work again. Duplicated copies of two birth certificates, two emigration certificates, two health certificates, two entry warrants. Copies in triplicate of marriage certificates for Earth Government, Sirius Government and Space Service Record Office. One original copy for the bride.

And so it went on, every conceivable problem great or petty, at all hours without let-up. Upon landing after a long run, it was considered normal for the captain to be the only one to stagger down the ramp, whirly-minded with constant nerve-testing and serious lack of sleep. Sometimes he was tempted to take action to demote himself, except that—

"I ask you, Jules, not to disgust me."

The *Fantome* came down at Bathalbar, on the planet Dacedes, system of Sirius. The run had numbered two hundred eighty-five Earth-days.

Landing formalities over, Captain Jules Rioux left the ship, wandered hazily to Mama Kretschmer's. That was routine and in accordance with best psychological advice.

A ship's commander needs deep, potent sleep and plenty of it. But first he must expunge from his mind all thoughts of the vessel, the journey, and everything pertaining thereto. He must so condition himself mentally that he will slumber like a child, happily, right around the clock. The preliminary technique was to discard past problems and walk into one's own heaven.

Mama Kretschmer, a big-bosomed hausfrau from Bavaria, nodded familiarly, said, "Der Kapitan Roo. I am pliss. You vant der sem as effer?"

"If you please, Madame Kretschmer."

He went into the back room. The front one, big, crowded and noisy, held commanders who'd got in several days ahead and already were feeling their oats. The back room, soundproofed, with heavily cushioned reclining chairs, contained three semicomatose officers of his own rank. He did not speak to these. They offered no greeting, seemed unaware of his entry. They were knocking at the doors of paradise.

In short time Mama brought him a glass of navy rum, neat, warmed to blood heat, spiked with a few drops of oil of cinnamon. He lay back, settled himself comfortably and sought for the land of peace.

The spiced rum glowed within his bowels, fumed into his head. The silence bore down upon his eyelids. Slowly, ever so slowly, he moved away from this time of exhaustion and walked into that other world.

Women with broad, rosycheeked peasant faces, little lacework caps on their hair, baskets on their arms. Long iron trays sliding over pineash and coming out loaded with loaves, long ones, flat ones, curly ones, plaited ones.

A chatter of feminine voices reciting village gossip amid an ineffable fragrance of pinesmoke and fresh-baked bread.

Heav'n, heav'n.

Eric Frank Russell (1905-)
Born in Sandhurst, England, Eric Frank Russell began publishing
science fiction stories in the late 1930s. He won the 1955 Hugo
Award for "Alamagoosa", judged the best science fiction story of the
year.

"I wonder if we'll ever really find out
about Men—I mean *really* find out
what made Men different from us
Robots—"

men are different

Alan Bloch

I'm an archaeologist, and Men are my business. Just the same, I wonder if we'll ever find out about Men—I mean *really* find out what made Men different from us Robots—by digging around on the dead planets. You see, I lived with a Man once, and I know it isn't as simple as they told us back in school.

We have a few records, of course, and Robots like me are filling in some of the gaps, but I think now that we aren't really getting anywhere. We know, or at least the historians say we know, that Men came from a planet called Earth. We know, too, that they rode out bravely from star to star; and wherever they stopped, they left colonies—Men, Robots, and sometimes both—against their return. But they never came back.

Those were the shining days of the world. But are we so old now? Men had a bright flame—the old word is "divine," I think—that flung them far across the night skies, and we have lost the strands of the web they wove.

Our scientists tell us that Men were very much like us—and the skeleton of a Man is, to be sure, almost the same as the skeleton of a Robot, except that it's made of some calcium compound instead of titanium. Just the same, there are other differences.

It was on my last field trip, to one of the inner planets, that I met the Man. He must have been the last Man in this system, and he'd forgotten how to talk—he'd been alone so long. Once he learned our language we got along fine together, and I planned to bring him back with me. Something happened to him, though.

One day, for no reason at all, he complained of the heat. I checked his temperature and decided that his thermostat circuits were shot. I had a kit of field spares with me, and he was obviously out of order, so I went to work. I turned him off without any trouble. I pushed the needle into his neck to operate the cut-off switch, and he stopped moving, just like a Robot. But when I opened him up he wasn't the same inside. And when I put him back together I couldn't get him running again. Then he sort of weathered away—and by the time I was ready to come home, about a year later, there was nothing left of him but bones. Yes, Men are indeed different.

Alan Bloch
We know that Alan Bloch is a Man from the planet called Earth—at least we think *we know! Further information about him is mysteriously unavailable. "Men Are Different" appeared in* 50 Short Science Fiction Tales *(1963), edited by Isaac Asimov and Groff Conklin.*

Charles and J-1001011 are on a
space mission of destruction. Man
and machine become a super-efficient instrument of death.

Frightening? Yes, especially when
Charles is the *machine*, J-1001011
the *man*.

city of yesterday
Terry Carr

"Wake up," said Charles, and J-1001011 instantly sat up. The couch
sat up with him, jackknifing to form his pilot's seat. J-1001011 noted
that the seat was in combat position, raised high enough to give him
an unobstructed vision on all sides of the planetflier.

"We're in orbit around our objective," said Charles. "Breakout and
attack in seven minutes. Eat. Eliminate."

J-1001011 obediently withdrew the red-winking tube from the
panel before him and put it between his lips. Warm, mealy liquid fed
into his mouth, and he swallowed at a regular rate. When the nour-
ishment tube stopped, he removed it from his mouth and let it slide
back into the panel.

The peristalsis stimulators began, and he asked, "Is there news of
my parents?"

"Personal questions are always answered freely," said Charles,
"but only when military necessities have been completed. Your briefing for this mission takes precedence." A screen lit up on the flier's
control panel, showing a 3-4 contour map of the planet they were orbiting.

J-1001011 sighed and turned his attention to the screen. "The
planet Rhinstruk," said Charles. "Oxygen 13.7%, nitrogen 82.4%,

plus inert gases. Full spacewear will be required for the high altitude attack pattern in effect on this mission."

The image on the screen zoomed in, selected one continent out of three he had seen revolving below, continued zooming down to near planet level. Charles said, "Note that this is a totally enemy planet. Should I be shot down and you somehow survive, there will be no refuge. If that happens, destroy yourself."

"The target?" the pilot asked.

"The city you see below. It isn't fully automated, but its defenses will be formidable anyway." On the screen J-1001011 saw a towered city rising from a broad plain. The city was circular, and as the image sharpened with proximity he could make out individual streets, parkways . . . and beam emplacements. The screen threw light-circles on seven of these in all.

"We will have nine fliers," said Charles. "These beams will attempt to defend, but our mission will be simple destruction of the entire city, which presents a much larger target than any one of our fliers. We will lose between three and five of us, but we'll succeed. Attack pattern RO-1101 will be in effect; you'll take control of me at 30,000 feet. End of briefing."

The pilot stretched in his chair, flexed muscles in his arms and hands. "How long was I asleep?" he asked.

"Eight months, seventeen days plus," said Charles.

That long! A quarter-credit for sleep time that would give him over two months on his term of service, leaving him . . . less than a year, Earth standard. J-1001011 felt his heart speed up momentarily, before Charles' nerve-implants detected and corrected it. The pilot had been in service for nearly seven subjective years. Adding objective sleep time, it came out to over nineteen years. The sleep periods, during Hardin Drive travel between star systems, ate up his service term easily for him . . . but then he remembered, as he always did, that his parents, whoever and wherever they were, would be getting older at objective time rate on some planet.

Nineteen years. They should still be alive, he thought. He remembered them from his childhood, on a planet where colors had been real rather than dyed or light-tinted, where winds had blown fresh and night had fallen with the regular revolution of the planet.

He had had a name there, not a binary number—Henry, or Hendrick, or Henried; he couldn't quite remember. When the Control machines had come for him he had been ten years old, old enough to know his own name, but they had erased it. They had had to clear his memory for the masses of minute data he'd need for service, so the machines had stored his personal memories in neat patterns of microenergy, waiting for his release.

Not all of them, though. The specific things, yes: his name, the name of his planet, its exact location, the thousand-and-one details that machines recognize as data. But not remembered sights, smells, tastes: flowerbursts of color amid green vegetation, the cold spray of rainbowed water as he stood beside a waterfall, the warmth of an animal held in the arms. He remembered what it was like to be Henry, or Hendrick or Henried, even though he couldn't remember the exact name of the person he had been.

And he remembered what his parents were like, though he had no memory at all of *their* names. His father: big and rangy, with bony hands and an awkward walk and a deep, distant voice, like thunder and rain on the other side of a mountain. His mother: soft and quiet, a quizzical face framed by dark hair, somehow smiling even when she was angry, as if she weren't quiet sure how to put together a stern expression.

By now they must be . . . fifty years old? Sixty? Or even a *hundred* and *sixty,* he thought. He couldn't know; he had to trust what the machines told him, what Charles said. And they could be lying about the time he spent in sleep. But he had to assume they weren't.

"Breakout and attack in one minute," Charles said.

The voice startled him momentarily, but then he reached for his pressure helmet, sealed it in place with automatic movements, machine-trained muscle patterns. He heard the helmet's intercom click on.

"What about my parents?" he asked. "You have time to tell me before we break out. At least tell me if they're still alive."

"Breakout and attack in thirty seconds and counting," said Charles. "Twenty-eight, twenty-seven, twenty-six . . ."

J-1001011, human pilot of a planetflier named Charles, shook his head in resignation and listened to the count, bracing himself for the coming shock of acceleration.

It hit him, as always, with more force than he had remembered, crushing him back into the chair as the planetflier rocketed out of the starship's hold along with its eight unit-mates. Charles had opaqued the pilot's bubble to prevent blinding him with sudden light, but the machine cleared it steadily as it drove downward toward the planet's surface, and soon the man could make out the other fliers around him. He recognized the flying formation, remembered the circular attack pattern they'd be using—a devastating ring of fliers equipped with pyrobombs. Charles was right. They'd lose some fliers, but the city would be destroyed.

He wondered about the city, the enemy. Was this another pacification mission, another planet feeling strong in its isolation from the rest of GalFed's far-flung worlds and trying to break away from central regulation? J-1001011 had been on dozens of such missions. But their attacks then hadn't been destruct-patterns against whole cities, so this must be a different kind of problem. Maybe the city was really a military complex . . . even a stronghold of the Khallash. If they really existed.

When men had first made contact with an alien race a century and a half before, they had met with total enmity, almost mindlessly implacable hatred. War had flared immediately—a defensive war on the part of the humans, who hadn't been prepared for it. And in order to organize the loose-knit Galactic Federation efficiently, they'd computerized the central commands . . . and then the middle echelons . . . and finally, a little over a century ago, the whole of GalFed had been given to the machines to defend.

Or so he had been taught. There were rumors, of course, that there were no Khallash any longer, that they'd been destroyed or driven off long ago . . . or that they'd never existed in the first place, that the machines had invented them as an excuse for their own control of GalFed. J-1001011 didn't know. He'd never met the aliens in battle, but that proved nothing, considering the vastness of space and the many internal problems the machines had to cope with.

Yet perhaps he would meet them now . . . in the city below.

"Thirty thousand feet," said Charles. "Attach your muscle contacts."

The pilot quickly drew from the walls of the compartment a network of small wires, one after the other, and touched each to magnetized terminals on his arms, hands, legs, shoulders. As he did so he felt the growing sensation of airflight: he was becoming one with the flier, a single unit of machine and man. Charles fed the sensory impressions into his nervous system through his regular nerve-implants, and as the muscle contacts were attached he could feel the flier's rockets, gyros, pyrolaunchers all coming under his control, responding instantly to movements of his body's muscles.

This was the part that he liked, that almost made his service term worth it. As the last contact snapped into place, he *became* the planetflier. His name was Charles, and he was a whole being once more. Air rushed past him, mottled fields tilted far below, he felt the strength of duralloy skin and the thrust of rockets; and he was not just a flesh-and-blood human wombed in his pilot's compartment, but a weapon of war swooping down for a kill.

The machines themselves don't appreciate this, he thought. Charles and the rest have no emotions, no pleasures. But a human does ... and we can even enjoy killing. Maybe that's why they need us—because we can love combat, so we're better at it than them.

But he knew that wasn't true, only an emotional conceit. Human battle pilots were needed because their nervous systems were more efficient than any microminiaturized computer of the same size and mass; it was as simple as that. And human pilots were expendable where costly mechanization wouldn't be.

"Control is full now," he said; but Charles didn't answer. Charles didn't exist now. Only the computer aboard the orbiting starship remained to monitor the planetflier below.

In a moment the starship's voice came to him through Charles' receptors: "All human units are ready. Attack pattern RO-1101 will now begin."

The city was below him, looking just as it had on the contour map: wide streets, buildings thrusting up towards him, patches of green that must have been parks ... or camouflage, he warned himself. The city was the enemy.

He banked into a spiral and knifed down through the planet's cold air. The other fliers fell into formation behind him, and as the starship cut in the intercommunications channels he heard the voices of other pilots:

"Beautiful big target—we can't miss it. Anybody know if they're Khallash down there?" "Only the machines would know that, and if they'd wanted to tell us, they'd have included it in the briefing."

"It looks like a human city to me. Must be another rebel planet."

"Maybe that's what the Khallash want us to think."

"It doesn't matter who they are," J-1001011 said. "They're enemy; they're our mission. Complete enough missions and we go home. Stop talking and start the attack; we're in range."

As he spoke he lined his sights dead-center on the city and fired three pyrobombs in quick succession. He peeled off and slipped back into the flight circle as another flier banked into firing trajectory. Three more bombs flared out and downward, the second flier rejoined the pattern.

Below, J-1001011's bombs hit. He saw the flashes, one, two, three quick bursts, and a moment later red flames showed where the bombs had hit. A bit off center from where he had aimed, but close enough. He could correct for it on the next pass.

More bombs burst below; more fires leaped and spread. The fliers darted in, loosed their bombs and dodged away. They were in a complete ring around the city now, the pattern fully established. It was all going according to plan.

Then the beams from the city began to fire.

The beams were almost invisible at a distance, just lightning-quick lances of destructive energy cutting into the sky. Not that it was important to see them—the fliers couldn't veer off to evade them in time, wouldn't even be able to react before a beam struck.

But the planetfliers were small, and they stayed high. Any beam hits would be as much luck as skill.

They rained fire and death on the city for an hour, each flier banking inward just long enough to get off three or four bombs, then veering out and up before he got too close. At the hour's end the city below was dotted by fires, and the fires were spreading steadily. One of the planetfliers had been hit; it had burst with an energy release that buffeted J-1001011 with its shock wave, sending him momentarily off course. But he had quickly righted himself, re-entered the pattern and returned to the attack.

As the destruction continued, he felt more and more the oneness, the wholeness of machine and man. Charles the other-thing was gone, merged into his own being, and now he was the machine, the beautiful complex mass of metals and sensors, relays and engines and weaponry. He was a destruction-machine, a death-flier, a super-efficient killer. It was like coming out of the darkness of some prison, being freed to burst out with all his pent-up hatreds and frustrations and destroy, destroy. . . .

It was the closest thing he had to being human again, to being . . . what was the name he had back on that planet where he'd been born? He couldn't remember now; there was no room for even an echo of that name in his mind.

He was *Charles*.

He was a war-machine destroying a city—that and only that. Flight and power occupied his whole being, and the screaming release of hatred and fear within him was so intense that it was love. The attack pattern became, somehow, a ritual of courtship, the pyrobombs and destruction and fire below a kind of lovemaking whose insensitivity gripped him more and more fiercely as the attack continued. It was the only kind of real life he had known since the machines had taken him.

When the battle was over, when the city was a flaming circle of red and even the beams had stopped firing from below, he was exhausted both physically and emotionally. He was able to note dimly, with some back part of his brain or perhaps through one of Charles' machine synapse-patterns, that they had lost three of the fliers. But that didn't interest him; nothing did.

When something clicked in him and Charles' voice said, "Remove your muscle contacts now," he did so dully, uncaring. And he became J-1001011 again.

Later, with the planetfliers back in the hold of the starship and awaiting the central computer's analysis of the mission's success, he remembered the battle like something in a dream. It was a red, violent dream, a nightmare; and it was worse than that, because it had been real.

He roused himself, licked dry lips, said, "You have time now, Charles, to tell me about my parents. Are they alive?"

Charles said, "Your parents do not exist now. They've just been destroyed."

There was a moment of incomprehension, then a dull shock hit J-1001011 in the stomach. But it was almost as if he had been expecting to hear this—and Charles controlled his reaction instantly through the nerve-implants.

"Then that was no Khallash city," he said.

"No," said Charles. "It was a human city, a rebel city."

The pilot searched vaguely through the fog of his memories of home, trying to remember anything about a city such as he'd destroyed today. But he could grasp nothing like that; his memories were all of some smaller town, and of mountains, not the open fields that had surrounded this city.

"My parents moved to the city after I was taken away," he said. "Is that right?"

"We have no way of knowing about that," said Charles. "Who your parents were, on what planet they lived—all this information has been destroyed in the city on Rhinstruk. It was the archives center of the Galactic Federation, storing all the memory-data of our service humans. Useless information, since none of it will ever be used again —and potentially harmful, because the humans assigned to guard it were engaged in a plot to broadcast the data through official machine communications channels to the original holders of the memories. So it became necessary to destroy the city."

"You destroyed an entire city . . . just for that?"

"It was necessary. Humans perform up to minimum efficiency standards only when they're unhampered by pre-service memories; this is why all your memory-data was transferred from your mind when you were inducted. For a while it was expedient to keep the records on file, to be returned as humans terminated their service, but that time is past. It has always been a waste of training and manpower to release humans from service, and now we have great enough control in the Federation that it's no longer necessary. Therefore we're able to complete a major step toward totally efficient organization."

J-1001011 imagined fleetingly that he could feel the machine's nerve-implants moving within him to control some emotion that threatened to rise. Anger? Fear? Grief? He couldn't be sure just what was appropriate to this situation; all he actually felt was a dull, uncomprehending curiosity.

"But my parents . . . you said they were destroyed."

"They have been. There is no way of knowing where or who they were. They've become totally negligible factors, along with the rest of your pre-service existence. When we conrol all data in your mind, we then have proper control of the mind itself."

"He remembered dark trees and a cushion of damp green leaves beneath them, where he had fallen asleep one endless afternoon. He heard the earthquake of his father's laughter once when he had drunk far too much, remembered how like a stranger his mother had seemed for weeks after she'd cut her hair short, tasted smoked meat and felt the heat of an open hearth-fire. . . .

The nerve-implants moved like ghosts inside him.

"The central computer's analysis is now complete," Charles announced. "The city on Rhinstruk is totally destroyed; our mission was successful. So there's no more need for you to be awake; de-activation will now begin."

Immediately, Pilot J-1001011 felt his consciousness ebbing away. He said, more to himself than Charles, "You can't erase the past like that. The mission was . . . unsuccessful." He felt a yawn coming, tried to fight it, couldn't. "Their names weren't . . . the important. . ."

Then he couldn't talk any more; but there was no need for it. He drifted into sleep remembering the freedom of flight when he was Charles, the beauty and strength of destroying, of rage channeled through pyrobombs . . . of release.

For one last flickering moment he felt a stab of anger begin to rise, but then Charles' implants pushed it back down inside. He slept.

Until his next awakening.

Terry Carr (1937-)
Terry Carr's interest in science fiction began as a schoolboy in Oregon after he read When Worlds Collide, *which had been misfiled in the school library, under "astronomy". He now writes and edits science fiction novels and short stories.* World of Kor *is one of his most popular novels.*

To the stranger on the desolate
rocky island the bloodflowers are
beautiful, a fragile form of life.
But he doesn't know that when the
bloodflowers appear again they will
bring *death* . . .

bloodflowers

W. D. Valgardson

Danny Thorson saw Mrs. Poorwilly before he stepped off the freight
boat onto Black Island. He couldn't have missed her. She was fat and
had thick, heavy arms and legs. She stood at the front of the crowd
with her hands on her hips.

"You the new teacher?" Mrs. Poorwilly said.

"Yes, I'm—"

Mrs. Poorwilly cut him off by waving her arm at him and saying,
"Put your things on the wheelbarrow. Mr. Poorwilly will take them up
to the house. Board and room is $50 a month. We're the only ones
that give it. That's Mr. Poorwilly."

Mrs. Poorwilly waved her hand again, indicating a small man who
was standing behind an orange wheelbarrow. He had a round, red
face, and his hair was so thin and blond that from ten feet away he
looked bald.

Danny piled his suitcases and boxes onto the wheelbarrow. He
was tired and sore from the trip to the island. The bunk had been too
short. The weather had been bad. For the first three days of the trip
he hadn't been able to hold anything down except coffee.

When the wheelbarrow was full, Mr. Poorwilly took his hands out
of his pockets. They were twisted into two rigid pink hooks. He slipped them through two metal loops that had been nailed to the han-
dles of the wheelbarrow, then lifted the barrow on his wrists.

At the top of the first rise, Mr. Poorwilly stopped. As if to reassure Danny, he said, "Mrs. Poorwilly's a good cook. We've got fresh eggs all winter, too."

Danny glanced back. Mrs. Poorwilly was swinging cases of tinned goods onto the dock. Her grey hair blew wildly about her face.

They started off again. As there were no paths on the bare granite, Danny followed Mr. Poorwilly. They walked along a ridge, dropped into a hollow. The slope they had to climb was steep, so Danny bent down, caught the front of the wheelbarrow and pulled as Mr. Poorwilly pushed. They had just reached the top when they met an elderly, wasted man who was leaning heavily on the shoulder of a young girl as he shuffled along.

Danny was so surprised by the incongruity of the pair that he stared. The girl's black hair fell to her shoulders, making a frame for her face. She looked tired, but her face was tanned and her mouth was a warm red. Her cheeks were pink from the wind. She stopped when she saw Danny.

The man with her made no attempt to greet them. His breath came in ragged gasps. His dark yellow skin was pulled so tightly over his face that the bone seemed to be pushing through. His eyes protruded and the whites had turned yellow. He gave the girl's shoulder a tug. They started up again.

When they had passed, Danny said, "Who was that? The girl is beautiful."

"Sick Jack and his daughter. It's his liver. Mrs. Poorwilly helps Adel look after him. She says he won't see the spring. He'll be the second. How are you feeling after the trip? You look green."

"I feel green. It was nine days in hell. The boat never quit rolling."

"Good thing you're not going back with them, then." Mr. Poorwilly twisted his head toward the dock to indicate who he meant. "Sunrise was red this morning. There'll be a storm before dawn tomorrow."

Mr. Poorwilly slipped his hands back into the metal loops. "Sorry to be so slow, but the arthritis causes me trouble. Used to be able to use my hands but not anymore. It's a good thing I've got a pension from the war. Getting shot was the best thing has ever happened to me."

Danny noticed a small, red flower growing from a crack in the rock. When he bent down to get a better look, he saw that the crack was filled with brown stems. He picked the flower and held it up. "What is it?"

"Bloodflower," Mr. Poorwilly replied. "Only thing that grows on the island except lichen. Shouldn't pick it. They say it brings bad luck. If you cut your finger or make your nose bleed, it'll be OK."

Danny laughed. "You don't believe that, do you?"

"Mrs. Poorwilly says it. She knows quite a bit about these things."

When they reached the house, Danny unloaded his belongings and put them into his bedroom. Mr. Poorwilly left him and went back to the dock for the supplies Mrs. Poorwilly had been unloading.

While the Poorwillys spent the day sorting and putting away their winter's supplies, Danny walked around the island. What Mr. Poorwilly said was true. Nothing grew on the island except lichen and bloodflowers. Despite the cold, patches of red filled the cracks that were sheltered from the wind.

The granite of the island had been weathered smooth, but there was nowhere it was truly flat. Three-quarters of the island's shoreline fell steeply into the sea. Only in scattered places did the shoreline slope gently enough to let Danny walk down to the water. To the west the thin blue line of the coast of Labrador was just barely visible. Two fishing boats were bobbing on the ocean. There were no birds except for some large grey gulls that rose as he approached and hovered in the air until he was past them. He would have liked to have them come down beside him so he could have touched them, but they rose on the updrafts. He reached toward them and shouted for them to come down, then laughed at himself and continued his exploring.

Except for the houses and the fish sheds, the only other buildings were the school and the chicken roost behind the Poorwillys. All the buildings were made from wood siding. Because of the rock, there were no basements. Rock foundations had been put down so the floors would be level.

Most of the houses showed little more than traces of paint. The Poorwillys' and Mary Johnson's were the only ones that had been painted recently. Danny knew the other house belonged to Mary Johnson because it had a sign with her name on it. Below her name it said, "General store. Post office. Two-way radio."

Danny explored until it started to get dark, then went back to the

Poorwillys.

"Heard you've been looking around," Mrs. Poorwilly said. "If you hadn't come back in another five minutes, I would have sent Mr. Poorwilly to bring you back."

"There's no danger of getting lost." Danny was amused at her concern.

"No," Mrs. Poorwilly agreed, "but you wouldn't want to slip and fall in the dark. You're not in a city now with a doctor down the street. You break a leg or crack your skull and you might have to wait two, three weeks for the weather to clear enough for a plane to come. You don't want to be one of the three."

Danny felt chastised, but Mrs. Poorwilly dropped the subject. She and Mr. Poorwilly spent all during supper asking him about the mainland. As they talked, Mrs. Poorwilly fed her husband from her plate. He sat with his hands in his lap. There were no directions given or taken about the feeding. Both Mr. and Mrs. Poorwilly were anxious to hear everything he had to tell them about the mainland.

When he got a chance, Danny said, "What'd you mean 'one of the three'?"

"Trouble always comes in threes. Maybe you didn't notice it on the mainland because things are so complicated. On the island you can see it because it's small and you know everybody. There's just 35 houses. Somebody gets hurt, everybody knows about it. They can keep track. Three, six, nine, but it never ends unless it's on something made up of threes."

"You'll see before the winter is out. Last month the radio said Emily died in the sanatorium. TB. Now Sick Jack's been failing badly. He's got to be a hard yellow and he's lost all his flesh. He dies, then there'll be one more thing to end it. After that, everything will be OK."

Mrs. Poorwilly made her pronouncement with all the assuredness of an oracle. Danny started on his dessert.

"Mr. Poorwilly says you think Adel's a nice bit of fluff."

Danny had started thinking about the book on mythology he'd been reading at summer school. The statement caught him off guard. He had to collect his thoughts, then he said, "The girl with the long dark hair? I only caught a glimpse of her, but she seemed to be very pretty."

"When her father goes, she'll be on her own," Mr. Poorwilly said.

"She's a good girl. She works hard."

"Does she have any education?"

"Wives with too much education can cause a lot of trouble," Mrs. Poorwilly said. "They're never satisfied. The young fellows around here and on the coast have enough trouble without that."

Danny tried not to show his embarrassment. "I was thinking in terms of her getting a job on the mainland. If her spelling is good and she learned to type, she could get a government job."

"Might be that she'll go right after her father. No use making plans until we see what the winter brings." Mr. Poorwilly turned to his wife for confirmation. "It's happened before."

Mrs. Poorwilly nodded as she scraped the last of the pudding from the dish and fed it to her husband.

"What you want is what those people had that I was reading about. They used to ward off evil by choosing a villager to be king for a year. Then so the bad luck of the old year would be done with, they killed him in the spring."

"They weren't Christians," Mr. Poorwilly said.

"No," Danny replied. "They gave their king anything he wanted. A woman, food, gifts, everything, since it was only for a year. Then when the first flowers bloomed, they killed him."

"Must have been them Chinese," Mr. Poorwilly said.

"No. Europeans. But it was a long time ago."

"Have you ever ridden on a train?" Mrs. Poorwilly asked. "Mr. Poorwilly and I rode on a train for our honeymoon. I remember it just like yesterday."

Mr. and Mrs. Poorwilly told him about their train ride until it was time to go to bed. After Danny was in bed, Mr. Poorwilly stuck his head through the curtain that covered the doorway. In a low voice, he said, "Don't go shouting at the sea gulls when you're out walking. Most of the people here haven't been anywhere and they'll think you're sort of funny."

"OK," Danny said. Mr. Poorwilly's head disappeared.

The next day Mrs. Poorwilly had everyone in the village over to meet Danny. As fast as Danny met the women and children, he forgot their names. The men were still away fishing or working on the mainland. Mr. Poorwilly and Danny were the only men until Adel brought Sick Jack.

Sick Jack looked even thinner than he had the day before. The yellow of his skin seemed to have deepened. As soon as he had shaken Danny's hand, he sat down. After a few minutes, he fell into a doze and his daughter covered him with a blanket she had brought.

Mrs. Poorwilly waited until Sick Jack was covered, then brought Adel over to see Danny.

"This is Adel. She'll come for coffee soon, and you can tell her about the trains and the cities. She's never been off the island."

Adel blushed and looked at the floor. "Certainly," Danny said. "I've a whole set of slides I'm going to show Mr. and Mrs. Poorwilly. If you wanted, you could come and see them."

Adel mumbled her thanks and went to the side of the room. She stayed beside her father the rest of the evening, but Danny glanced at her whenever he felt no-one was looking at him.

She was wearing blue jeans and a heavy blue sweater that had been mended at the elbows and cuffs with green wool. It was too large for her so Danny assumed that it had belonged to her father or one of the other men. From what Mrs. Poorwilly had said, Danny had learned that Adel and her father were given gifts of fish and second-hand clothing. When the men went fishing, they always ran an extra line for Sick Jack.

In spite of her clothing, Adel was attractive. Her hair was as black as he had remembered it and it hung in loose, natural waves. Her eyes were a dark blue. Underneath the too-large sweater, her breasts made soft, noticeable mounds.

She left before Danny had a chance to speak to her again, but he didn't mind as he knew he'd see her during the winter.

For the next two weeks, busy as he was, Danny couldn't help but notice the change in the village. The men returned at all hours, in all kinds of weather. Mostly they came two and three at a time, but now and again a man would come by himself, his open boat a lonely black dot on the horizon.

Most of the men brought little news that was cheerful. The fishing had been bad. Many of them were coming home with the absolute minimum of money that would carry them until spring. No-one said much, but they all knew that winter fishing would be necessary to keep some of the families from going hungry. In a good year, the winter fishing provided a change in diet for people sick of canned food. This year the fishing wouldn't be so casual.

By the end of September the weather had turned bitterly cold. The wind blew for days at a time. The houses rocked in the wind. Danny walked the smallest children to their homes. The few days the fishermen were able to leave the island, there were no fish. Some of the men tried to fish in spite of the weather, but most of the time they were able to do little more than clear the harbour before having to turn around.

The evening Sick Jack died, Danny had gone to bed early. The banging on the door woke him. Mr. Poorwilly got up and answered the door. Danny heard the muttered talk, then Mr. Poorwilly yelled the news to Mrs. Poorwilly. They both dressed and left right away. Danny would have offered to go with them, but he knew that he would just be in the way so he said nothing.

Mrs. Poorwilly was back for breakfast. As she stirred the porridge, she said, "She's alone now. We washed him and dressed him and laid him out on his bed. She's a good girl. She got all his clothes out and would have helped us dress him, but I wouldn't let her. Mr. Poorwilly is staying with her until some of the women come to sit by the body. If the weather holds, we'll have the funeral tomorrow."

"Why not have the funeral while the weather stays good? It could change tomorrow."

"Respect," Mrs. Poorwilly said. "But it's more than that, too. I wouldn't say it to her, but it helps make sure he's dead. Once just around when I married, Mrs. Milligan died. She was 70. Maybe older. They rushed because the weather was turning. They were just pushing her over the side when she groaned. The cold did it. She died for good the next week, but since then we like to make sure."

Danny went to the funeral. The body was laid out on the bed with a shroud pulled to its shoulders. Mary Johnson sang "The Old Rugged Cross." Mrs. Poorwilly held the Bible so Mr. Poorwilly could read from it. Adel sat on a kitchen chair at the foot of the bed. She was pale and her eyes were red, but she didn't cry.

When the service was over, one of the fishermen pulled the shroud over Sick Jack's head and tied it with a string. They lifted the body onto a stretcher they had made from a tarpaulin and a pair of oars. The villagers followed them to the harbour.

They laid the body on the bottom of the boat. Three men got in. As the boat swung through the spray at the harbour's mouth, Danny saw one of the men bend and tie an anchor to the shrouded figure.

Mrs. Poorwilly had coffee ready for everyone after the service. Adel sat in the middle of the kitchen. She still had a frozen look about her face, but she was willing to talk.

Sick Jack's death brought added tension to the village. One day in class while they were reading a story about a robin that had died, Mary Johnson's littlest boy said, "My mother says somebody else is going to die. Maybe Miss Adel now that her father's gone."

Danny had been sharp with him. "Be quiet. This is a Grade Three lesson. You're not even supposed to be listening. Have you done your alphabet yet?"

His older sister burst out, "That's what my mother said. She said—"

Danny cut her off. "That's enough. We're studying literature, not mythology. Things like that are nothing but superstition."

That night Danny asked about Adel. Mrs. Poorwilly said, "She's got a settlement coming from the mine where he used to work. It's not much. Maybe $500 or $600. Everybody'll help all they can, but she's going to have to get a man to look after her."

During November, Danny managed to see Adel twice. The first time, she came for coffee. The second time, she came to see Danny's slides of the mainland. Danny walked her home the first time. The second time, Mrs. Poorwilly said, "That's all right, Mr. Thorson. I'll walk with her. There's something I want to get from Mary Johnson's."

Danny was annoyed. Mrs. Poorwilly had been pushing him in Adel's direction from the first day he had come. Then, when he made an effort to be alone with her, she had stepped between them.

Mrs. Poorwilly was back in half an hour with a package of powdered milk.

Danny said, "I would have got that for you, Mrs. Poorwilly."

"A man shouldn't squeeze fruit unless he's planning on buying," she replied.

Adel walked by the school a number of times when he was there. He got to talk to her, but she was skittish. He wished that she was with him in the city. There, at least, there were dark corners, alleyways, parks, even doorsteps. On the island, you couldn't do anything without being seen.

At Christmas the villagers held a party at the school. Danny showed his slides. Afterwards they all danced while Wee Jimmy played his fiddle. Danny got to dance with Adel a good part of the night.

He knew that Mrs. Poorwilly was displeased and that everyone in the village would talk about his dancing for the rest of the year, but he didn't care. Adel had her hair tied back with a red ribbon. The curve of her neck was white and smooth. Her blouse clung to her breasts and was cut low enough for him to see where the soft curves began. Each time he danced with one of the other women, Danny found himself turning to see what Adel was doing. When the party was over, he walked Adel home and kissed her goodnight. He wanted her to stay with him in the doorway, but she pulled away and went inside.

Two days before New Year's, Mrs. Poorwilly's prediction came true. The fishing had remained poor, but Michael Fairweather had gone fishing in a heavy sea because he was one of those who had come back with little money. Two hundred yards from the island his boat capsized.

Danny had gone to school on the pretext of doing some work, but what he wanted was some privacy. He had been sitting at the window staring out to sea when the accident happened. He had seen the squall coming up. A violent wind whipped across the waves and behind it a white, ragged line on the water raced toward the island. Michael Fairweather was only able to turn his boat halfway round before the wind and sleet struck.

Danny saw the boat rise to the crest of a wave, then disappear, and Michael was hanging onto the keel. Danny bolted from the room, but by the time he reached the dock, Michael had disappeared.

The squall had disappeared as quickly as it had come. Within half an hour the sea was back to its normal rolling. The fishermen rowed out of the harbour and dropped metal bars lined with hooks. While one man rowed, another held the line at the back of the boat. As Danny watched, the boats crossed back and forth until it was nearly dark.

They came in without the body. Danny couldn't sleep that night. In the morning, when a group of men came to the Poorwillys, Danny answered the door before Mr. Poorwilly had time to get out of his bedroom. The men had come for the loan of the Poorwillys' rooster.

Mrs. Poorwilly nestled the rooster in her jacket on the way to the dock, then tied it to Mr. Poorwilly's wrist with a leather thong. Mr. Poorwilly stepped into the front of the skiff. The rooster hopped onto the bow. With that the other men climbed into their boats and followed Mr. Poorwilly and the rooster out of the harbour.

"What are they doing?" Danny asked.

Mrs. Poorwilly kept her eyes on the lead boat, but she said, "When they cross the body, the rooster will crow."

Danny turned and stared at the line of boats. In spite of the wind, the sun was warm. The rooster's feathers gleamed in the sun. Mr. Poorwilly stood as still as a wooden figurehead. The dark green and grey boats rose and fell on the waves. Except for the hissing of the foam, there was no sound.

Danny looked away and searched the crowd for Adel. He had looked for a third time, when Mrs. Poorwilly, without turning, said, "She won't come for fear the current will have brought her father close to shore. They might bring him up."

All morning and into the afternoon the boats crossed and recrossed the area in front of the harbour in a ragged line. No-one left the dock. The women with small babies didn't come down from their houses, but Danny could see them in their doorways.

As the day wore on, Danny became caught up in the crossing and recrossing of the boats. None of the men dragged their hooks. The only time the men in the rear of the boats moved was to change positions with the men at the oars.

When the cock crew, the sound caught Danny by surprise. The constant, unchanging motion and the hissing of the spray had drawn him into a quiet trance. It had been as if the boats and he had been there forever.

The sound was so sharp that some of the women cried out. The men with the iron bars covered with hooks threw them into the sea, and shoved the coils of rope after them. They didn't want to pass the spot where the cock crew until the hooks were on the bottom. The bars disappeared with little spurts of white foam. Danny could hear the rope rubbing against the side of the boat as it was pulled hand over hand.

"It's him," Mrs. Poorwilly said. "God have mercy, they've got him."

Danny turned back. It was true. Instead of a white shroud, the men were pulling a black bundle into the boat.

The funeral was bad. Marj Fairweather cried constantly and tried to keep the men from taking the body. As they started to leave, she ran to the dresser for a heavy sweater, then sat in the middle of the floor, crying and saying, "He'll be so cold. He'll be so cold."

In spite of Marj, the tension in the community eased after the funeral was over. People began to visit more often, and when they came they talked more and stayed longer.

Adel came frequently to the Poorwillys. When she came, she talked to the Poorwillys, but she watched Danny. She wasn't open about it, but when Danny looked at her, she let her eyes linger on him for a second before turning away. She had her colour back and looked even better than before. Most of the time, Danny managed to walk her home. Kissing her was not satisfactory because of the cold and the bulky clothes between them, but she would not invite him in and there was no privacy at the Poorwillys. In spite of the walks and goodnight kisses, she remained shy when anyone else was around.

The villagers had expected the weather and the fishing to improve. If anything, the weather became worse. Ice coated the boats. The wind blew night and day. Often, it only stopped in the hour before dawn.

Then, without warning, Marj Fairweather sent her children to the Poorwillys, emptied a gas lamp on herself and the kitchen floor, and lit a match.

This time there was no funeral. The entire village moved in a state of shock. While one of the sheds was fixed up for the children, Marj's remains were hurried to sea and dumped in the same area as her husband's.

The village drew into itself. The villagers stayed in their own houses. When they came to the door, they only stayed long enough to finish their business. The men quit going to the dock. Most of them pulled their boats onto the island and turned them over.

A week after the fire, Danny arrived to find his room stripped of his belongings. Mrs. Poorwilly waited until he had come into the kitchen. "Mr. Poorwilly and I decided to take two of the Fairweather children. We'll take the two youngest. A fourteen-year-old can't take care of six kids."

Danny was too stunned to say anything. Mrs. Poorwilly continued. "Some of us talked about it. We hope you don't mind, but there's nothing else to do. Besides, there's going to be no money from the mine. Adel needs your board and room worse than we do. We'll keep the Fairweather children for nothing."

When Danny didn't reply, Mrs. Poorwilly added, "We got help moving your things. We gave Adel the rest of this month's money."

Danny hesitated for a moment, but there was nothing to say. He went outside.

He knocked at Adel's door. She let him in. "Mrs. Poorwilly says you're to stay with me now."

"Yes, she told me," Danny said.

Adel showed him to his bedroom. All his clothes had been hung up and his books had been neatly piled in one corner. He sat on the edge of the bed and tried to decide what to do. He finally decided he couldn't sit in the bedroom for the next five months and went back into the kitchen.

The supper was good, but Danny was too interested in Adel to pay much attention. In the light from the oil lamp, her eyes looked darker than ever. She was wearing a sweater with a V-neck. He could see the soft hollow of her throat and the smooth skin below her breastbone. Throughout supper he told her about the mainland and tried to keep his eyes above her neck.

The next morning when he went to school, he expected to see a difference in the children's attitudes. Twice he turned around quickly. Each time the children had all been busy writing in their notebooks. There was no smirking or winking behind their hands. At noon, he said, "In case any of you need to ask me something, there's no use your going to the Poorwillys. I'm staying at Miss Adel's now."

The children solemnly nodded their heads. He dismissed them and went home for lunch.

Adel was at home. She blushed and said, "The women at the sheds said I should come home early now that I've got you to look after. Since the men aren't fishing there isn't much to do."

"That's very good of them," Danny replied.

Danny and Adel were left completely alone. He had expected that some of the villagers would drop by, but no-one came to visit. Danny

and Adel settled into a routine that was disturbed only by Danny's ir-
ritation at being close to Adel. Adel shied away from him when he
brushed against her. At the end of the second week, she accepted
his offer to help with the dishes. They stood side by side as they
worked. Danny was so distracted by Adel's warmth and the constant
movement of her body that the dishes were only half dried.

Danny put his hand on Adel's shoulder and turned her toward him.
She let him pull her close. There was no place to sit or lie in the
kitchen so he picked her up and carried her to the bedroom. She
didn't resist when he undressed her. After he made love to her, he fell
asleep. When he woke up, Adel had gone to her own bed.

Danny took Adel to bed with him every evening after that, but during the night she always slipped away to her own bedroom. At the
beginning of the next week, they had their first visitor. Mrs. Poorwilly
stopped by to see how they were doing. They had been eating supper when she arrived. Normally, they would have been finished eating, but Adel had been late in coming from the fish sheds. The
weather had improved enough for the men to go fishing. Mrs. Poorwilly accepted a cup of coffee and sat and talked to them for an hour.

It was as if her coming had been a signal. After that, villagers dropped by in the evenings to talk for a little while. They nearly always
brought something with them and left it on the table. Danny had
wanted to protest, but he didn't know what to say that wouldn't em-
barrass their visitors so he said nothing.

Adel stopped going back to her own bed. Danny thought about
getting married but dismissed the idea. He was comfortable with
things the way they were.

The day Danny started to get sick he should have known something was wrong. He had yelled at the children for no particular reason. When Adel had come home, he had been grouchy with her. The
next day his throat had been sore, but he had ignored it. By the end
of the day, he was running a temperature and his knees felt like water.

Adel had been worried, but he told her not to call Mrs. Poorwilly.
Their things had become so mixed together that it was obvious they
were using the same bedroom.

For the next few days he was too sick to protest about anything.
Mrs. Poorwilly came frequently to take his temperature and to see

that Adel kept forcing whisky and warm broth into him. All during his sickness Danny was convinced that he was going to die. During one afternoon he was sure that he was dead and that the sheets were a shroud.

The crisis passed and he started to cough up phlegm, but he was so weak that it was an effort for him to lift his head. The day he was strong enough to sit up and eat in the kitchen, Mrs. Poorwilly brought him a package of hand-rolled cigarettes.

"Nearly everyone is coming to see you tomorrow. They'll all bring something in the way of a present. It's a custom. Don't say they shouldn't or they'll think you feel their presents aren't good enough."

Danny said that he understood.

The school children came first with hand-carved pieces of drift-wood. He admired the generally shapeless carvings, and after the first abortive attempt carefully avoided guessing at what they were supposed to be.

After the children left, the McFarlans came. Mr. McFarlan had made a shadow box from shingle. He had scraped the shingle with broken glass until the grain stood out. Inside the box he had made a floor of lichen and pebbles. Seagulls made from clam shells sat on the lichen.

His wife stretched a piece of black cloth over the end of a fish box. On it she had glued boiled fish bones to form a picture of a boat and man.

Someone brought a tin of pears, another brought a chocolate bar. One of the men brought half a bottle of whisky.

Each visitor stayed just long enough to inquire how Danny felt, wish him well and leave a present on the table. When the last visitor had gone, Danny was exhausted. Adel helped him to bed.

He felt much better by the end of the week, but when he tried to re-turn to work, Mrs. Poorwilly said, "Mary Johnson's doing a fine job. Not as good as you, of course, but the kids aren't suffering. If you rush back before you're ready, everybody will take it that you think she's doing a poor job. If you get sick again, she won't take over."

Adel returned to work at the sheds, but the women sent her home. The weather had held and there was lots of fish, but they said she should be at home looking after Danny.

At first it was ideal. They had little to do except sit and talk or make love. Danny caught up on his reading. They both were happy, but by the end of March their confinement had made them both restless.

To get out of the house, Danny walked to Mrs. Poorwilly's. While they were having coffee, Danny said, "I guess everyone must have got the flu."

"No," Mrs. Poorwilly replied, "just some colds among the children. Adel and you making out all right?"

"Yes," Danny said.

"Her mother was a beauty, you know. I hope you didn't mind moving, but these things happen."

"No, I didn't mind moving."

They sat for five minutes before Danny said, "Could I ask you something? I wouldn't want anyone else to know."

Mrs. Poorwilly nodded her assent.

"Mary Johnson is doing such a good job that I thought I might ask her to radio for a plane. Maybe it would be a good idea for me to take Adel to the mainland for a week."

"Any particular reason?"

"Yes. If she wants, I'll marry her."

"Haven't you asked her?"

Danny shook his head. It had never occurred to him that she might say no.

"Wait until you ask her. The superintendent will want a reason. You'll have to tell him over the radio and everyone will know. You wouldn't want to tell him and then have her turn you down."

Adel was standing at the window when he returned. He put his arms around her. "You know, I think we should get married."

Adel didn't answer.

"Don't you want to marry me?" he asked.

"Yes. I do. But I've never been off the island. You won't want to stay here always."

"We can stay for a couple of years. We'll go a little at a time. We can start with a week on the mainland for a honeymoon. We'll go somewhere on a train."

That evening he went to Mary Johnson's. Mary tried to raise the mainland operator, but the static was so bad that no contact could be made. Danny kept Mary at the radio for half an hour. He left when she promised to send one of the children with a message if the radio cleared.

Danny returned the next night, but the static was just as bad. Mary promised to send for him as soon as the call went through.

A week went by. The weather continued to improve. Danny checked the thermometer. The temperature was going up a degree every two days.

At the end of the week he returned to Mary's. The radio wasn't working at all. One of the tubes needed to be replaced. He left. Half-way home he decided to go back and leave a message for the plane. The radio might work just long enough for a message, but not long enough for him to be called to the set. When he came up to the house, he was sure that he heard the radio. He banged on the front door. Mary took her time coming. When she opened the door, he said, "I heard the radio. Can you send a message right away?"

Mary replied that he must have just heard the children talking.

Danny insisted on her trying to make the call. She was annoyed, but she tried to get through. When she had tried for five minutes, Danny excused himself and left.

He walked part-way home, then turned and crept back over the rock.

The windows were dark. He lay in the hollow of rock behind the house until the cold forced him to leave.

In the morning, he went to the dock to talk to the fishermen. He offered to pay any one of them triple the normal fare to take him down the coast. They laughed and said they would bring him some fresh fish for supper.

When he had continued insisting that he wanted to leave, they said that a trip at this time of year was impossible. Even planes found it difficult to land along the coast. A boat could be crushed in the pack ice that was shifting up and down the shore.

Danny told Adel about the radio and the boats. She sympathized with him, but agreed with the men that it was hopeless to try and make the trip in an open boat.

"Besides," she said, "the freight boats will be coming in a month or so."

True to their word, the fishermen sent a fresh fish. Danny tried to pay the boy who brought it, but he said that he had been told not to accept anything. Danny had put the money into the boy's hand. The boy had gone, but a few minutes later he returned and put the money in front of the door.

Late that afternoon, Danny walked to the dock. After looking around to see that no-one was watching, he bent down and looked at the rope that held one of the boats. He untied it, then tied it again.

He returned to the house and started gathering his heavy clothing. When Adel came into the room, she said, "What are you going to do?"

"I'm leaving."

"Is the plane coming?"

"I'm taking myself. I've had enough. I'm not allowed to work. You're not allowed to work. Everyone showers us with things they won't let us pay for. I try to use the radio, but it never works." He turned to face her. "It always worked before."

"Sometimes it hasn't worked for weeks," Adel replied. "Once it was six weeks. It's the change in temperature."

"But it works. The other night I heard it working. Then when I asked Mary Johnson to call, she said it was just the children talking."

"Mary told me," Adel said. "You made her very upset. She thinks you're still not feeling well."

"I'm feeling fine. Just fine. And I'm leaving. I don't know what's going on here, but I'm getting out. I'm going to get a plane and then I'm coming back for you."

"You said we could leave a little at a time."

"That was before this happened. What if something goes wrong? Three people have died. One of them died right before my eyes and I couldn't do anything about it. What if we needed a doctor? Or a policeman? What if someone took some crazy notion into his head?"

Danny took Sick Jack's nor'westers off a peg. He laid out the clothes he wanted and packed two boxes with food. He lay awake until three o'clock, then slipped outside and down to the boats.

The boats were in their usual places. He reached for the rope of the first boat. His hand closed on a heavy chain. Danny couldn't believe it. He jumped onto the boat and ran his hand around the chain. He climbed out and ran from boat to boat. Every boat was the same. He tried to break the chains loose. When they wouldn't break, he sat on the dock and beat his hands on the chains. When he had ex-

220

hausted himself, he sat with his face pressed into his hands.

In the morning, Mary sent one of the boys to tell Danny that the radio had worked long enough for her to send a message. It hadn't been confirmed, but she thought it might have been heard. For the rest of the day, Danny was elated, but as the days passed and the plane did not appear, he became more and more depressed. Adel kept saying that the plane would come, but Danny doubted if it would ever come.

The weather became quite mild. Danny walked to the dock every day. The chains were still on the boats. He had spent an hour on the dock staring at the thin blue line that was the mainland and was walking back to Adel's when he noticed that the snow had melted away from some of the cracks in the granite. The cracks were crammed with closely packed leaves.

He paused to pick a leaf. *April the first,* he thought, *April the first will come and we'll be able to go.* Then, as he stared at the small green leaf in his hand, he realized that he was wrong. It was weeks later that the first freight boat came.

The rest of the day he tried to make plans for Adel and himself, but he could not concentrate. The image of thousands and thousands of bloodflowers kept spilling into his mind.

W.D. Valgardson (1938-)
W.D. Valgardson's first story collection, Bloodflowers, *was published in 1973. The title story was chosen one of the Best American Short Stories in 1971. An Icelander by birth, Valgardson has lived in remote northern settlements in Canada. This has provided him with the settings for most of his hard-hitting stories.*

acknowledgements

"Poison", ©1950 by Roald Dahl, from *Someone Like You,* Alfred A. Knopf, Inc., 1950, is reprinted by permission of the publisher.

"A Shocking Accident" by Graham Greene, from *May We Borrow Your Husband? & Other Comedies of the Sexual Life.* Copyright 1957 by Graham Greene. Reprinted by permission of The Viking Press, Inc.

"The Hour of Letdown" from *The Second Tree From The Corner* by E.B. White, copyright 1951 by E.B. White, originally appeared in *The New Yorker.* Reprinted by permission of Harper & Row, Publishers, Inc.

"An Ounce of Cure" by Alice Munro, from *Dance of the Happy Shades*, is reprinted by permission of McGraw-Hill Ryerson Limited.

"Tiresome Company" by Jacques Ferron, from *Tales from the Uncertain Country*, House of Anansi Press Limited, copyright 1972, translation by Betty Bednarski. Reprinted by permission of the publisher

"Wanda Hickey's Night of Golden Memories" by Jean Shepherd first appeared in Playboy magazine; also published in a collection of the same title. Reprinted by permission of the publisher, Doubleday and Company, Inc.

"The Gunfighter" from *Miracle at Indian River* by Alden Nowlan, ©1968 by Clarke, Irwin & Company Limited. Used by permission.

"A Man Called Horse" ©1950 by Dorothy M. Johnson, from *A Man Called Horse (Indian Country)*, appeared originally in *Collier's.* Reprinted by permission of McIntosh and Otis, Inc.

"Out of the Rain" from *Somebody Else's Summer* by Ted Wood. ©1973 by Clarke, Irwin & Company Limited. Used by permission.

"Mr. Know-All" ©1924 by W. Somerset Maugham, from *The Complete Short Stories of W. Somerset Maugham*, Doubleday and Company, 1932, is reprinted by permission of the publisher.

"First Confession" by Frank O'Connor, from *The Stories of Frank O'Connor*, Alfred A. Knopf, Inc., 1951, is reprinted by permission of the publisher and A.D. Peter and Company.

"Snow" by Gwendolyn MacEwen is reprinted from *Noman* by permission of Oberon Press

"The Man With the Heart in the Highlands" by William Saroyan, from *The Man With the Heart in the Highlands and Other Stories*, Dell, 1968, is reprinted with the permission of the publisher.

"The Connection", ©Andreas Schroeder, from *The Late Man*, Sono Nis Press, Delta, B.C., 1971, is reprinted by permission of the publisher.

"Heav'n, Heav'n" by Eric Frank Russell is reprinted by permission of the author and his agents, Scott Meredith Literary Agency, Inc., 580 Fifth Avenue, New York, New York 10036.

"Men Are Different" by Alan Bloch is reprinted by permission of the author.

"City of Yesterday" by Terry Carr is reprinted by permission of Henry Morrison, Inc.

"Bloodflowers" by W.D. Valgardson is reprinted from *Bloodflowers* by permission of Oberon Press.

Every effort has been made to trace the ownership of copyright material used in this book and to make full acknowledgement for its use. The publishers will welcome any information that will allow them to correct errors or omissions in the acknowledgements.

Design: Michael van Elsen
Photographs: Birgitte Nielsen

Typesetting: Computype Limited
Printing and Binding: The Bryant Press Limited

Printed and bound in Canada
90 CG 83